ADRIFT

M. A. HUNTER

First published in Great Britain in 2023 by Boldwood Books Ltd.

Cover Design by 12 Orchards Ltd

Cover Photography: Pexels and Shutterstock

This book is a work of fiction and, except in the case of historical fact, any resemblance to actual persons, living or dead, is purely coincidental.

Every effort has been made to obtain the necessary permissions with reference to copyright material, both illustrative and quoted. We apologise for any omissions in this respect and will be pleased to make the appropriate acknowledgements in any future edition.

A CIP catalogue record for this book is available from the British Library.

Paperback ISBN 978-1-80549-543-7

Large Print ISBN 978-1-80549-539-0

Hardback ISBN 978-1-80549-538-3

Ebook ISBN 978-1-80549-536-9

Kindle ISBN 978-1-80549-537-6

Audio CD ISBN 978-1-80549-544-4

MP3 CD ISBN 978-1-80549-541-3

Digital audio download ISBN 978-1-80549-535-2

Boldwood Books Ltd
23 Bowerdean Street
London SW6 3TN
www.boldwoodbooks.com

For all those with a dream: never stop chasing it!

1

PRESENT DAY

Sometimes it's the scars we can't see that take the longest to heal. That's why I can't help my mind wandering as I stare out at the sea, so blue and endless, hiding a thousand secrets of its own, but none as great as the one that claws at the farthest embers of my memory. It laps gently beside us as the party rages above the surface. It's all I can see in every direction. We could scream blue murder and there isn't a soul who would hear us. Why then do I feel like I can hear something calling to me from the dark depths? A warning that danger is lurking.

'You ready for a fresh one, my brother?' I hear Harry's singsong Dublin accent gently break through my thoughts, as he reaches for the brown bottle I've been nursing for the last hour.

I don't want to tell him that I'm already feeling light-headed, so when Harry pulls the bottle from my grip, I do my best to plaster on a grateful smile.

He turns to face the others and shouts over the rock music pumping out of the Bluetooth speaker. 'May I remind you, gentlemen, that this is supposed to be a stag do for our good friend Fergus? There is an icebox bursting with Guinness, this pish you lads call beer, and enough vodka to go blind on in the galley, and I'm not going to be the only one suffering at sunrise.' He waits until their voices die down. 'Now can we all get fucking wasted, please?'

A roar of laughter and excitement breaks from those splashing about in the hot tub, and Harry stumbles towards the hatch into the galley in search of fresh supplies. The yacht rocks from side to side, but I seem to be the only one ill at ease. The air is a cocktail of sun lotion, rotting fish, and testosterone.

It's only a couple of days, I remind myself.

There was a time I would have done anything for these guys. I shiver at the memories, which are trying to scratch their way through.

A shadow passes in front of my eyes, followed by that of a bikini-clad Sophie dropping onto the cushioned bench beside me. 'This really is a piece of paradise, isn't it?'

I imagine being alone on a yacht of alpha males might make most women feel vulnerable or at risk, but not Sophie; she's shown so many times that she's more than capable of holding her own. She's always been regarded as 'one of the lads' and is probably the only woman my sister would be comfortable with allowing to come away with her future husband. And I'm certain if any of the rowdy group tried to take advantage, Sophie would soon put them back in place.

But I'm not so sure I'd regard this as paradise. A long weekend with university friends and an unlimited supply of warm weather and alcohol sounded perfect when Harry first suggested it, but now we're here, it's every bit as awkward as I feared it might be. Can I ever be at ease when so much water has passed under the bridge? Nobody has mentioned *that* night, but it's all I can think about. I shouldn't have come.

I watch as Sophie leans backwards, closes her eyes, and allows the sun's warm rays to wash over her. At thirty-two, she and I are the oldest of the group, but despite Sophie being a week younger than me, she's always been the matriarch, pulling the strings. And I'm surprised she agreed to come on this extended stag weekend, knowing that alcohol would be flowing freely. Maybe she's testing her new sobriety. Or maybe there's another reason. I can't ignore the voice in the back of my head reminding me that the Garden of Eden had snakes in the grass.

'It certainly is paradise,' I say when I realise she's looking over, awaiting a response.

'I've not always been a fan of Harry's plans,' Sophie continues, a bead of sweat escaping from behind her fringe and running the length of her slim face, 'but on this occasion, I'm prepared to admit he's pulled it out of the bag.'

As if on cue, Harry reappears from the galley, with five bottles of lager poking through his fingers and that cheeky grin I remember so well. He glides effortlessly across the deck, dispersing the bottles, while keeping one eye on Elena, our yacht's hostess for the next three days.

She catches him looking at her, and smiles back, her face as golden brown as the arms poking out of the short sleeves of her white shirt. Is she already falling under his spell as so many others before have? Unsurprisingly, Harry's eye isn't the only one she's caught since we boarded four hours ago. Elena is native to the islands in this area, but she has a decent grasp of English, and from the way she hasn't yet complained about the noise and Harry's and Rhys's outrageous flirting, I'd say she's used to hosting stag parties for excitable Brits. I won't be mentioning her presence here to my sister.

The captain, Joaquín, who looks more than capable of handling himself in a fight, pulls on a handle, and the engines quieten, slowing our trajectory. Harry moves closer to Elena, and whilst I can't hear exactly what he's saying, I've no doubt the lines are tried and tested and as sweet as honey. She certainly isn't rebuffing his advances. Her long jet-black hair is tied neatly in a ponytail, and in any other circumstances she could be mistaken for a catwalk model or siren. Certainly out of both of our leagues, but Harry's never been one to shy away from a challenge. Joaquín watches on, but makes no effort to interrupt.

I force myself to look away and press the dripping bottle of lager to my forehead, but it offers scant consolation from the burning heat.

I notice Rhys is shooting daggers at Harry and Elena. It's a look I've seen before, and the breath catches in my throat as I recall the night I was on the receiving end of that glare. I stand and quickly move across to Harry, pulling him away and over to the bench, plonking him beside Sophie. I look back to check that Rhys is happier now, but can't see him in the hot tub. Then I spot him disappearing into the galley, presumably hurrying after Elena, who's probably gone to prepare snacks to soak up some of the alcohol.

'Can I get you another orange juice, Soph?' Harry asks, his eyes fixed on the galley steps.

'Thanks, but I'm fine,' she replies, reaching for the sun lotion and squirting a generous amount into the palm of her hand. 'Either of you two want a top-up?'

As if on cue, Harry unfastens the garish blue and yellow Hawaiian shirt he's been wearing since we met at the airport, and flexes his biceps.

Sophie rolls her eyes. 'If you think muscles and manscaping impress me, you're going to be disappointed. You might have more luck with our hostess – that's if Rhys doesn't get there first. Pretty sure he'd win in a pissing contest too.'

Harry clutches his gut as if wounded, but his face breaks into his usual careless grin. 'Well, you know, you and me never did hook up in the house, so maybe it *is* time you discovered what you've been missing. Pete here will tell you I never leave a woman unsatisfied.'

He slaps me on the back, and I nearly drop the bottle, but before I can respond, he moves away, bored of such mundane conversation, crosses the aft, and steps down into the hot tub, clinking his bottle with Fergus and Christophe.

'I think I'm good at the moment, thanks, Soph,' I say. 'Do you want me to do your back?'

'Please.' She shuffles around on the cushion, and passes me the bottle.

I tuck her ginger plait over her shoulder, and apply the lotion, massaging it into her fair, freckled skin. I remember a few times when we lived together, when she'd sunbathe in the back garden, and wasn't so careful, ending up resembling a walking lobster. There were so many warning signs back then that I should have paid more attention to, but with the pressure of it being our final year, and everything else that went on... I shake my head, not wanting to be drawn back there. In truth, this is the first time we've all been together in years, and I'm surprised they all agreed to reunite for Fergus's final weekend of freedom. Credit to Harry for convincing them.

'Oh, wow you have the hands of a god,' I hear Sophie say, and realise the lotion has soaked in, and I'm just massaging her shoulders absent-mindedly.

My cheeks blaze as I lower my hands. 'Sorry. You're all done.'

'Don't apologise! That was possibly the best massage I've ever had. If you weren't already spoken for, I'd be giving serious consideration to dragging you below deck.'

It's her turn to blush, and I desperately want to fight against the awkward silence that suddenly grows. There's way too much history to overstep that boundary. And besides, Carly and I are happy, and our troubles feel far behind us.

We both look away, striving to find anything to break the tension. It's Sophie who is first to speak. 'It's great to see the old gang back together again. Who'd have thought we'd all be thriving ten years on?'

My stomach lurches as Rhys returns to the deck and climbs back into the hot tub. He doesn't mention what he's been up to with Elena, and although Harry gives him a questioning look, Rhys keeps his lips closed in a tight smile. Maybe Sophie is right about the potential pissing contest; I'll have to make sure Harry doesn't get in over his head.

My phone vibrates on the cushion beside me, and I smile when I see my sister's face. I accept the video call, and my heart warms instantly when I see Carly next to her, dancing. The muddy fields of Somerset are visible just over their shoulders.

'Finally, someone who's prepared to answer their phone. Hello, big brother, is my fiancé having a good time?'

I look over to Fergus, tempted to call him over and let them speak, but he has his back to me, and with the others hanging on to his every word, I imagine he's regaling them with one of his many anecdotes about growing up in the rugged Highlands. Of all the men my sister could have chosen to fall in love with, why did it have to be Fergus? She always had a string of admirers when we were growing up. I don't know if it's the shock of uncontrollable fiery hair, his bear-like girth, or because I can never tell when he's withholding the truth, but my skin crawls when I see them together.

I turn the phone's screen round instead and point it in the direction of the hot tub. 'I think you can say that.' I call out his name but either he doesn't hear or isn't interested, so I eventually turn the screen back to my face. 'And are you ladies having a great time at the festival?'

I can see they're both wearing glow stick necklaces and sipping from cans of supermarket-brand lager.

'Glasto is immense!' Carly shouts out, and again I'm so relieved that my girlfriend and sister have become such close friends. I wish Fergus and I could be as close.

I'm certainly not envious of our opposing destinations. Despite the lurking threat of seasickness, I'd choose the yacht over a weekend in a muddy field any day of the week.

Something catches my sister's attention, and she disappears from the screen, leaving me to stare into the beautiful brown eyes of the only woman I've ever truly loved. I want to tell her as much when Sophie suddenly snatches the phone from my grasp, and takes it around the others gathered in the hot tub so each can say hi to my better half. They've all known Carly almost as long as me. Of course, one of them has known her longer, and it still rankles even after a decade of love and intimacy.

I shake the memory away, determined to try to let the past rest. It needs to stay buried.

Harry takes control of the phone and introduces Carly to Elena, who has now reappeared on deck. I wish he hadn't, though. I would never cheat on Carly, but I know she has insecurities and I don't want anything to spoil her weekend either. The yacht quakes as Joaquín restarts the engine, and opens the throttle.

I stand unsteadily and go to collect the phone from Harry before disappearing into the galley, wanting to speak to Carly privately.

There are six cabins stretching out to the left and right of me, and I head down to my room – the last one on the right where the yacht's Wi-Fi is strongest – and close the door behind me.

'How are you doing? How's the weather?'

Her eyes dart to the darkening clouds overhead, and she wrinkles her nose. 'Supposed to chuck it down later, but that's part of the fun.'

I don't agree but keep it to myself.

'Looks sunny where you are, though,' she continues.

'It's gorgeous here. You'd love it!'

'What happened to the storm that was supposed to be heading *your* way?'

I think about the long-range weather forecast I'd checked when packing. 'No sign of it yet. If we're lucky, it should just hit the mainland.'

'That's a relief,' she says. 'I can't think of anything worse than being trapped on a boat in rough sea.'

'You'd love this yacht if you saw it too,' I continue. 'I've no idea how Harry got such a good deal for it.'

'I'm glad you're having a good time. I just wanted to call and tell you I love you.'

My heart could burst. I'm about to reciprocate when the silence is broken by an ear-splitting alarm.

2

PRESENT DAY

I race out of my room, still clutching my phone, as my whole body convulses. My heart is racing. I don't cope well in emergency situations. Is there a fire on board? Something worse?

'What the hell is that noise?' I just about hear Carly say as I race into the galley, but I don't stop to tell her I have no idea.

Sprinting up the stairs, I count four of the group leaning over the back of the yacht: Fergus's hairy back and tattoo sleeve, Christophe's black trunks and olive-skinned legs, Sophie's rainbow-coloured sarong, and Harry's pasty white sparrow legs.

I can't see Rhys anywhere.

'Man overboard!' Sophie shrieks, hurrying to the port side to grab the orange ring-shaped lifebuoy. She hurls it out into the water.

Joaquín has already stopped the engine, and is hurrying down from the raised platform; I can only assume Elena's the one who sounded the alarm. She rushes to join the others, looking over the edge. It's now I realise the music has stopped. A deathly silence fills the air as the ground bobs. It reminds me of just how isolated we are out here.

'I'll have to call you back,' I tell Carly, quickly ending the call, and throw my phone onto the cushioned bench.

I squeeze between Harry and Christophe, and see Rhys splashing his arms, trying to keep his head above the water. The lifebuoy floats just out of his reach. We must have been travelling at some knots when he hit the water, as he's a good ten or so metres behind us.

I don't understand why he doesn't just grab the ring and swim back. Out of the whole group, he's the only one who's maintained any real level of physical fitness, running half marathons every couple of months.

Despite Sophie's obvious concern, it doesn't seem to be a feeling shared by the rest of the group. Fergus can't seem to stop laughing.

'Don't thrash about,' Joaquín calls out. 'Grab the ring.'

Rhys throws his arms out, but his fingertips brush against the edge of the plastic, inadvertently pushing it further away. His head dips below the water, and when it emerges, he is coughing and spitting out water. I genuinely think he might drown if someone doesn't get to him.

I don't think twice, lifting my leg over the safety rope, but then I feel Joaquín's clammy fingers coil around my arm.

'No, I will go. I am responsible. You must all stay on the yacht.' He looks back to Rhys, and holds out his arm, fingers splayed. 'Try to keep still. I'm coming.'

He pulls the white shirt over his head, revealing carefully sculpted abs, before yanking off his white shoes and socks and diving over the edge. He glides through the water, quickly swallowing up the distance between Rhys and the yacht. He grabs the lifebuoy in one motion as he passes it and quickly tucks it over Rhys's arms, just as his face disappears below the waterline again.

Joaquín tugs him back up, and ensures the lifebuoy is tucked below his armpits, before surveying the top of the sea.

What's he looking for?

Slipping one arm around the orange ring, he paddles with his free arm, dragging Rhys back with him. The motion is awkward, and water splashes up at us as we all continue to lean over. I don't know how much seawater he's swallowed, but his face is an unhealthy shade of green.

Would it really be that bad if we had to end the party early to head back to shore and get him medical treatment?

They finally make it back to the stern, and Joaquín puts his arms around Rhys's waist, lifting him out of the water, beckoning for us to get hold of his hands. I grab one, and Harry grabs the other, and between us we manage to pull him up and back over the safety rope. We lie him down on the cushioned bench, and turn back to offer the same help to Joaquín, but he's already got his feet on the swim platform, pulling himself up and over.

Elena has fetched towels for the two of them. She pushes past Fergus and Christophe, and drops to her knees beside Rhys. 'We need to sit him up,' she says, placing her hands on his shoulders, and manoeuvring him into a sitting position. 'Tuck your head between your knees, and cough up any excess water.'

He does as he's told, and I turn away at the sound of his retching.

'What happened?' I whisper to Sophie, who's watching on without breathing.

She must not have heard me as she doesn't respond. I look next to Christophe and Fergus, whose faces are finally taking in the significance of the situation. Fergus meets my gaze and he opens his mouth to speak, but he has no words. I've seen that look of terror in his eyes before, and that posture: he's wrapping his hands around his body as if maintaining an invisible forcefield that can deflect any harm.

When his retching stops, I look back to Rhys. Harry has found a bottle of mineral water, which he hands over, encouraging him to take a drink.

'I-I'm fine,' he says to us all with haggard breath. 'I just need my inhaler.'

Joaquín stands, his shorts wet through.

'Thank you,' Rhys splutters, blood rushing to his cheeks. 'You saved my life.'

'You'll be okay,' Elena tells him, tucking a clump of stray hair behind her ear. 'But you should all know it isn't safe to swim here.' She steps back and turns slightly, so she can address the whole group. 'There are sharks that inhabit this stretch of water.'

The breath catches in my throat. Did she just say sharks? My eyes dart to the horizon, searching for dorsal fins poking through the water.

Rhys could have died.

'Tomorrow we will arrive at Paradise Cove,' Joaquín announces. 'It will be safe to swim there, but not here. Please, please, please, nobody else get into the water until I say it is safe.'

Is that what happened? Did Rhys jump into the sea to get Elena's attention? Given how much he was struggling to keep his head above the water, I can't believe he'd voluntarily choose to jump in. But does that mean he fell? The safety rope is high enough that it would take quite a jerk or stumble to go over.

I look around the gathered group, all of them now looking shocked by what has happened, but maybe it's the news of our razor-teethed neighbours that has caused the blood to drain from all of their faces.

Joaquín stares at us individually to ensure we have all understood and will heed his warning, before heading back towards the hatch down to the galley and cabins beyond.

I hand Rhys the untouched bottle of lager Harry gave me earlier. 'Are you all right? What happened?'

He opens his mouth to speak, but then his brow furrows, and he takes a swig from the bottle. 'I must have just leant over too far. Lucky I didn't end up as a shark's dinner.'

Fergus wraps a protective arm around his shoulders and drags him back towards the hot tub, where Sophie and Christophe help him into the warm water.

'I just need to phone Carly back and let her know everything's okay,' I tell them. The whole episode has left a sour taste in my mouth, and I need some space. 'It might be good if we eat something soon as well.'

Harry applauds my suggestion. 'There's loads of bits and pieces in the galley. I'll check with Elena if we can just help ourselves.' He turns to the others, a forced smile on his face. 'This is supposed to be a party, remember? Who's in charge of music?'

Christophe raises his hand and fiddles with his phone. A moment later, the sound of Oasis replaces the eerie silence, and even Rhys looks as though he's finally relaxing. He splashes handfuls of warm water over his cheeks, and allows his shoulders to sink below the water.

Harry passes me a fresh bottle of lager. 'Sláinte!'

I clink the bottle against his, and then head towards the corridor of cabins, grabbing my phone from the bench on the way. When I'm inside my room, I let out a small sigh of relief and lean against the closed door. I don't want to think about what could have happened to Rhys had Joaquín not jumped in to save him.

I haven't seen any sharks, and my geographical knowledge isn't strong enough to know whether predator sharks really do lurk in these waters. If we were in the United States or Australia,

I'd have probably guessed for myself. The grave look on Elena's face suggests that she wasn't just trying to frighten us.

I used to be a fairly strong swimmer, but I'm not sure I'd trust my muscle memory in a race with a bloodthirsty shark. I shudder at the thought.

I need to clear my mind, so I video call Carly, who answers immediately.

'Is everything okay?' she asks, the concern clear in her tone. 'What was that alarm?'

'Everything's okay. Rhys fell overboard and had to be rescued, but he's fine now.'

I don't want to mention the threat of sharks, in case she tells my sister.

'Oh, gosh, he fell overboard? Poor Rhys.'

An image of the two of them flashes behind my eyes and I try to move past it. 'He's fine now,' I repeat. 'Probably just trying to show off in front of the hostess.'

'I doubt it,' she scoffs. 'He can't swim.'

I don't want to ask how she could know such a fact after ten years, and try to reassure myself that they aren't still in touch. I know they don't follow one another on social media, but I've never checked whether Carly still has his phone number. After what happened between them, it's been easier to lose touch with him. Given he's said barely two words to me since we boarded, I guess the feeling's mutual. Fergus is still close to both him and Christophe, according to my sister, but I guess they wouldn't be here if they weren't.

'So do you have your own room on board?' Carly asks next, maybe sensing my own insecurities resurfacing.

'Actually, it's called a cabin,' I correct, as I pan the phone around the room for her to see, 'and yes, I have it all to myself. In fact, if you're up for it, I could lock the door and then you and I could—'

'Keep it in your trousers, my love; there's no way I am having phone sex with you while in a field full of strangers in Somerset. I'll make it up to you when I'm back.'

I know she's right, and I'm embarrassed to have even suggested it. 'Spoilsport! Okay, well, I better get back up on deck. I love you.'

She blows a kiss, which I pretend to catch. 'Love you more.'

I end the call and drop onto the double bed, stretching out my arms and legs as if making a snow angel. Harry really did pull out all the stops for this holiday, and I must make sure to thank him properly. He's gone to great effort to make us feel comfortable.

So, I need to stop thinking about what happened in that house. What *we* did.

A regular whirring sound suggests the boat's engines have started up again, and the noise is enough to prevent me from falling asleep. I do hope Joaquín isn't planning to sail during the night; I'm not sure sleep would be possible with this constant rumble.

Standing, I can hear voices just outside my cabin, and I'm about to slide open the door when I hear Rhys shushing whoever he's with. I pause when I hear my name.

'Don't let on to Pete, okay? Promise me. I don't want him to tell Fergus and ruin the weekend.'

'Okay, okay, I won't,' I hear Sophie whisper back. 'But are you saying you were pushed?'

'One minute I was staring out at the water, then I felt a bump, and then I was flailing. I looked at him when I got out, and his face was the picture of innocence; he didn't even apologise.'

I press my ear closer to the door, curious to know who they're talking about.

'You're saying he pushed you? Do you want me to have a word with him?'

'No, no, I don't want anything to spoil the trip. I'll wait till we dock tomorrow, and then I'll have it out with him once and for all.'

I remain glued to the door, desperate to know who they were talking about, but I hear them move away after Harry calls out, announcing lunch is ready.

3

PRESENT DAY

Several hours have passed since Rhys was rescued from the water, but it's hard to keep track of time when the alcohol is flowing so freely and everyone present is determined to make the most of the glorious sunshine. I've been carefully supplementing my lager intake with long sips from a bottle of mineral water I've carefully secreted behind one of the cushions. Given the temperature, the others should be taking a leaf out of my book to prevent themselves from becoming dehydrated. All except Sophie, of course, who hasn't once yielded to temptation. I never thought I'd see the day when she'd be able to decline alcohol. But even as our eyes meet now, she looks like she's having a great time, and is giggling as much as the rest of us. It can't be easy for her; nine months sober and being put in this environment. I've never been prouder.

I haven't been able to stop thinking about what I overheard: *You're saying he pushed you?*

The *he* in question could be anyone, and yet I can't imagine any of the group deliberately pushing Rhys into open water. Christophe wouldn't be top of my list of suspects. Christophe, who had to work so hard to fit in at university; Christophe, who claims he survived the slums of the Parisian suburbs, even though I know his parents paid for him to be privately educated; Christophe, who is constantly seeking Fergus and Rhys's approval.

That then brings me to Fergus: the man my sister has vowed to devote the rest of her life to. Given our own personal history, I was worried how he might react to me tagging along, and I probably wouldn't have come if Simone hadn't begged me to keep an eye on him. She swears she trusts him, but also she knows how easily he can be led when he's around Rhys and Christophe.

And that leaves Harry, but I can't imagine why he would want to see Rhys go overboard. Even their shared interest in Elena wouldn't be enough. Harry has always been self-assured when it comes to his sexual proclivities, and he won't be seeing Rhys as an actual rival. And besides, I've known Harry for a long time; he doesn't have a malicious bone in his body.

But how well can I say I really know any of these guys any more? We drifted apart after university, though that was only natural given we came from different points of the compass. I wasn't surprised when Harry didn't go home to Dublin after graduation. He always said he would end up in London, and it was great having such a good friend so close. I hadn't realised he and Fergus were still so friendly until my sister told me Fergus had asked him to be best man. I'd assumed he would have called on Woody or one of the others he was so close to.

Since lunch, I've been watching Rhys closely, looking to see if he's giving away any clues as to who he believes is responsible, but like a great poker player, he's playing his cards close to his chest. The way he's laughing and joking with the group, nobody would guess there's any animosity there. And if I hadn't overheard him whispering with Sophie, I'd be none the wiser either. What is it they say about keeping friends close?

The sky has now reached the level of heady darkness where

we need to switch on the lights fixed into the yacht's gunnel – the rim of the boat that surrounds the hull. Joaquín keeps referring to parts of the yacht with their official names, and it's hard to keep up. I've learned that the front of the yacht is the bow. There are two sun loungers there, despite that end being where the ride is bumpiest. Where we're gathered now is the stern, where the sunken hot tub is, though Joaquín has covered it with a wooden board, creating more room for us to spread out, and to prevent any more 'accidental' tumbles.

Elena approaches now, all talk of the dangers of the surrounding waters forgotten.

'Gentlemen, excuse me,' she says, waiting until we're all looking at her. 'It is now nine o'clock, and too dark to continue. Joaquín will drop the anchor here, and get us started at first light. We're slightly behind schedule, but we should be able to make up the time if we get moving by seven. Tomorrow we will dock at Paradise Cove, where the waters are warmer and you'll be able to safely swim and make use of the private beach. Joaquín will radio in our coordinates, and then we'll leave you to it.'

Harry raises his arm into the air. 'Hold on, if there are only six cabins, where are you two planning to sleep?'

I look away. He's incorrigible.

'There is a V-berth in the bow. Our things are in there.'

Ah, I had wondered what was behind that locked door at the end of the corridor. Their room must be V-shaped to be right in the bow. Does that mean they're an item?

Harry looks disappointed with the answer, but I also know he won't give up that easily. Elena bows her head, and departs to undertake her duties. As she leaves, Rhys's eyes do not leave the tight curve of her bottom once.

'Whose turn is it next?' Fergus asks, drawing our attention

back to the game of truth or dare that we've been playing for more than an hour.

'It's Pete's,' Sophie says, her eyes twinkling mischievously at me. 'I'll ask. Truth or dare?'

The dares so far have been relatively tame, but it would be just my luck to get one that, fuelled by too much booze, is awkward or dangerous.

'Truth,' I declare, immediately wincing, pretending I already regret the decision.

Sophie's smile widens to the point where I think I may actually have made the wrong choice. 'Obviously, we all know how much you love Carly, and what a sweetheart she is,' she says, 'but in the interests of upping the stakes, here goes: if Carly were to cheat on you with one of us – a stupid one-night stand, let's say – do you think you could forgive and forget?'

My mood sours in an instant. I glare at Sophie, but I don't see any spite in her eyes.

And yet she's tapped into my darkest fear.

'Come on, Soph, play fair,' I hear Harry leap to my defence. 'Ask him something else.'

'I'm not suggesting Carly ever would – or any of us, for that matter,' Sophie clarifies, her eyes still twinkling. 'I just want to know how Pete would react. Is he a lover or a fighter?'

My gaze immediately falls on Rhys, but he is deep in conversation with Fergus. I don't want them to see how much the question is troubling me, and if I don't answer it, the forfeit is to down two shots of tequila, which I'm determined not to do.

I straighten, put on my sternest face, and take a deep breath. 'Who is it I'm forgiving? Carly or the dickhead amongst you who seduced her?'

Sophie claps her hands together as she erupts into laughter. 'Did someone say fight? I love that you never back down from a challenge. The question was whether you could forgive Carly, but since you ask, could you forgive the guilty party amongst us?' She wriggles her eyebrows playfully.

She's raised the stakes again, but given I feel certain Carly would never betray me in that way, my response is simple. 'I'd cut his fucking balls off, and make him eat them.'

Sophie leaps to her feet, grabbing my hand and pulling me up, holding my arm aloft. 'And that, my friends, is how you play the game!' She pulls me into a hug and whispers into my ear. 'I'm sorry, I was just teasing. You know you mean the world to me.'

We separate awkwardly and she retakes her seat. Am I misreading the signals, or was that a come-on? There's never been anything more than friendship between Sophie and me, and I thought that was what we both wanted. She's attractive, but I've always kind of thought of her as a sister, in the same way Harry is like my brother.

My cheeks are ablaze, even though the sun has set, and there is a cool breeze blowing beneath the blanket of infinite black sky.

Christophe clears his throat. 'Fergus's turn next, and I get to ask the question.'

Fergus's head snaps round.

'Truth or dare, Fergus?' Christophe asks, his deep voice dripping with a sense of menace I've not heard before. I don't like the sinister turn this game has suddenly taken on.

Fergus briefly glances at me, before replying, 'Dare.'

Christophe stands as I reclaim my seat, and looks around for a suitable challenge. 'Okay, your dare, Fergus, is to make out with someone on board this ship.'

I sense this challenge isn't just about making Fergus uncomfortable; both Rhys and Harry are staring longingly up at the cockpit, where Elena is in conversation with Joaquín.

'Um, no way,' Fergus says, without even looking in Elena's

direction. 'I'm getting married, and I'm not about to throw that away for the sake of a silly game.'

'Oh, come on, don't be a killjoy,' Christophe scoffs. 'What happens on board stays on board. Simone will never find out, and Pete isn't the sort to tell tales, are you?'

I don't know how much Christophe has had to drink, but he's liable to get punched if he doesn't tone it down.

'No,' Fergus says firmly, before I have chance to interject.

I don't understand why Christophe is being so aggressive, but maybe he's just lashing out, after the tough time Fergus gave him at university. I would have expected him to have left that level of pettiness in the past.

'Well, you know the rules,' Christophe says, raising the bottle. 'Two shots of tequila.'

Fergus snatches the bottle from him and puts it to his lips, his eyes watering as he knocks back the spirit and grimaces. I'm not certain he won't heave it straight back up, as his cheeks take on a shade of green. 'If you'll excuse me, I'm going to go and call Simone.'

He leaves without another word. I feel I should go after him for Simone's sake, but my path is blocked by Rhys's sudden leaping up.

'I don't mind accepting Fergus's challenge for him,' he says, again eyeing Elena, who now appears to be watching our game play out.

'No trades,' Harry says firmly, glaring at him. 'Anyway, it's my turn. Who's going to ask me a question? I'm more than happy to sing you a couple of verses of "Danny Boy".'

I rest my hand on his wrist. 'Why don't we play a different game now, hey?'

He isn't listening. 'I'll take a dare. Who's got one for me?'

Rhys turns back to face us, his eyes narrowed. 'I have one if you think you're man enough?'

'Bring it on,' Harry snarls back.

'Well, given I've already taken a swim with the sharks today, your dare is to do the same.'

'No,' I interject, almost spitting out the sip of water I just took. 'That's a ridiculous dare. Come on, Rhys, the rules are nothing dangerous, let alone life-threatening.'

'I didn't mean in the open water,' he says defensively. 'I meant in the shark cage.'

My mouth drops. 'The shark cage?'

'There's one under the boat,' he says, his eyes fixed on Harry's. 'Elena told me about it earlier. There's goggles and breathing apparatus as well. So the dare is to spend five minutes in the shark cage.'

I turn to Harry. 'You don't need to do this. Let's call it a night, and remember that we're here to celebrate, not wind each other up.'

'Five minutes?' Harry clarifies, standing and rolling his neck and shoulders until there's a loud crack. 'Bring it on.'

Rhys claps his hands together excitedly and heads off to ask Elena.

I turn to Harry. 'This is madness,' I whisper. 'Nobody is going to think any less of you if you take the shots instead.'

He fixes me with a pitying stare. 'It's a cage: it's not like the sharks can get at me. I'm not letting him show me up in front of Elena. Relax. I've got this.'

I've known Harry for more than a decade, and I know he won't listen to reason, so I only have one card I can play. 'Well, if you're going in, I'm going with you.'

He frowns with disapproval. 'Ah, that's sweet. You're worried about me, but I don't need you to hold my hand.'

I lift myself onto my toes so we're the same height. 'It's like

Soph said: I never back down from a challenge.'

Harry knows how obstinate I can be, and doesn't argue.

Elena tries to talk us out of it, warning that it'll be too dark to see anything down there, even with the boat's underwater lighting, but neither of us is going to back down. So she helps us put on our masks and air tanks, and explains how to breathe with them. And then we watch as Joaquín cranks a handle, and the cage appears on the starboard side of the yacht.

'The water will be fairly cold,' he says, 'so I don't want the two of you in there for more than five minutes. Don't stay still, keep moving to keep the blood flowing, and when you have had enough, pull on this rope.'

A thin yellow cord hangs between his fingers and disappears into the dark, murky water inside the cage.

Harry lifts his legs over the safety rope and sits down on the edge of the gunnel, before lowering himself into the water, his light brown curls quickly disappearing beneath the surface.

When I'd said I would go with him, I'd expected him to refuse and down the shots, but it's too late for me to back out now. I can see how much Rhys is enjoying this, and I think back to what I overheard in the corridor. If he believes Harry pushed him, then this dare would be his perfect revenge, but I can't believe that Harry would have it in him to push Rhys into the water. What would he have to gain from it?

I'm already shivering as the night temperature continues to drop, and I probably should have asked Joaquín if I could have borrowed a wetsuit, but it's too late for all that now. Taking several breaths through the nozzle in my mouth, I silently count to five, and then ease myself over the edge. By the time I realise how surprisingly cold the water is, it's already over my head. I gasp and inadvertently spit out the nozzle.

Panic sets in, and I continue to sink, the weight of the air tank dragging me further into the murky darkness. Where the hell is that yellow cord Joaquín was holding?

A flash of light moves out from behind me, and as I tense, wondering what kind of creature has managed to squeeze through the thick metal bars of the cage, I feel warm hands on my arms, and then Harry is there, pressing the nozzle back between my lips. I'm forced to swallow the water that gets into my mouth from the sides, and gag as the salt burns my throat, but after several settling breaths, my shoulders begin to relax. Harry gives me a look, asking if I am okay, and I thrust out a reassuring thumb.

Elena was right that we can barely see past the bars of the cage. The occasional colourful fish swims past, offers a curious look, and continues on its way.

Harry must see how I'm starting to turn to ice, and rubs his hands along the length of both his arms, encouraging me to do the same. Elena did warn us to keep moving, and Harry is doing exactly that. He begins to perform somersaults, first forwards and then backwards. I used to be able to execute handstands in the swimming pool, but with nothing to rest my hands against, I don't attempt it here. I'm just keen for the five minutes to pass so we can get out and claim the moral victory.

I want to ask Harry whether he did push Rhys into the water, but we have no way of verbally communicating with each other.

Maybe it was an accident. If Rhys was too close to the edge, or maybe peering over trying to see the rudder, and Harry was close by and didn't see him, a sudden shift in the water could have meant he might bump into Rhys. I could imagine that happening, but surely Harry would have known this and offered him an apology. It doesn't make sense.

Harry has now swum to the far side of the cage, and has poked his arm through the bars, pretending that something has grabbed hold of him and is trying to pull him through. For a moment, I actually fall for the bluff, and as I move closer, he quickly pulls his arm back and mimes a gut-wrenching laugh. I wave my finger to show my displeasure, but only for a moment as I see the rapidly approaching eyes and razor-sharp teeth of the beast over Harry's shoulder.

It slams nose-first into the cage, and the whole structure shakes around us. I jerk backwards, the nozzle dropping from my mouth again. I grab Harry and pull him towards me in case the shark manages to prise the bars apart.

When I volunteered to get into this cage, I never actually believed I'd come face to face with a predator, and now I just want out. I scan the murky water above our heads until I spot the yellow cord, and I tug on it with all my might. I don't care if our five minutes isn't up, there's no way I'm spending another second in this water.

I have to keep swallowing as my lungs slowly run out of air, and it's a relief when the cage emerges from the water. As soon as Joaquín lifts the lid, we scramble out.

'Whoa, whoa, whoa,' Sophie says, helping me climb back over the safety rope. 'You look like you've seen a ghost.'

I suck in deep gasps of breath and slide the straps of the air tank from my shoulders, letting it clunk down against the wooden deck. 'Sh-shark,' I just about manage to sputter.

'No way,' she mouths, her eyes widening with excitement. 'You actually saw one? That's so cool.'

Harry is next over the rope and confirms my statement. 'A big bugger as well. The fecker must have been at least six feet long.'

Towels are fetched and wrapped around the two of us as we struggle to get warm. When I'm offered wine, I don't hesitate in necking it, and hold the glass out for a refill. I'm going to need something to help me sleep after that scare.

I look for Elena to see if she can tell us what kind of shark it was, but she doesn't appear to be nearby. And then I spot her up in the cockpit, her lips locked with Rhys's. And that's when I realise the real reason Rhys dared Harry to go in the cage: not as some kind of revenge, but so he could make his move on Elena. Harry has noticed them too, a look of anger flashing across his face.

'Plenty more fish in the sea,' I say, adding a chuckle.

He meets my stare, and shrugs. 'Sharks too, it would seem.'

He reaches for the bottle of wine, puts it to his lips and is just about to climb into the hot tub, joining Christophe, when Fergus comes bounding out of the hatch beneath the deck, a look of abject terror on his face.

'The Wi-Fi's cut out,' he screeches, his eyes searching out whoever might be responsible. 'Simone was just about to tell me something – something awful has happened to them – and the call disconnected.'

I move forward, all thoughts of the shark evaporating. 'What's happened? Are they all right? Are she and Carly okay?'

Elena must have heard the complaint, as she prises Rhys from her, and says she will see if she can fix the router.

Fergus follows her down through the hatch, venting his frustration as he does so, while I hunt for my own phone to try to call Carly, even though I know that with the Wi-Fi down, and no signal this far out to sea, I have no way of getting hold of her. I slump onto the cushioned bench.

Sophie joins me, a sombre look on her face.

'It sounds like the start of a horror story, being miles from anywhere and no means of communicating with the outside world,' she says without a hint of irony.

The last thing we need is for our fear to be heightened, but it's what she says next that chills me to the bone.

4

TEN YEARS AGO

'This must be the place,' Harry says, pulling a cigarette from behind his ear and sparking it up.

I study the text message on my phone. 'This is where she said.'

I double-check I've got the date and time right, and although we're a couple of minutes early, there's no sign of the Sophie Williams who was advertising for roommates.

'I think it's nice,' Harry declares with no clue of what the inside is like.

Given the overgrown lawn and unkempt hedge, I'm not getting my hopes up. It's not the worst place we've seen since we started house-hunting. That award is reserved for the studio flat where the double bed pulled out of the wall. The landlord with the jam-jar glasses and nasty whiff of BO advertised it as a two-bed apartment, and when we asked where the second of us would sleep, he expected we'd share the bed. And he'd had the nerve to want £500 a month.

Given that Harry is dressed in torn skinny jeans, and a T-shirt which hasn't seen the inside of a washing machine for more than a week, I guess beggars can't be choosers.

'It's nearly midday, maybe she's inside?' I suggest, heading up the uneven flagstone path.

After using the door knocker, I listen for any sound of movement, but the place must be empty. Moving to the side of the house, I'm surprised by how far back it appears to stretch. From the front, it looks like a standard three-bedroom detached house, but I may have underestimated it.

'Oh, good, you're here.' A voice carries from the road. 'I take it you're Pete and Harry?'

The young woman extends her hand and we both shake it.

'Pete,' I say. 'And you're Sophie?'

Harry is ogling her as he does every new woman who crosses his path, but she doesn't seem the least bit interested, which is a relief. I've seen how wrong tenancy agreements can go when there are relationships between the housemates. And knowing how promiscuous Harry can be, we'd be safer in an all-male house, though that comes with its own difficulties.

'That's right,' Sophie responds. 'I'm glad you found the place. I know it's a bit off the beaten track, but there's actually a footpath that runs along the back that leads straight through to the Highfield campus, and it's accessible from the rear garden. It's about a five-to-ten-minute walk, depending on your speed. And there are plenty of buses from there that will take you into the centre of Southampton. Shall we go in?'

She's so self-assured that I immediately sense I'm going to like Sophie Williams. We follow her back to the front door, and she inserts a key and lets us in.

'There are six bedrooms in total, two down here, three on the first floor, and one is a loft conversion. There's a shower and toilet on this floor, through the kitchen at the back, and a larger bathroom on the first floor.' She opens a door immediately to her right. 'This is the lounge-diner, which has access to basic cable television – no sport or movies. The broadband is ultra-fibre, and the Wi-Fi signal is strong in all rooms apart from the downstairs bathroom and the cellar.'

The room is bigger than my parents' front room back home, with a large corner sofa, big enough to comfortably sit at least five, with two separate reclining armchairs in the opposite corner. There is also a long table and chairs at one end. The television on the wall must be at least fifty inches in size. Maybe I really have underestimated this place.

Sophie leads us back out of the room, and along the corridor, using a separate key to unlock the next door on the right. 'This is bedroom one. The double bed and desk are standard in all of the rooms, as is an Ethernet port for wired internet. Bedroom two across the hall is virtually identical to this one, with a view of the front garden. The landlord isn't green-fingered but I reckon I can talk him into going halves on a gardener.'

'Are there smoke alarms fitted in all of the bedrooms too?' I ask, pointing at the small white box on the ceiling.

She nods encouragingly. 'And each room requires a key to gain entry, for security purposes.'

The bedroom is only fractionally smaller than the lounge-diner, and is far bigger than I was expecting. Having lived in halls of residence for two years, I'm used to barely having enough room to spin around without bumping into something. This is a definite upgrade.

The kitchen at the rear of the property is long and narrow, with an electric oven and hob that have seen better days, and a tall American-style fridge-freezer. I count six double cupboards, each with space for a padlock if required. There is a small square table with four chairs.

Sophie leads us up to the first floor, where the rooms are identically sized to those downstairs, just with different views from the windows. The bathroom looks like it could do with a good scrub, but I'm not put off by the prospect of a bit of hard work. It strikes me as a home in need of a little TLC, and I can already picture myself living here.

'Now, I've already signed up three of my friends – Christophe, Rhys, and Fergus – who I'll introduce you to later and I'm sure you'll get on fine with them. We're all part of the university's lacrosse team, but don't worry, we're not all stereotypical jocks.'

That's a relief to hear, but I had assumed our potential new housemates would have been here to meet us. I'm not sure I'm comfortable agreeing to live with strangers. That said, given the slim pickings we've seen, we can't allow this place to slip through our fingers.

'Fergus and Rhys see themselves as the alphas, but both are pretty sweet once you get to know them. It'll be funny, actually, if the two of you *do* move in. We'll have an Englishman, Welshman, Scotsman, and an Irishman. We'll practically be a lame joke from the eighties. It ought to make watching the Six Nations more interesting, especially as Christophe grew up in Paris.'

'Rhys is on my course,' Harry says quietly. 'He was the one who mentioned you were searching for housemates. I'm surprised you couldn't find two more from your lacrosse team.'

'Well, there were a pair who were interested, but they're in a relationship, and I don't know about you, but in my experience it's best not to have relationships between housemates.'

Her eyes drop to her feet, as if there's more she wants to say, but is holding back.

'We could be the exception to the rule,' Harry says, puffing out his chest. I'm not convinced he's joking.

'You were the first to message me,' Sophie continues, ignoring his comment, 'so if you're interested, then I'll refuse the other interested parties.'

'Five men and only two bathrooms?' I say, in an effort to ease the tension. 'It could get tribal.'

'We haven't chosen rooms yet,' Sophie adds, 'as we figured it would be better to wait until everyone's seen the place and then draw lots or something. To be honest, I don't care which room I get as they're virtually identical anyway.' She pauses and looks from Harry to me. 'I tell you what, I'll give you a couple of minutes to chat about it, and then you can give me your answer. No pressure. As I said, there's plenty more interest in the place.'

'Can I just check that the rent is only £400 a month?' I ask as she turns to leave.

She nods, a big smile on her face. 'Including utilities. You won't find a better price in Southampton for a place like this.'

Harry frowns. 'Why *is* it so cheap, though? The size, the proximity to the campus... did someone die here or something?'

Sophie looks horrified. 'Heavens, nothing like that. Truth be told, the landlord is... how do I put this diplomatically? He's a bit... odd.'

My ears prick up. 'Odd how?'

'Actually, *odd* is probably not the right word. Listen, Raymond is one of the lacrosse coaches. He's a tough taskmaster and as far as I understand it, this was his mother's house, until she went into a hospice and died some years back. She was very meticulous, but I guess the thought of living here without her is just too painful for him or something.'

I can't help picturing Norman Bates in the rocking chair in *Psycho*, and I have an overwhelming desire to politely decline and hit the trail, but she's right that we won't find better digs for the price, and it is only a year.

'He rents the place out to students every year, but he's quite picky about the quality of tenant. He won't let it to first or second years because he doesn't want it to get trashed. Like his mother, he's a bit particular about things, and there are certain rules we have to agree to abide by, but it's no big deal.'

'Sounds too good to be true,' Harry mutters, eyes wandering from room to room as if he's trying to work out which of them appeals to him the most.

'Raymond's got a bit of a reputation for being creepy, but I think he's just a lonely old man who doesn't know how to properly socialise. I took pity on him a couple of months ago and we got chatting and he told me about this place. He said I could have it for the year for £2,400 a month, so I figured I'd fill it and split the cost.'

I narrow my eyes; it still sounds almost too perfect. 'He could probably make double that.'

She nods. 'I know. He actually asked for three grand a month originally, but I managed to negotiate it down on the condition that I agree to have dinner with him.' She pulls a disgusted face. 'It's a necessary evil for a place like this. I'll just have to get steaming drunk before I go.'

'Anything else we should know about?' Harry asks.

'As I mentioned, there are one or two stipulations as part of the contract, but nothing obscene. I'll try and fish it out for you so you can take a gander.' She pulls out her phone, which is ringing. 'Would you excuse me for a moment? I just need to deal with this.'

She heads up the stairs to the loft room and closes the door. I beckon for Harry to follow me down to the kitchen so we won't be overheard.

'What do you think?'

'Are you freaking kidding me? It's the best place we've looked at, and if we get rooms on the same floor, it'll be just like being back in halls, but with much more space. Think of the parties we'll be able to host. We'll be the hottest ticket in town.

Just think about all those young and willing freshers flocking here.'

I don't remind him that I've just started seeing Carly, nor that, in our final year, we should be studying harder and partying less.

'And the creepy landlord doesn't bother you?'

'Listen, if this guy likes to dress up as his dead mother and wander the corridors, I'm okay with that.' He laughs and slaps me on the back. 'But listen, if you're not down with it, then we'll hit the road. I'm not going to force you into a place, especially as it was my fault we lost our old one.'

There's a knock at the door, and Sophie steps in, carrying a bottle of wine and a corkscrew. 'Well? Are we celebrating?'

I look at Harry and although he shrugs nonchalantly, I can see the excited twinkle in his eyes.

'We're in,' I say, unable to stop myself smiling.

'Yay!' Sophie twists the corkscrew into the bottle. 'There should be some glasses in the cupboard above the sink.'

Harry goes to the cupboard to fetch the glasses, while I move to the back door, and stare out into the wide overgrown garden, spotting the gate in the rear fence.

'Do you mind if I have a look in the garden?' I ask.

'No, key should be in the door,' Sophie says, as she extracts the cork, and sloshes wine into the three glasses Harry is holding.

I take one as it's passed to me, unlock the door and step out into the warm sunshine. The tall grass dampens the hem of my jeans as I move through it towards the gate, which is fitted with a shiny new padlock.

I can't wait to tell Carly about the bargain we've just secured. I'm currently earning £800 a month, working part-time in the supermarket, which means with the low rent for this room, I might actually be able to start saving some money.

I turn to head back to the house when I hear a whimpering

sound. At first, I can't see where it's coming from, but as I move towards it, I soon spot the small kitten lying in the tall grass.

'Hello there,' I say, before I realise it's whimpering in pain.

Balancing my glass on a mound of earth, I pull blades of grass away from the kitten and soon realise it's trapped in some sort of wire mechanism. It tries to shrink away as I move my hands closer, and I hush soothingly, trying to tell it that I'm not going to hurt it. The wire is barbed and has been twisted into a sort of noose, with the other end secured to a hook in the ground. I put my hands around the kitten delicately and move it to rest between my legs, allowing me to carefully widen the noose. I cut my finger in the process, but it slips off the kitten's neck, and the poor thing jumps away with relief.

The kitten isn't wearing a collar, but I can see red welts where the barbs must have punctured its skin. I'm not going to let it go without treatment. If I'm lucky, its owners were smart enough to microchip it.

I snuggle the kitten close to me as I collect my glass from the ground and stand, wondering what kind of sick person would create something so cruel.

5

PRESENT DAY

'It reminds me of the night of the blackout,' Sophie says, and the hairs on the back of my neck stand.

I don't think Christophe and Harry can have heard her as they're still splashing about in the hot tub, but I see the way Rhys shakes his head before heading down into the galley.

I pull Sophie closer to me. 'Why the hell would you bring *that* up now?'

She pulls herself free of my grip, and rubs at her wrist gingerly. 'I just meant...' She lowers her eyes. 'I'm sorry, I didn't mean anything by it.'

As I look out to the horizon, it certainly does seem as black and endless as when a storm knocked out power across the campus, but I don't want to be reminded of it – and she knows why better than anyone else.

'Forget I mentioned it,' she says quickly. 'How about we drink to absent friends instead?'

Is she deliberately trying to sink the mood? Woody is noticeably missing from this reunion, and I assumed someone would have offered an explanation as to why he wasn't invited, but it seems I'm not the only one trying to focus on the present.

'You should have brought Carly with you,' she says next. 'Get the whole gang back together.'

'She's on Simone's hen do at Glasto,' I say evenly, 'but you should give her a call when we're back. I'm sure she'd love to catch up.'

'Have you two set a date for your big day yet? Feels like you've been together forever.'

We get asked this question so often that I now have an automated response ready to regurgitate. 'We're happy as we are. I love her, and she loves me. We always said we would have a long engagement, and it's not like the world has been settled enough recently to actually host a wedding, has it? Throw in all those postponed weddings due to the pandemic, and it just doesn't feel like the right time.' It's not exactly the truth. If I had my way, Carly and I would have set a date by now, but she wants to take it slow, and I'm okay with that. 'We have a mortgage together, which is a bigger commitment. I have a friend who practises family law, and he reckons it takes less time and money to get divorced than it does to get out of a mortgage contract.'

I realise how cold this sounds so decide to flip the conversation.

'What about you? Are there no eligible bachelors you have your eye on?'

She narrows her eyes. 'You know what they say: all the best ones are married... or gay.'

I start as Harry slaps me on the shoulder. 'What's the craic? Am I interrupting something?'

I shake my head. 'No, all good here. You all right?'

'Apart from not having a drink in my hand. Can I get you two anything?'

'I'll go,' Sophie says quickly. 'I need to use the toilet anyway.'

She slips away, and it feels like it's a deliberate move to avoid any more awkward questions. She doesn't look back as she descends the steps into the galley.

Harry takes her place on the bench. 'What's the story, horse? Sorry, were the two of you in the middle of something? Didn't mean to be a third wheel.'

'Not at all.'

'Because if you were thinking about... you know... far from it for me to get in your way.' I don't follow at first, until he wiggles his eyebrows, and adds, 'What happens at sea stays at sea.'

Harry's my best friend, but he knows I don't agree with that thinking. Cheating is cheating, and I abhor it in all its forms.

'No, Harry,' I say firmly. 'I was just checking that Soph was okay. So, if you want to try it on with her, be my guest.'

He looks at me ruefully. 'That ship sailed a long time ago. Didn't I tell you I made a move back when we were in the house?'

I shake my head, though I can't say I'm surprised, recalling how promiscuous Harry was in those days; probably still is.

'It wasn't long after we moved in, but she made it very clear that she wasn't interested in hooking up, even for a casual, no-strings kind of thing. I told her how considerate a lover I am, but she left me on me tod. I got the impression that she was secretly holding a torch for someone else, though she's never admitted as much.'

My cheeks burn. I try to steer the conversation away from where I sense it is heading. 'I'm surprised Woody's not here.'

'Couldn't get hold of the fecker. The number I had for him is out of service, and he never responded to the mountain of emails I sent. I told him exactly where we were headed and when, but not a peep back. I asked Fergus if he could have a word, but he said not to bother.'

Simone's not mentioned anything about Fergus falling out with Woody, and as far as I was aware, they were still thick as thieves, but then again, Simone and I aren't as close as we once were; not since she and Fergus got together.

Sophie returns with two glasses and a bottle of Jameson's that she hands over to Harry. He pours us each a generous measure and passes me a glass. 'Sláinte!'

'Cheers,' I respond, clinking my glass against his.

'I assume you've planned something obnoxiously embarrassing for Fergus tomorrow?' Sophie asks.

Harry cocks a solitary eyebrow. 'Rest assured, I have a suitcase full of props to really get this party started. Once we dock at Paradise Cove, he'll realise what a terrible mistake he's made in asking me to host his stag party.'

I don't even want to think about where Harry's twisted imagination has taken him, but I can imagine Fergus is going to find himself naked and restrained at some point over the coming days. I'll do my best to make sure Fergus remains safe, thinking back on my promise to Simone, but there's also a part of me looking forward to seeing him humbled once and for all.

Sophie slaps her hands against the cushion. 'I think I'm going to turn in for the night. I'll see you both in the morning.'

Harry leans forward. 'Remember, if you get lonely later, I'm in the cabin between Pete and Fergus.' He winks, but she doesn't respond.

'Seriously, dude,' I warn him after she's left, 'you'd best not plan any dodgy pranks when you're my best man.'

He holds out his hand, and I slap mine into it. 'You know I wouldn't dare get on the wrong side of your Carly. Besides, you haven't asked me to be your best man yet, and I don't know if I'm available on that day. I might be busy washing my hair.' He runs a hand through the thick head of curls and pouts.

'Of course you're going to be my best man. Who else would I ask?'

'Well, that's true, there aren't many others who would put up with your lack of social skills and way-too-sensible attitude.'

He clinks his glass against mine again, and sips the whiskey.

I can feel Christophe staring at us from the hot tub, but when I look over, he quickly averts his eyes.

I lean closer to Harry so I can whisper. 'Tell me I'm being crazy, but is there a weird vibe on board?'

He leans in too. 'Not that I've noticed. What do you mean?'

I don't want to mention what I overheard Rhys telling Sophie in the corridor, nor the fact that Rhys and Christophe have barely said two words to me since I arrived.

'I don't know, it's just... forget about it, I'm probably just being paranoid.'

He wraps an arm around my shoulders and presses his forehead against mine. 'Listen, once we dock in Paradise Cove tomorrow, what say you and I ditch these others and make the most of the resort? All-inclusive food and drink, sun, sea and sand – let's treat it like the lads' holiday we always talked about but never quite organised?'

I nod and force myself not to look as Christophe climbs out of the hot tub and stomps towards the galley.

6

TEN YEARS AGO

'Where the hell is Fergus?' Sophie sighs, checking her watch for the umpteenth time, her steady pacing of the kitchen-diner increasing with every passing minute.

'I'm sure he'll be here,' I offer reassuringly, but in truth, I have no idea where he is.

In the two weeks since Harry and I moved in, I'd assumed I would have bonded best with Fergus, given we occupy the two ground-floor rooms, but it hasn't been the case. I never really see him, with him not emerging from his room until after I've hurried off to the campus for seminars or lectures, and he doesn't seem to return until the early hours most days – and I only know this because he's rarely quiet when he does make it in, despite Sophie's repeated reminders. During the week, he keeps the hours of a vampire, and each weekend he's either watching or playing sport with his best friend Woody, who treats the place as his own.

'Was I not clear when I told everyone to meet in the kitchen at six?' she asks, glaring at each of the four of us in turn.

The question is rhetorical, but I still feel compelled to answer. 'We all knew. Maybe he's just been held up by work or something.

Why don't we get started and then I can fill him in when he gets here?'

I've not seen Sophie looking so ill at ease since we took that timid kitten to the vet for treatment, later learning – thanks to the microchip in its neck – that it belonged to a neighbour. The poor thing hasn't been back to the garden in the weeks since, and I've completed a thorough search to ensure no similar archaic devices are present.

Sophie finally stops pacing and takes a seat at the table. She drains the remainder of what was in her wine glass, and takes a deep breath, the tension in her shoulders easing. 'This party tonight: we have to do it in the right way. God forbid Raymond ever finds out we've organised a housewarming.'

'It's technically a garden party,' Rhys interjects, misreading the situation. 'The rules are we're not allowed a "house party". What it is, is: if we keep everyone in the garden, then we have nothing to worry about.'

Sophie raises a sceptical eyebrow. 'That's exactly why I wanted to speak with you all before people start arriving. We have to make sure nobody gets inside the house. We've only invited a few people, so the garden should be more than big enough for everyone not to feel like sardines.'

I notice the others break eye contact with Sophie, and she picks up on it immediately. 'We made a list of who we were going to invite,' she says evenly. 'You did all stick to that list, right?'

I actually only invited Carly and she was on Sophie's approved list, so I know I haven't broken my promise, but I'm not sure the same can be said for the others in the room, and there's no way of knowing who Fergus invited as he still hasn't returned.

'Harry?' she says in the deep, disapproving tone that instantly makes me think of my father the day he caught me smoking.

Harry's head bobs as he searches for somewhere to focus his eyes, anywhere that keeps Sophie out of his periphery.

'Christ on a bike!' he blurts out. 'Okay, so maybe I went a bit beyond what we agreed, but there's this girl on my course I've been desperate to get to know better, and she said she had a sister visiting from Newcastle, and so I said she could come too, and—'

The table shakes as Sophie slams her palm on the top. 'And the rest of you?'

Rhys gulps audibly, and Christophe turns away, lowering the oven door to check on whatever he's baking. Sophie pours the remains of the rosé into her glass.

'I'm sure it'll be fine,' I say, with a calm I'm not feeling. 'We'll keep the patio doors locked, and then nobody will be able to get inside. We'll get everyone to come in through the gate at the bottom of the garden.'

'We can't prevent people using the bathroom?' Harry counters.

'The hell we can't,' Sophie snaps back. 'If they need to pee, they can go across to the trees beyond the rear fence; God knows enough winos have probably done far worse there. He ripped up the tenancy agreement with the last residents because they had a party and didn't ask permission.'

'You need to relax, Soph. There's no way Raymond can know we're having a party. It'll be fine.'

Sophie glares at him, but doesn't say anything.

Harry sighs. 'Okay, how about we keep the door to the rest of the house closed, and lock each of our rooms?'

The front door slamming echoes along the hallway, and Fergus appears in the doorway, nodding at each of us. 'What's going on here then? WI meeting, is it?'

Sophie's face darkens, but I jump into the firing line. 'We're having the house meeting Sophie asked us to attend, remember?'

He seems to pick up on the hint. 'Oh, aye, sorry I'm late... lecture overran.'

The fact that Fergus and Christophe are on the same course and the latter has been home for over an hour already clearly shows Fergus's lie, but thankfully Sophie chooses to ignore it.

'We're just setting ground rules for tonight,' she says. 'We've all agreed that nobody is allowed beyond the kitchen. That okay with you?'

He shrugs nonchalantly and crosses the room towards the patio. He already has a cigarette between his lips and a shiny silver lighter in his hands when Sophie asks where he's going.

'For a smoke. That all right with you, Mam?'

'What about the house meeting?'

He shrugs again, reaching for the door handle. 'I haven't invited anyone anyway, so if there's trouble, it'll have nothing to do with me.'

Sophie looks as though she might chase after him and drive her glass into his throat, so I rest my hand on hers. 'Relax, everything is going to be fine. We'll do what Harry suggested and keep everyone from breaching this room. We've filled a bin with ice, and beer and wine, and it's a warm evening, so most will want to be outside anyway. Besides, you said Raymond isn't even around this weekend, and we'll have the place spick and span before Monday.'

Her eyes glisten in the artificial light, searching my face for any trace of deceit. I pull my hand away, and smile reassuringly.

'Usual rules apply too,' she says to the room. 'No smoking in the house, and I don't want any of your male friends hitting on me.' She stands and scoops up her glass, a little unsteady on her feet. 'I need to go and get changed.'

She's wearing a crimson mini dress and a cream pashmina, so I assumed she was already dressed.

Rhys and Harry follow her out of the room and three sets of feet on the stairs can soon be heard. I stand and move across to Christophe, who is busy rolling out pastry.

'You need a hand with anything?'

He's seen how much of a struggle it is for me to cook anything beyond pasta and a jar of pesto, and shakes his head politely.

'What's all this in aid of, anyway? It's only a few students, who probably aren't expecting food.'

He pushes the glasses up his nose with a floury finger. 'But the way to a woman's heart is through the stomach, no?'

I don't correct him.

'Aye, that's exactly what will tempt a wee lassie,' Fergus calls out from the patio door. 'A virgin who's never even been with a woman.'

The cloud of smoke that follows Fergus as he comes back in is overpowering, and I have to step away as he nears Christophe and picks up a piece of the mozzarella that has been sliced in preparation for the pizza.

Fergus opens and closes the lid of the metal lighter as he encroaches on Christophe's space as if waiting for some reaction, before boredom takes over and he heads off to his room.

* * *

I watch Rhys chatting away to a group of four women, and wish I had his confidence. He has them hanging on his every word. I've never been able to walk over to a stranger and strike up a conversation. Whenever I'm introduced to someone new, my mouth dries up, and my brain goes to sleep. If Carly hadn't approached me at that wedding, we wouldn't have spoken, certainly wouldn't have danced, and I wouldn't have given her my number. I do hope she hurries up, otherwise I'm going to be Billy-no-mates for the rest of the night. I can't see Harry amongst the thirty or so people dancing.

Then there's a tap on my shoulder, and a breathless Christophe is standing behind me.

'Have you seen Soph?'

I casually wave my hand around the garden. 'I'm sure she's here somewhere. Why? What's going on?'

'You need to find her. Tell her Raymond is here, and he is pissed off.'

He heads back in through the patio doors without another word, and I move further into the garden, into the partial darkness, scanning faces, looking for Sophie. When I find no sign of her, I head back in, up the stairs and knock on her door, before passing on Christophe's message.

'Shit! How the bloody hell did he find out about the party?'

'I don't know, but maybe he's here for a different reason. If we can keep him in the front room, he might never find out we have people in the garden.'

She scowls at me. 'If he's here, he already knows. He was supposed to be away this weekend. Shit, shit, shit.'

She pushes me out of the way and hurries down the stairs and into the living room, plastering on a warm and welcoming smile.

'Raymond, what a pleasant surprise,' she says too loudly. 'To what do we owe this pleasure?'

This is my first encounter with Raymond Grosjean, and even I can feel the anger oozing out of his every pore. He's wearing a black leather biker's jacket, which looks about two sizes too big and emphasises his emaciated frame. His thinning hair hangs long and uncombed around his face, framing the rough skin of his red cheeks. I can't tell whether his face is always this shade of radish or it's just as a result of our actions.

'You broke rule one.' His deep Cornish brogue resonates.

Sophie holds up a finger in challenge, but he isn't willing to listen, raising his own hand to cut her off before she even tries to talk her way out of trouble.

'You knew the stipulations when you signed the agreement.'

It's at this moment that I realise I don't actually know what these stipulations are. Sophie made reference to there being certain rules when she first showed Harry and me around the place, but she's never actually produced a list of them for us to see.

She sighs dramatically. 'You're right, we knew the stipulations.' She pauses, and then moves her hand to his arm, walking her index and middle fingers down to his hand. 'But I'm sure there's some kind of arrangement you and I can come to, to resolve this hiccough.'

His glare softens as he meets her eyes.

'Why don't you and I go and iron out the details in my room?' she says, pressing her tiny hand into his, and pulling him towards the door, reaching for the open bottle of Scotch on the sideboard as she does so.

My stomach turns.

I step forward and block her path to the door and whisper, 'You don't have to do this.'

She rests a hand on my cheek. 'It's okay. I'm fine. Trust me.'

I look to Christophe, willing him to say something, but he seems comfortable with what's about to happen. The staircase creaks as she leads him up.

I can't picture anything but Sophie trying to seduce Raymond, and my stomach turns. It's a relief when the doorbell sounds, and I open it to see Carly on the doorstep with a bottle of white in one hand, a bottle of red in the other.

'I wasn't sure what to bring for a housewarming,' she says,

leaning forward and pecking me on the cheek. 'Are you all right? You look peaky.'

I throw my arms around her shoulders and kiss her. 'All the better now that you're here. Come on in and I'll introduce you to the others.'

Christophe is no longer in the lounge-diner, so I lead Carly through the house and into the garden where I find him standing beside Fergus and Rhys, presumably filling them in on what's just happened.

'Guys, this is Carly,' I say, hugging her close. 'Carly, this is Fergus.'

She hands him the two bottles. 'It's nice to meet you.'

'And this is Christophe,' I continue. 'And finally, this is Rhys.'

She leans in as if she's about to kiss his cheek, but then thinks better of it and offers him her hand. He shakes it limply, but the whole exchange is just plain awkward.

'It's nice to meet you, Rhys,' she says with less enthusiasm.

'Crackin',' he says, but even in the dim light I can see his cheeks flushing.

I can't say why, but there's something not right about this.

'Can I get a glass of wine?' Carly asks, taking my hand and pulling me away from the others.

'Sure,' I say, leading her to the ice bucket, and reaching for a bottle and a fresh plastic glass.

She takes a long swig before squeezing my hand. 'Do you want to dance?'

She doesn't wait for me to respond, just takes my hand and drags me towards the patch of grass where others are dancing to the music. She holds me close, slowly circling, but it feels as if we're being watched. When I turn to look, I see Rhys's stare burning a hole in the back of Carly's head.

7

PRESENT DAY

I wake with a start and the sense that something isn't right. Sitting up in bed, I strain my eyes to see anything, not recognising my whereabouts until I remember I'm in the cabin on board the yacht. There is a small glow leaking out from behind the drawn blind, but barely enough to see past the foot of the bed. I reach for my phone where it's charging on the nightstand and see it's a little after seven. I'm surprised Joaquín hasn't started the engines yet, but maybe he was late rising after Rhys pounced on Elena last night. In fact, I'm sure there was a thumping sound that just woke me, so perhaps the two of them are just starting to get organised.

I lie still as the yacht gently buffers from side to side. I definitely couldn't get used to living on a boat. I'm managing to keep the nausea at bay with over-the-counter medication, and I know we've been lucky enough to avoid any rough sea so far. Bring me the safety and comfort of our two-bedroom apartment in the city any day.

I reach for the phone again, keen to know whether Carly's messaged, but as I unlock my screen, I see the Wi-Fi is still down, and the message I sent to her hasn't been delivered. There's still no mobile signal either. I feel guilty that I told Fergus everything would probably be back up and running by the time we woke up. The mood really soured last night, as he was so worried about whatever Simone was about to tell him before the line died. Knowing how dramatic my sister can be, coupled with the fact that Carly didn't call me, I'm sure it's nothing to be worried about. It was reassuring to see how deeply he cares for Simone, though. Maybe he really has changed from the overbearing, fiery bully I remember from university.

Even so, I can't just lie here and wait for his anger to boil, so I push back the thin sheet and locate a pair of shorts and a T-shirt, which I slip into. In the mirror, my dark brown hair looks as though I've been dragged backwards through a hedge, so I quickly brush through it with my fingers. I'll never be the most handsome guy on board, but it will do.

I unlock my door and slide it open as quietly as I can for fear of waking any of the others. Remembering what they were like when we lived together, sleep deprivation and hangovers is not a healthy cocktail. My head doesn't feel too bad this morning, though my mouth is as dry as the Sahara.

I make my way to the galley, find a used glass that I rinse under the tap and then fill with cold water. I drain and refill it, before climbing up the galley steps and through the open hatch onto deck. Joaquín and Elena are nowhere to be seen, which explains why I can't hear the engine.

The remains of last night's drinking session greet me. Empty tubes of Pringles lie scattered on the deck floor, along with empty wine and beer bottles, and a deck of cards. Having located a black bin liner beneath the sink in the galley, I wait until I'm back on deck before shaking it open and slowly fill it with our litter. I catch sight of the empty raised cockpit. I'm sure Joaquín said we would need to be sailing by seven if we were to make up time, but it's already past that; the bright orange sun is almost totally clear of the horizon.

Where on earth are they? Would it be rude for me to knock and wake them? If Paradise Cove is as relaxing as Harry suggested, I'd hate to miss any of our allotted time there. Just stepping back onto dry land is a respite my body would appreciate.

'Morning,' I hear Sophie say in a loud whisper, as she stifles a yawn and emerges from her cabin. She's dressed in an oversized chequered shirt, the buttons unfastened, revealing perfectly toned abs. It seems giving up alcohol isn't the only health kick she's on. I hope the open shirt isn't for my benefit, but after what she whispered last night, I can't be sure. I don't want to hurt her feelings, but equally it'll only be worse if I inadvertently lead her on.

'Morning. Sleep well?'

She nods. 'Like a lamb. You?'

I nod. 'I'm looking forward to getting back on dry land, though.'

'I have some wrist bands for travel sickness if you'd like to borrow them?'

'Thanks. I should be fine once we dock.'

She smiles at me. 'It's funny, you know, when I first acknowledged my alcohol dependency, I was terrified that I'd never be able to drop off to sleep naturally. There were periods before I was prepared to admit I had a problem where I would drink every day for weeks, just to ensure I would be able to fall asleep and get a few hours before I had to be up for work. And I'm not going to say the first few days of sobriety weren't tough, but I now cherish my sleep-filled nights. I used to wake up two to three times a night to have a drink or pee, and now most nights I sleep right through.' She yawns again. 'In fact, I'd probably still be asleep if I hadn't heard that thumping sound. Did you drop something?'

'No.' I frown. 'I've been as quiet as a mouse, but now that you mention it, I think something woke me up as well. No idea what, though, as we appear to be the only two to have surfaced so far.'

She laughs. 'Poor Elena. We probably should have warned her about Rhys's voracious appetite.' She suddenly catches herself. 'Sorry, I didn't mean—'

'Forget about it,' I say, straining a smile so she knows I'm not offended. 'Wi-Fi's still down. Do you reckon we could locate the router and try to fix it before Fergus rises? He'll be like a bear with a sore head if he doesn't get hold of my sister.'

'Sure. Any ideas where it is?'

I haven't seen anything resembling a router since we boarded.

'I know that the signal is strongest in my cabin,' I say, 'so I'd estimate it's more likely to be at the bow of the boat.'

She stretches her arms over her head and yawns once more, before playfully slapping herself around the face. 'Once we've switched it off and on again, my vote is fresh coffee, and cracking open that packet of croissants I saw Elena stashing in the galley.'

I hadn't realised how hungry I was, but the mention of coffee and pastries is met with a gurgle of agreement.

Sophie leads the way through the hatch and galley, towards the V-berth, which Elena said was where she and Joaquín would be sleeping. It would make sense for the router to be kept where she can undertake any necessary maintenance, I suppose. Sophie knocks on the door to the berth. We stand waiting for either Joaquín or Elena to emerge, but there's no sound from within. Sophie tries the door handle, but it's locked.

'Elena might still be with Rhys,' she says, squeezing past me in the narrow space and moving towards the last door on our right, closest to the bathroom.

She tries the handle but it doesn't move, so she proceeds to knock until Rhys calls out, 'I'll be there in a minute.'

Rhys slides the door open, one hand precariously across his

genitals, and rubs sleep out of his eyes with the other. 'What do you want?'

I avert my gaze. 'Sorry to wake you,' I say, 'but we were hoping Elena might be able to fix the router before Fergus gets up. Also, the captain said he wanted to set sail at seven, but it's nearly half past and we're still not moving.'

He blinks several times and stifles a yawn, trying to process the information. 'I'm not being funny, but Elena's not in here.'

'What do you mean she's not in there?' Sophie asks, trying to peer through the gap in the doorway. 'We saw you drag her in last night, and don't forget these walls are paper thin. I'm pretty sure even the sharks heard the two of you going at it.'

Rhys smiles proudly at this. 'Fair dos. She *was* in here, obviously, but left ages ago. I got up and went to the toilet around three and she'd already gone. I assume she's in her room. Go try banging down her door, will you?'

He moves to slide the door closed, his interest lost.

'We already tried her room, but there's no answer,' I say quickly, pressing my hand to the closing door.

He frowns at this. 'Oh, well, have you checked in the cockpit? If she's not in her room, she must be helping the captain.'

The hairs stand on the back of my neck, but I try to ignore them. 'She's not on deck.'

Rhys's eyes fly to Harry's cabin door. 'I'm not being funny, but if she's hooked up with that leprechaun now, I'll—'

Oh, no, I hope she didn't sleep with Rhys and then stop by Harry's for a second booty call.

Sophie manages to restrain Rhys long enough for me to get to Harry's cabin first. I try the handle and it opens, but Harry is alone in bed. He stirs as he hears Rhys's noises of struggle. He's chomping at the bit to get in.

'What's the craic?' he asks, sitting up, his eyes barely open.

'You haven't seen Elena by any chance, have you?'

He flops back onto his pillow. 'Try Rhys's room. It was him she went off with.'

'She's not in Rhys's room and she's not answering the door to the V-berth.'

Hearing the debate, Christophe and Fergus open their doors.

'Do either of you know where Elena or Joaquín are?' Sophie asks.

Both shake their heads.

'What's going on?' Fergus asks. 'What time is it?'

'About half past seven.' I sigh. 'We should have set sail half an hour ago, and there's no sign of our captain and hostess.'

Christophe squeezes into the corridor and knocks on the door to the V-berth. 'Elena? You are in there?'

We all wait to hear a response, but there's nothing.

'What if she's banged her head and passed out?' Fergus asks.

'We have no choice but to barge the door down to check,' Sophie says, reasoning, but Rhys is quick to leap to her defence, claiming Elena has a right to privacy.

A moment later, we hear the sound of the latch sliding open inside the V-berth, but when the door opens, it isn't Joaquín or Elena, but Christophe.

'How did you...?' I begin to ask.

'There's window access to the deck above.' He points at the source of light in the low ceiling of the berth. 'I opened it and dropped in. They're not in there, though.'

We look at each other in turn; with Christophe's track record, none of us are surprised that he managed to get into the room. But where the hell can Joaquín and Elena have gone? And why would they go without leaving at least a note to advise why?

'By the way,' Christophe continues, 'did one of you have anything to do with dropping the anchor?'

The question throws me at first. 'No. Joaquín said he was lowering it last night so we wouldn't float away.'

'That's kind of my point,' Christophe says. 'The anchor is gone. The chain is broken, and I think maybe we have been adrift for some time.'

8

TEN YEARS AGO

I'm exhausted when I return from work, and am immediately put out by the sound of revving engines and yelling coming from the front room. I'm not surprised to find Fergus spread out on the sofa, the lights off, save for the large-screen television in the corner, displaying F-1 highlights. There's a girl on the other couch beside Christophe.

With a strong head cold and having spent the last six hours stuck on a busy checkout at my part-time job, my intention was to come home, pop a couple of painkillers and hit the sack. So much for best-laid plans.

I knock gently on the door, but neither Fergus, Christophe, nor the stranger seem to hear me, so I knock louder. I hate to be a killjoy, but I'm due back at the supermarket first thing, and I'm shattered.

'Hey, Fergus, do you think you could lower the volume a bit? I was hoping to grab an early one.'

He looks up, and ushers me inside, reducing the volume. 'What'd you say?'

I move further into the room, vaguely recognising the girl, but unable to place from where.

'Just that I'm looking to hit the sack, so was asking if you guys can keep it down a bit?'

'Sure, sure, oh, by the way, this is Woody from our lacrosse team. I dinnae think the two of you have met yet. Woody and his girlfriend were going to move in with us originally, but then Soph vetoed the idea.'

This is awkward. I recall Sophie mentioning another couple being interested, and now I feel like an imposter. I'm never great at meeting new people, but the fact that he probably knows more about me than I do about him has me on edge. Woody is half the size of Fergus, but still towers over me in height and mass. With his bulging biceps, a chiselled jawline, and long highlighted hair, it wouldn't surprise me to learn that he models in his spare time. He offers a hand, but doesn't stand up. I shake it because I feel obliged to do so, and try not to wince as he squeezes hard.

'Woody?' I say to fill the awkward silence. 'As in the cowboy from *Toy Story*?'

He doesn't look amused.

'It's a nickname,' he says with an American accent – west coast. California, maybe? 'My name's James Woods, but everyone just calls me Woody for short.'

I nod, remaining standing, racking my brain for something I can say that won't make me look like the socially awkward buffoon I am. 'So, were you named after the actor James Woods then?'

He stares back at me blankly.

'You know, he was in *Casino* with Robert De Niro and Sharon Stone? He was also in a tonne of other films, but can't think of any titles.'

The look of confusion remains on Woody's face, but he nods. 'Yeah, exactly.'

'For fuck's sake,' Fergus suddenly yells, drawing all of our attention to what's unfolding on the television. 'Don't do that! Why the fuck is he pitting now? He's lapping quicker than the rest and should build up more of a gap. I canny believe it!'

I'm familiar with F-1, but it isn't a sport I follow, and am just about to wish them all good night, when Fergus turns and looks at me. 'Grab a seat, and help yourself to a beer,' he says, pointing at the box of cans on the carpet near my feet.

I don't know how to respond, and just want to go to my room, but Fergus grabs my arm and drags me down to the seat beside him, before passing me a can from the box. Christophe watches on. Is that envy in his eyes?

'Woody was just telling us a story he heard about the coach.' They must pick up on my confusion, as Fergus quickly adds, 'Raymond Grosjean.' He looks over to Woody. 'Tell him what you were telling us about your mate.'

Woody sits forward, the flashing lights of the television casting a haunting flicker across his face, with only his eyes properly visible. 'I have this buddy who has a sister who used to live here. She was one of six girls, all on the same nursing course, or something. Anyway, my buddy told me they were absolutely terrified of creepy old Raymond and his even creepier mother. They reckoned this old house was haunted by a dead spirit.'

My eyes scan the area of the room directly in front of me. I catch Christophe staring at me, but his skin is pale, his eyes wide as if fraught with worry.

'She would tell my buddy – her brother – how all sorts of weird shit would happen when nobody else was around. Things would get moved in locked rooms, strange noises in the middle of the night, that kind of thing. And Raymond always seemed to know what was going on, as if he was in communication with some spirit inside the place. It got to the point where they couldn't stand it any more and asked to cancel the lease.'

I think back to the night of the housewarming and how Raymond turned up uninvited when he was supposed to have been away for the weekend.

'After she moved out, she tried to complain to the university but they wouldn't listen, so she did some digging of her own. She couldn't find any mention of him online. No digital footprint whatsoever, which is weird in itself in this day and age. Then she stumbled upon a news story from back in the sixties talking about a Raymond Grosjean *Senior*, whose body had been discovered at the foot of the stairs of this very house. He wasn't a drinker, and was in fairly good health, so the police investigated and his wife – Dorothy Grosjean – fell under suspicion, but they couldn't prove she had anything to do with it. The case remains unsolved to this day. Raymond Junior was eight years old, and it's alleged he was the one to find his father's body. That's got to leave you pretty fucked up, if you ask me.'

'Maybe it was the kid who pushed his old man down the stairs,' Fergus adds quietly. It's enough to make me jolt. 'What do you reckon, Pete? Is this place haunted by the old man's ghost?'

In my periphery, I can see him grinning at Woody, and I realise now this is nothing more than a ploy to try to freak me out. Maybe it's possible the pair of them have hatched this story to convince me and Harry to move out so Woody and his girlfriend can take our place.

I look at Christophe again to see if he's in on the act, but his brow is furrowed, and his eyes won't stop scanning the room.

'Are you all right?' I ask.

He doesn't answer. Instead, he stands and stomps out. I hear him hurry up both flights of stairs and then slam the door to the attic room.

Fergus erupts with laughter, extending his can towards Woody, who smashes his own can against it. 'I told you he'd freak out!' he roars. 'What a wet blanket!'

'Man, I thought you were gassing me when you said he suffered with panic attacks.' Woody chuckles. 'Do you think we should check on him?'

I think back to the few times I've spoken with Christophe. I thought he was just shy and awkward, but now that I think about it, it could just have easily been social anxiety. I'm about to excuse myself when Fergus barks at the television again.

'I feckin' knew he shouldn't have pitted! What's wrong with that bampot?' He turns back to face us, muting the television in frustration. 'If you ask me, all this talk about anxiety attacks is pish. Peoples need to stop being so melodramatic.'

I want to pull him up on his out-of-date attitude, but something holds me back. My own anxiety about confrontation, maybe?

'S'all mind over matter if yous ask me,' Fergus continues, waving his hand dismissively. 'I had a friend who was clinically diagnosed with depression, managed to cure himself just by putting his mind to it. According to my old man, there was no such thing as mental health during the Second World War and people there survived the Blitz and the constant threat of death. They just bloody well got on with things. Imagine if war broke out now; there'd be no bairns left to fight because they'd all be running off to seek a doctor's note.'

I want to tell him that many people's poor mental health goes undiagnosed for far too long, but I know I'll be fighting a losing battle. Instead, I stretch my hands above my head, and wish them a good evening, before departing. But once I'm inside and the door is locked behind me, I can't stop thinking about what Woody said: *They reckoned this old house was haunted by a dead spirit.*

9

PRESENT DAY

We all hurry to the deck, but there isn't room for all of us to squeeze around to the bow, so I hang back at the stern with Harry, while the rest go to check the bow. When I was cleaning the main deck moments ago, I hadn't noticed we were drifting, but sure enough, there's definite movement as the others hurry to the front to witness the broken anchor chain.

I'm feeling nauseous, but can't bear the thought of food. *There must be a simple explanation*, I tell myself. *Now is not the time for panic.*

'Do you think there could be another room we haven't checked?' Harry asks. 'You know, like a cellar or something?'

Flashes of blood on the cellar staircase rise to my mind's eye, and I have to chase them away.

'I don't think yachts work like that,' I reply absently.

'What about an engine room? Presumably yachts get serviced like a car would, so there must be some means of getting to the engine. What if they're down there now and aren't even aware we're looking for them?'

'I think they'd have heard us calling for them by now.'

'But what if they're trapped? Or bumped their heads and passed out?'

Harry's imagination is getting the better of him, and I put a comforting arm around his shoulder, and sit us on the bench. 'I'm sure nothing bad has happened to them.'

His hand shoots to his mouth and he gasps. 'What if they fell overboard and have been eaten by a shark?'

I picture the razor-sharp teeth of the blue shark from last night. Could Joaquín have been up here getting ready to set sail when a shark charged the yacht, causing him to topple in? There was a noise that woke me, but that can't be it. He showed yesterday he's a strong swimmer, and wouldn't we have heard him screaming had he been attacked? And what about Elena?

It also doesn't explain why the anchor chain has been cut. There's only one explanation for that, as far as I can deduce: someone wanted to leave us drifting.

Rhys is the first to return, and I've never seen him looking so pale. 'Christophe was right: the anchor is gone. Looks like the chain has been unclipped from the boat, rather than actually cut. God knows where it is now. Presumably at the bottom of the sea.'

Fergus and Sophie are next to return to the deck, equally bemused.

I fix my stare on Rhys. 'What time did you last see Elena?'

'I already told you: I woke up around three and she wasn't in my room.'

'Was it just before three, or after? Please try and remember exactly what time it was.'

He puffs out his cheeks. 'I woke up, and realised the space beside me was cold, so I just assumed she'd gone back to her own room – so nobody would judge her for what we'd done. I thought fair dos. I decided to get up and grab a drink of water because I was thirsty, like. I went to the galley and grabbed a bottle of mineral water from the fridge, had a few sips, and went to the toilet. I got back into bed, and I glanced at my phone. I think it said 3.10.'

'Did you see or hear anything else when you were in the galley?'

He shakes his head, before snapping his fingers together, remembering something. 'Someone was snoring really loudly.' He stares at Fergus, but doesn't say his name. 'Apart from that, nothing.'

'Did you see if the door to the V-berth was open or closed?'

He shakes his head and shrugs. 'I didn't notice. I was half asleep.'

'But you didn't hear anybody moving about on deck?'

'No. Anyway, the hatch was closed and locked from inside, so there couldn't have been anyone out there.'

My eyes widen. 'The hatch was open when I got up just after seven, which means someone must have opened it.' I look at each of my friends individually, waiting for one of them to speak up, but I only see stony faces staring back at me. 'So not a single one of you opened the hatch and came up on deck?'

Christophe comes over. 'I know I didn't. I was asleep until I heard you all talking in the corridor.'

I take a breath, trying to engage the rational side of my brain. 'So we're saying Elena hasn't been seen since some time before three, allowing for the bedsheet to have cooled. Did anyone hear someone else moving about during the night?'

Fergus raises his hand into the air. 'I also got up to use the bathroom. I think it must have been just after Rhys, as the tank was filling back up from just being flushed. I didn't check the time specifically, but it felt like I'd been asleep for a fair while.'

'I can't think of any reason why Elena would disconnect the anchor,' I say, 'so let's park that for a second, and try and work out where she and Joaquín have gone. There's no obvious land nearby, and given how serious he was when warning us about swimming, I don't imagine they've gone for a paddle, so what does that leave?'

Sophie stands and stares at the back of the boat. She gradually raises her arm and points. 'The dinghy and outboard are gone.'

All of our heads snap round. She's right: the inflatable dinghy which we were supposed to be using to get from the yacht to Paradise Cove is no longer there.

'The wee shites have abandoned us?' Fergus barks. 'Bloody typical!'

'I'm sure they didn't abandon us,' I scoff, though anything is possible. 'Well, at least that explains how they've vanished into thin air. They must have taken the dinghy for some reason. Maybe they realised we were missing something, or Joaquín found some kind of mechanical issue with the yacht, and he's gone to find something to repair it.'

I don't believe the words as they tumble from my mouth, and I don't think Sophie is prepared to buy it either, based on her pout. There's no reason for them both to have left without at least leaving a note to explain where they are. And with us adrift, how on earth would they find their way back? No, something definitely doesn't add up, but I don't want to think about the reasons for that.

'Why wouldn't they tell us, or leave us a note?' Sophie says, echoing my thoughts.

'Maybe they thought they'd be back before any of us surfaced?' I respond, trying to make sense of the situation. 'We were certainly packing it away last night and it was gone one before most of us headed in.' I glance at Rhys as the obvious exception. 'Maybe they've made an emergency dash to get extra fuel and have been held up for some reason.'

It's the most rational, if not realistic, conclusion to draw.

'Well, that's just not bloody on!' Harry seethes. 'We've paid for a long weekend aboard this yacht, including the day in Paradise Cove, and they're acting the maggot.' He stands, his face glowering. 'I'm going to call the company and give them a bloody good piece of my mind!'

We part as he stomps off towards the hatch, skipping down into the galley in the direction of his room.

'Phoning the shore is probably a good shout,' I concur. 'Maybe they can explain where they are and when they'll be back. Or maybe they'll be able to phone and find out what's going on.'

I don't mention that my hypothetical scenario still fails to explain why they would disconnect the anchor before leaving us. For all we know, Joaquín could have disconnected it last night when he said he was mooring us for the night. What if they scarpered as soon as Elena left Rhys's room?

How long have we been adrift?

Harry comes storming back up the steps. His face is so red, I'm half-expecting to see steam burst from his ears. It's then I remember a call to shore is impossible without a signal.

But instead of commenting on this, he squares up to Christophe. 'Where is it, you thieving gobshite?'

Christophe starts. 'Where's what?'

'My phone, obviously.'

'How on earth should I know where *your* phone is?'

'Because it's not in my room where I left it, and you're the only klepto on board.'

'Well, I haven't taken it,' Christophe proclaims. 'I don't do that any more.'

'Wait here,' I tell them. 'You can use mine. Maybe we can make an emergency call.'

I head towards the hatch and hurry down the steps, along the corridor and to my cabin. Neither my phone nor charger are on the nightstand where I left them. I drop to my knees and check on the floor in case I inadvertently knocked it when I got out of bed, but there's no sign. The bed itself is built into the floor, so there's no space beneath it where it could have fallen.

I stand and try to replay this morning's events through my mind. I definitely did check my phone's display, because that's how I knew there was no Wi-Fi. Then I left it plugged in while I went in search of Elena and Joaquín, and tidied up the main deck. I haven't returned to my cabin until now. Has someone been inside?

I join the others back on deck. 'My phone is missing too.'

All eyes fall on Christophe once again. He was also the last to return from the bow of the yacht. Could he have slipped back through the window access into the V-berth, taken our phones and reappeared with none of us being the wiser?

'I haven't touched your bloody phones!' he shouts. 'Check my cabin if you don't believe me.'

Harry doesn't need telling twice, charging below deck with the others in tow. Harry is first back out, having searched Christophe's cabin. 'What have you done with them?'

Christophe looks to me for support. 'I haven't taken anyone's phones, I *swear*! This is nothing to do with me.'

'Our phones are gone as well,' Sophie says when she, Rhys and Fergus return.

I drop onto the bench, unable to keep my hands from trembling. I don't do well when I feel like I'm not in control, and I don't want to have a full-on anxiety attack in front of them. Harry knows I'm on medication to ease the symptoms, but I don't want the rest to know, least of all Fergus, with his outdated theories. I close my eyes and focus on my breathing.

'If this is someone's idea of a joke, it's nae funny,' Fergus says. 'I need to know if Simone is okay.'

'We should search all of the rooms,' Sophie says. 'As well as the bathroom, galley, and V-berth. They can't just disappear into thin air.'

She heads back below deck with Harry, Rhys and Fergus. Christophe remains on deck, leaving just the two of us.

'I swear this is nothing to do with me, Pete. I know I used to... I used to have a problem, but I've sought professional help for that. It's been years since I've felt the compulsion. You have to believe me. I wouldn't do anything to ruin this weekend.'

I can't answer as the invisible walls around me are starting to cave in.

No, not now.

'Pete, are you okay? You're breathing strangely.'

Grant me the serenity to accept the things I cannot change, the courage to change the things I can, and the wisdom to know the difference.

I silently recite the words over and over, focusing my breaths on each of the beats.

'There's no sign of them anywhere,' I hear Sophie say.

I open my eyes and see she's crouched beside me.

'And there's something else. I just checked the yacht's radio equipment, to see if we could reach the shore that way, but it's been sabotaged. Someone doesn't want us calling for help.'

10

TEN YEARS AGO

Carly's growling snore wakes me from my own peaceful slumber, and even as I try to nudge her into shutting up, the relentless snarl continues unabated. Well, if I can't beat her, I might as well join her, so I throw an arm around her chest, and press the side of my head against the top of hers, so that it's between my neck and shoulder. Her body is warm against mine and I feel more content than I've ever been.

I probably should be thinking about getting out of bed soon anyway; judging by the light peeking through the gap between the curtains, I'm sure my alarm will sound any minute. I give her a squeeze, before rolling back onto my side and reaching for my phone. I blink twice when I see the time.

Oh, shit, there must be some mistake.

I unlock my phone, but the 8.30 alarm I'm sure I set before we went out last night isn't on. How could I have made a mistake like this? I have a lecture in under an hour and I stink of cheap, sugary alcopops.

I nudge Carly. When she doesn't stir, I give her a full-on shove.

'What is it?' she says blearily, ending with a yawn.

'My alarm didn't go off. I need to shower and hightail it for a lecture. Don't you need to go home and change before your shift?'

She checks her watch, and covers her mouth with a hand as she yawns. 'Yeah, I should. I don't start until ten, so I've got time.'

I leap out of bed, grabbing my towel from where it's hanging on the radiator, as well as my room key.

'Hurry up,' I tell her when I spot she hasn't pushed back the duvet yet.

'Okay, okay. I'm going. Jeez, some wakeup call.'

I begin to remove my pyjamas, wrapping the towel around my waist and tying it in a knot to save time when I get upstairs. Once secured, I move back over to her. 'Listen, I'm sorry, but I need to get moving.'

She stands, and pulls me into a kiss, pressing her body against mine. 'We could always call in sick and go back to bed?'

She has no idea how tempted I am, and as her warm hands climb down the towel, tickling my waist, it's all I can do to keep myself from caving. But I can't because lecture attendance is being carefully monitored this year, and anyway, I don't want to miss out on anything, even though Intellectual Property Law is about as dry a subject as I've ever experienced. If I want to get into law school next year, I need to grade as high as I can. I'm up against some of the brightest students in the country and it's bad enough I'm already only being predicted a 2:1.

I push Carly's hands away. 'Not today. And you can't leave the streets unprotected.'

She turns her nose up, but doesn't keep pushing, instead heading over to the desk chair and collecting her clothes. 'Will I see you tonight?'

I clamp my eyes shut as I try to remember what day it is. 'Tonight? Um, it's Wednesday, right?'

Of course it's Wednesday, because Wednesday is the day I have an Intellectual Property Law lecture at half past nine.

'Um, no, sorry, I'm working tonight until ten, and then I need to make a start on my criminology assignment. It's due at the end of next week, and if I don't begin soon, I'll never get it done. Can we take a rain check?'

Now dressed, she comes over and plants a slobbery kiss on my cheek. 'Sure, no worries. Have a good day.'

Grabbing my shower gel, I head out of the room and hurry up the stairs. I climb into the bathtub, wincing at how cold it feels against my feet, before pulling the shower curtain closed. It takes a few seconds for the water to heat, but then the refreshing spray erupts out of the showerhead and helps clear all the stresses from my mind. Calmly, I think through the approaching day: first, a lecture, then I have half an hour's break before my criminology seminar, where our tutor is going to ask us all how much progress we've made on our assignments. I'll have to lie and hope he doesn't ask to see any of it. The completed assignment will count towards 10 per cent of my overall score for the course this year, so it isn't something I can simply ignore. After that, I think there's an hour's gap until a double lecture on International Criminal Law. I really am going to need all the caffeine I can get today, but I won't have time to make a coffee before I leave.

Washing the suds from my hair, I stop the taps and pull back the shower curtain. The room is filled with steam, and I realise that I forgot to switch on the extractor fan. Climbing out of the bath, I towel dry my hair and chest before tying the towel back around my waist. I open the window and put it on the latch. Hopefully any condensation should have escaped before anyone else wants to use the room.

I stop as I hear movement downstairs. Funny, I thought the place was empty. Tightening the towel around my waist, I clutch the bottle of shower gel to me and head downstairs and into the kitchen, but it's empty.

My mind again turns to the story Woody shared last week about his friend's sister's strange experiences in the house. In the cold light of day, I realise how preposterous a story it was, and that it was just him and Fergus trying to wind up Christophe.

All sorts of weird shit would happen... things would get moved in locked rooms, strange noises in the middle of the night, that kind of thing.

Proceeding along the hallway, I check the lounge-diner, but there's nobody in there either, so I must have misheard. But then I hear the sound of breaking glass and I know I didn't imagine that. As I step out of the room, I spot Fergus's door opening and realise he must have come back early for some reason.

I stop as I see Christophe appear in the gap, immediately recognisable by his side-parted dark hair.

'Oh, Christophe, it's you.'

He starts as he hears my voice and then shoves an arm behind his back. 'Oh, hey, I thought you'd already left.'

'My alarm didn't go off,' I explain, not that I should need to confirm my movements. I'm not the one leaving the wrong bedroom.

'I didn't realise Fergus was home,' I say, opting for the least controversial reason that Christophe would be emerging from his bedroom.

'Oh, um, he's not. I... um... I had to grab the lighter I lent him.' The arm appears from behind his back, and I spot the shiny silver lighter I recall Fergus playing with the night of the housewarming party. 'He said I should come and grab it whenever I need it back.'

I'm surprised Fergus would be okay with Christophe rifling through his room when he's not around, but then maybe they're closer than I realised. After all, I've only really known them a month, if that.

'Sure, of course,' I say bluntly because I'm dripping wet and need to get to my room and lecture.

He points at the staircase. 'I'd better get back upstairs. Are you heading in soon?'

'Yeah, as soon as I'm dressed. Are you going in today?'

'Not till after lunch. Catch you later.'

He disappears around the corner and I hear him hurry up the stairs, and then the creak of the staircase up to his room in the loft.

I quickly dress and check I've got everything I need. Pulling the bag onto my shoulders, I slide out of my door and place my keys in my pocket, but then I freeze.

I've never seen Christophe have so much as a puff of a cigarette. Why would he need a lighter?

I shake my head and remind myself it's none of my business, but then a second thought stops me in my tracks: Fergus is supposed to be away until the weekend, so how on earth did Christophe manage to get into his room?

11

PRESENT DAY

Sophie really is the harbinger of doom today. First the missing dinghy, and now the sabotaged radio. I'm dreading what disaster she's going to uncover next.

I allow her to pull me up from the bench and follow her up the three steps into the cockpit. The raised platform is supposed to give whoever is at the helm a better view over the bow of the yacht, but to be honest, from where I'm standing, I can't see past the pointed tip. Sophie points to the radio receiver, a handheld box with rounded edges that would fit snugly into the palm of my hand. She lifts it up and points at what remains of the curly black cable, which looks as though it has been severed with scissors or a sharp knife.

'Maybe we could rewire it back to the main body?' I suggest, as my brain tries to make sense of who is doing this to us.

I don't know the first thing about electrical engineering, but I once saw my dad replace the cable on our second-hand vacuum cleaner, and he didn't seem to struggle.

'All we need to do is find some tools,' I continue to blag. 'Has anyone seen a screwdriver, perhaps? Or some pliers?'

I wish I'd paid more attention when my dad had been tinkering. He'd know what to do right now. He was always so pragmatic, so level-headed. If I could just call him... but clearly the fact we are unable to communicate with the mainland is part of someone's plan.

Sophie follows my trail of thought, unclipping and lowering a hinged door in the main section of panel. 'I was thinking the same thing, and then I saw this.'

I bend forwards and inspect the cubby hole. Inside the darkness is a box the size of a Blu-ray player. I immediately spot the other end of the severed black cable poking out of the back, but it's only when Sophie extracts the box from the hole that I see what she means. The smell of burnt alcohol immediately fills my nostrils, and I feel a cold sweat escape from every pore.

'I guess the fact that there was only limited air inside the panel means the fire didn't last long, and because the door was closed, we didn't smell the burning. I guess with everything else going on this morning, it was easy to miss.'

Even though the large hardtop above the cockpit is providing valuable shade from the rising sun, my entire body is overheating.

Grant me the serenity to accept the things I cannot change, the courage to change the things I can, and the wisdom to know the difference, I silently recite, willing the nausea to stay away.

'Are you okay, Pete? You look kind of peaky.'

I feel Sophie catch me as I stumble backwards, and it's lucky she is there or I might have fallen back onto the deck. She leads me down the steps and over to the bench. I try to remember the instructions my therapist gave to me all those years ago.

Acknowledge five things you see around you; four things you can touch; three things you can hear; two things you can smell; one thing you can taste.

It isn't working. The wall of blue surrounding us is suddenly closing in on me, and the decking covering the hot tub seems to have rotated forty-five degrees to the right. Flashes of purple, yellow, and green blur at the edges of my vision.

Nausea builds at the back of my throat, but I stand; I don't want any of them to see me like this. I scan the immediate landscape for the hatch and stumble towards it, before losing my footing as the edges of my vision narrow further, as if someone has dropped a large net over me.

And then the terrifying darkness comes.

* * *

When I come to, I am back in my cabin, and can feel a cold, wet flannel stretched across my forehead and eyes. For the briefest of moments, I think it was all a dream. That in fact I'm back in the safety of my flat, and that it is Carly who is tending to my fever. Maybe I've simply developed COVID symptoms again, and rather than isolating herself, Carly is nursing me back to health.

But then I hear Harry and Sophie talking in whispered tones, though if they don't want me to hear, they're failing miserably.

'I had no idea he suffered with anxiety,' Sophie says, and I realise now that Harry has revealed my secret.

I should be angry at the betrayal, but in fairness, I didn't give him much choice. There's no alternative means of explaining my blackout.

'He's being treated for it, and I don't think the panic attacks are as regular as they once were.'

I detest the term 'panic attack'. What I experience isn't usually triggered by conscious worry or concern. They don't come often, but when they do, it feels like I'm dying. I cannot emphasise how authentic it feels. Each time it happens, I try to reassure myself that I'm not dying and that it will pass as it has every time before, but the symptoms grow and wring me to the point where death would be a welcome end to the torment. My heart races and it genuinely feels like it might explode and burst out of my chest. I've never experienced an actual heart attack, but I imagine it's not too dissimilar. The first time it happened, I was driving home from work. I was so alarmed that I had to pull over on the hard shoulder and call for an ambulance. The paramedics were calm and courteous as they explained that the agonising pain in my chest wasn't the result of an irregular arrhythmia, and that despite my protestations to the contrary, the discomfort and torture were not life-threatening.

I insisted on a second opinion and they took me to A&E, only for a doctor twice my age to repeat what they'd told me. Until that day, I'd always assumed Fergus was right and that anxiety attacks were merely figments of sufferers' imaginations.

I know now they're not.

It's like someone is pressing a pillow over my face, cutting off my oxygen supply, while someone else stands on my chest and slowly squeezes out every last molecule of air from my lungs. Then, while these two monsters are torturing me, someone else injects me with an overdose of adrenaline, and then proceeds to kick me until I'm black and blue.

Not even Carly knows how bad it can sometimes get. She knows I'm taking a daily dose of Sertraline to keep the symptoms at bay, but during each attack, I always force myself to leave the room.

'In this day and age, I don't understand why he's so keen to keep it a secret,' Sophie says next. 'We all have our own issues we're dealing with.'

'You remember what Fergus was like back in the day, especially how cruel he could be with Christophe whenever he had a wobble. I just don't think Pete wants to draw any unnecessary attention to his mental health.'

'Poor thing,' I hear Sophie say. 'You'd never know. He always seems to have it so together. I genuinely hold him and Carly up as the paradigms of success. After everything that happened... that night... Don't look at me like that. I know we're not supposed to talk about it, but it's not easy to pretend it didn't happen...'

No, no, no.

I force myself to sit upright, and the flannel drops into my lap. Harry is perched on the edge of the mattress beside me, and Sophie is standing at the foot of the bed.

'Hey there, bud,' Harry says, taking my hand in his. His skin is so cold in contrast to my own.

'You gave us a real scare there,' Sophie continues, offering me a sympathetic smile. 'How are you feeling now?'

Harry passes me a bottle of mineral water and I guzzle half of it in one go. The cool liquid brings welcome relief to my dry and craggy throat.

'You bumped your head when you collapsed,' he explains quickly. 'We told the others to wait on the deck and that we'd see you were okay. I didn't mention the reason for your fall to the others.' He lowers his eyes to his lap. 'I did tell Soph, though. I'm sorry, but I wanted to check with someone else that what we'd witnessed was a panic attack... and not something else.'

I wish he wouldn't call it that, but I nod to show my understanding. If it's only Sophie who's been let in on the secret, I can live with it. At least she won't treat me any differently; unlike Rhys and Fergus, who no doubt will see my condition as pure melodrama.

'Not that I want to trigger anything else,' Sophie says, dropping on to the edge of the mattress, 'but the radio is totally screwed. We have no way of contacting anyone. And there's still no sign of Elena or Joaquín.'

Nobody is saying it, but we're all now thinking Joaquín or Elena must have been the ones to disable the radio, before cutting us adrift, and abandoning ship.

'Rhys is taking it the hardest,' Sophie says. 'He feels like she used him.'

'He'll get over it,' Harry mutters. 'It's not like she's the first girl to only want a one-night stand with him.' He suddenly catches himself, and covers his mouth with his hand as he looks at me. 'Sorry, but you know what I mean.'

I know only too well, but I don't want to think about any of that either. 'Why would they do this to us?'

Both stare back at me blankly.

I focus my attention on Harry. 'You were the one who booked this trip, right?'

He nods, but his brow furrows.

'Where did you find the company? Did you see a legitimate website? Were there any other customer reviews? I'm not blaming this on you, just trying to understand how this could have gone so wrong.'

'It... Yes, I searched the company online, and the site looked impressive. Loads of images of people having fun. It was even mentioned in one of those top ten stag party review sites too. We just got stitched up with a dodgy captain and hostess, I guess.' He turns to Sophie for support.

'I saw the website too, Pete, and I don't think there was anything dodgy about it.'

'And what about our captain? Did the company tell you "Joaquín" would be looking after us?' I say, using air quotes in case his name was also fake.

'Yes, yes... If I had my phone, I could show you the email. They even sent a photograph of the two of them.'

There's no point in us hiding away and acting as if we haven't been totally screwed over. We need a plan of action; that's what my dad would say.

I shift myself off the bed. 'We need to talk to the others, and find a way back home.'

Sophie leads the way as she's closest to the door, with Harry and me following behind. Fergus, Rhys and Christophe are on the bench, two bottles of wine open, and they are bickering so hard that they don't even see the three of us approach.

'Well, for all we know, Pete could be the one behind all this,' I hear Christophe snap, his back to us. 'He was the first of us to wake, right? How do we know he didn't come up here and disable the radio, before cutting the anchor? Maybe he and Elena are in on this together, and she's waiting somewhere nearby to come and sail him into the sunset.'

He's slurring his words, even though it can't even be ten o'clock yet.

Fergus's wide eyes must draw his attention to us because Christophe spins round, clearly embarrassed to have been overheard.

'I wouldn't sabotage my future brother-in-law's party,' I say evenly, accepting that we're all on edge, and that Christophe's lashing out is just a coping mechanism. 'Clearly, Elena and Joaquín weren't the hosts we thought they were.'

'I reckon they're still on the yacht somewhere, hiding,' Fergus pipes up, gripping his glass so tightly it might actually crack.

His face is a mix of anger and desperation; it's now been more than twelve hours since his call to Simone was cut off. I could tell him that he's probably blowing her words out of proportion, but it wouldn't help, and I could just as easily be wrong. At least they're in the UK at an organised event with emergency services on standby.

'Where could they be, though?' Rhys asks. 'I'm not being funny, but we've checked every cabin and there are no obvious hiding places.'

'There is one place we haven't checked yet,' Christophe says quietly.

We all turn to look at him and he points at his feet.

'The shark cage. I just checked the breathing apparatus and one of the air tanks is missing.'

'He's right, he is,' Rhys concurs, supporting his best friend as he always does.

I hadn't even thought about the fact I haven't seen the air tanks and goggles this morning. The shark cage would also be the perfect place for them to hide undetected. They could have lowered themselves into the water and swum to the cage with none of us any the wiser. It would also have allowed one of them to sneak back on board and steal the phones.

Sophie must be reading my mind because she hurries to the cockpit and locates the mechanism Joaquín used to bring the cage to the surface last night. The motor whirs and gyrates, and the rest of us move to the starboard side as we wait for the cage to erupt through the sea, and for us to catch them in the act.

Rhys's ear-splitting anguish is the only sound as the cage appears, with Elena's lifeless body floating just beneath the lid.

12

TEN YEARS AGO

I'm exhausted when I make it back from the campus. My criminology professor – 'just call me Ed' – wanted each of us to pitch the subject of our assignments in a *Dragon's Den* environment, with the rest of the tutor group voting for and against the proposals. I was last to go, hoping that the bell would sound to end the class before they got around to me. It really hasn't been my lucky day. At least the extra time gave me the chance to scribble some notes about my chosen topic. When my turn came, I moved to the front of the room nervously and was about to get started when Ed told everyone to pay attention as my chosen topic is one close to his heart. He then proceeded to explain how he was part of the team that originally argued *against* my viewpoint in the courtroom.

I did my best to blag it, but his growing frown showed me just how badly I was doing. He asked me to stay behind after class, and then proceeded to pick through everything I'd said. He left me in no uncertain terms about just how much work I have to complete in the next nine days. It's just as well I gave Carly the brush-off about tonight, as I'm going to need to pull an all-nighter.

After the seminar, I was genuinely contemplating skipping the late afternoon International Criminal Law double lecture to come back here and start on my assignment, but then I bumped into Harry, and he convinced me to join him at the Student Union bar for lunch. I never should have agreed to split the two-for-one cocktails – it was only 11 a.m., after all – but I needed something to take the edge off, and Harry looked as though he needed the company. We chatted and he dragged me back from the brink, to the point where I felt more confident in my abilities to smash the assignment. And then I looked at my watch, and realised I'd already missed the first twenty minutes of the double lecture.

Harry tried to talk me out of hotfooting it over there and arriving noticeably late, but I told him it was better to be late than a no-show – but how wrong I was. I used the stairs up to the back of the lecture hall, hoping I could sneak in at the back undetected, but the pew I chose to sit at squeaked as I lowered it, and all the heads in the room turned and scowled at me. The most annoying part is that doddery old Professor Hugo McGregor probably wouldn't have even realised I wasn't there but for my squeaky chair. I swear they must deliberately not oil the back couple of rows to catch out late arrivals.

The last thing I need tonight is a four-hour shift on a supermarket checkout, but I daren't phone in sick so soon after I've returned from the summer break.

I've only just closed the door, falling into it under the weight of my rucksack, when I hear a commotion coming from Fergus's room. The hallway seems to shake as something slams into the wall. I was certain he was supposed to be away, but now I'm not so sure. If he is home, it would certainly explain how Christophe got into his room this morning. A second crash against the wall sets me on edge, and as much as I feel a duty to check that everything is okay, I don't have the time or the mental capacity to find out the cause of the noise.

I push myself from the front door, and tiptoe along the hallway, avoiding the squeaky floorboard near the radiator, only exhaling when I reach my door and slide the key into the lock. I swear it doesn't make a sound, but before I've depressed the handle, Fergus's door flies open and he stands in the gap, his face a ball of angst and sweat.

I force a thin smile and nod in his direction.

'Oh, it's you,' he says, the disappointment clear. 'You seen Rhys or Woody? I need to speak to them.'

The fact that Woody hangs around this place so much does make it feel like he's living here, but now doesn't feel the right time to mention it.

I shrug awkwardly. 'Sorry, I just got back. Have you tried Rhys's room?'

'Course I fucking have!'

I gulp, but don't respond. Deep down, I know that if I don't say anything, he'll eventually lose patience and go back into his room, and I'll be able to change into my uniform and leg it to the supermarket. But my conscience won't play ball.

'Is everything okay?' I hear myself ask before I can stop the words escaping.

Just go into your room before you're late for work.

'I thought you were going home to visit your parents.'

His eyes darken further, but he doesn't lunge for me, as I'm picturing in my head.

'Well, I guess that shows what you know. Listen, if you see Rhys, can you tell him I need a chat?'

It's a relief when he slams the door, and I'm able to slip into my room, throw off my bag and change into my work trousers and branded polo shirt. There's an odd smell I can't quite place, but I spray deodorant under my arms to cover it. I shouldn't have had those cocktails at lunch; I can already feel a headache brewing. I need the next four hours to pass as quickly as possible so I can get back to my assignment.

I'm just closing my door when something else slams into Fergus's wall. I picture Sophie having to charm Raymond when he learns of whatever damage Fergus is causing, and my conscience once again takes control of my body.

Knocking on Fergus's door, I brace myself for a barrage of abuse, but he's clearly got something on his mind.

He yanks the door open. 'What?'

I can't believe I'm doing this.

'Listen, I appreciate it's none of my business, and I'll understand if you tell me to sling my hook, but I wanted to check if there's anything I can do to help? Rhys might not be around, but I am. You know what they say about a problem shared being a problem halved.'

My shoulders tense as I anticipate his reaction, but rather than thumping me, he grabs hold of my shirt sleeve and drags me into his room.

Oh, God, he's going to kill me.

My eyes clamp tight as I await what won't be my first merciless beating at the hands of someone twice my size.

'You ever had one of those fucking awful days?' he says instead.

I open my eyes and see what looks like the outcome of a detonated bomb. Clothes are strewn left and right, the door to the fitted wardrobe is hanging by a single hinge, and the drawers are scattered across the floor and bed. I'd assume we've been burgled if I hadn't already seen that my room is exactly as I left it. Then I spot the cracked plaster where something – maybe a fist, judging by the fresh welts on Fergus's knuckle – has been slammed into it.

I could fill him in on my day, but I don't have the time and don't want to relive the embarrassment. 'We all have shit days sometimes, but what on earth could have happened to warrant this level of carnage?'

He surveys the room and for the first time the hint of a smile escapes. He slumps down on his bed in the only space visible.

'I was at my uncle's house when I got a call from the coach. He said he's heard rumours that I'm struggling on my course and if I don't pull my finger out, I'm booted off the team.'

As bad days go, this isn't even on the same scale as mine, I think, but don't say.

'People like me aren't meant to go to university. I only agreed to come because my uncle insisted. Since he took me in, he's worked his arse off to give me the best shot in life, and I don't want to let him down, but the coach is right: I am failing. It's nae that I don't want to try, but I'm nae an academic. Lacrosse has been the one thing I've succeeded at. Coach knows I'm the best player on the team, and he wouldn't risk the regional championship unless he was serious.'

He lowers his head, so I can't see the tears pooling in his eyes.

So, all of this mess and angst is because of our benevolent landlord Raymond. I glance at my watch, conscious that the bus will be arriving at my stop in a few minutes.

'You're taking film studies, right?' I say.

He nods. 'Aye. I figured it would just be sitting around watching movies and gassing about them, but there's more to it than that. The assignment for this term isn't even focused on British or US movies. We're supposed to pick a foreign language film and explain how it's influenced modern cinema, and I dinnae know where to start. I've been tryna get hold of Woody, but he isn't answering his phone.'

'Have you discussed it with your tutor?'

'Aye, and she tried to explain what she's looking for, but I still don't get it. She suggested I look at French cinema as that's the easiest comparison, but I don't speak French, and I hate reading subtitles. If I wanted to read, I'd take a book. You know?'

I really should be leaving, but my feet remain planted. 'Actually, I do know, and I might be able to help.'

Why am I still talking? Fergus has been nothing but a disruption with his late-night drunken returns and he hasn't gone out of his own way to show any interest in me or Harry.

'I studied French A-Level and an aspect of that involved early French cinema. Have you heard of the Nouvelle Vague?'

He stares back at me blankly.

'Okay, well, long story short, the earliest cinema pioneers were French, and they made significant advances in both technology and flare. Your tutor's right that a lot of their influence can still be seen in modern English language films. I have to get my arse to work right now, but I'd be happy to share what I know, and could help you to choose a suitable selection of films to compare if you'd like?'

He narrows his eyes, and I instantly sense I've overstepped. 'Why would you want to help me?'

I really don't have an answer.

'A friend in need is a friend indeed?' I say, cringing as the words tumble out.

He wrinkles his nose, but his cheeks are finally starting to return to a more natural shade. 'I dinnae suppose you also have veterinary skills you can share?'

I frown at the unusual question, until he nods at a small glass bowl on the corner of his desk. It's partly covered by the contents of one of the desk drawers, so I didn't spot it at first.

'Oh, you have a fish? I thought Soph said we weren't allowed pets.'

'We're not. I kept the tank under a blanket when I moved in. But when I got back today, I found him floating on top of the water. I've had him for two years and now he's dead, just like that. No explanation. One minute there, the next... As I said, it's been an awful day. And to top it off, I canny find my lucky lighter either.'

Christophe's face flashes before my eyes.

'What makes the lighter lucky?'

He stares down at his feet. 'It was my dad's. I remember him telling me when I was a kid how his grandfather had bought it during the Second World War, and he'd always felt it had brought him luck. It was passed down to my dad and then to me after he passed. My uncle had it cleaned up and inscribed with my dad's final words. And I've searched everywhere and canny bloody find it.'

I should tell him about what I witnessed this morning, but I don't want to upset him, and I'd rather confront Christophe directly than stir things up.

'I'm sure it will turn up,' I say instead.

I look at my watch again, realising I've now probably missed my bus and that will mean a bollocking from the duty manager.

'Thanks, Pete,' Fergus says, and I realise he's offered his hand out. 'I appreciate you helping me.'

I press my hand to his and he shakes it firmly.

'I should let you get on to work. I need to tidy up this mess.'

'You should clean your hand up too, and maybe see if there's a poster you can hang over the crack in the wall until we can get it patched up.'

I excuse myself and close the door behind me. I'm about to head to the front door when instinct tells me to check my own room again. Unlocking it, I enter, and sniff the air, now realising what that strange smell was: cologne. I don't use it, but I know someone who does. One thing's for sure: I'm going to need to keep an eye on Christophe and his light fingers.

13

PRESENT DAY

It's a relief when Fergus drags Rhys away from the side of the yacht, but his screeching barely subsides as he is led back to his cabin. At first, I don't want to believe that Elena is dead, but as her body bobs against the lid of the cage, I can see the saltwater splashing into her lifeless eyes. It's the first corpse I've seen in ten years, but it doesn't make it any easier.

The whirring of the motor stops, and Sophie appears beside me, gasping as she first sees Elena.

'What the...?' she gasps, grabbing my shoulders for support. 'Is she...?'

'I think so,' I say, unable to tear my eyes away. 'She's not wearing goggles or an oxygen tank, which suggests it wasn't her choice to get into the cage.' I don't add that the lack of spilled blood suggests she was still alive when she entered it.

Nobody speaks for what feels like an eternity, as the truth slowly dawns: somebody did this to her. Given Joaquín's and the dinghy's disappearance, he's the most likely candidate. The question is why, and is he planning to return?

Harry is the first to yell out. 'We need to call the coastguard or someone,' he says. 'We can't just wait here for him to return and finish us all off.'

I stare out at the horizon for any sign of where he could be hiding, but there's nothing but the sea and sky in all directions.

Sophie hurries back up to the cockpit and engages the motor again, and soon the lid of the cage and Elena disappear beneath the water line. We will need to release her body at some point, but for now it's easier to pretend she isn't there.

Christophe and Harry remain beside me, but neither speaks nor moves, and when I look at the pair of them, I see their skin is as pale as Sophie's.

The yacht shakes as something collides with the hull, and a moment later, Fergus charges out of the galley, waving one of the kitchen knives from the wooden block in our direction.

'All of you sit on the bench,' he commands.

His face is as red and uncontrolled as his hair.

Rhys stumbles out of the hatch next, a bloody gash just above his left eyebrow.

Fergus spins and waves the blade in Rhys's direction. 'You too: on the bench.'

We all oblige. I've never seen Fergus look so wired. He points the blade at each of us in turn, and despite not wanting to believe it, the manner with which he is thrusting the blade, I wonder whether maybe he could be the one who killed Elena. It's his aggressive temper that leaves me in constant fear about my sister's future. I shouldn't be surprised. Of the six of us, Fergus probably would have been my first pick as a killer.

I shake the thought from my head. What am I saying here? That a man I've known for more than a decade – a man my sister is planning to spend the rest of her life with – is a killer? It's preposterous. He's just reacting to the insane situation in the only way he knows.

Fergus rubs at his forehead with his knife hand, anger finally giving way to confusion, and I see Sophie starting to lift herself from the cushion. Is she seriously planning to try to disarm him?

I press my hand against her thigh and force her back down.

'Fergus?' I call out to bring his focus back to the group, and to discourage any other kamikaze attempts to regain control. 'You need to put the knife down, mate. Okay? There's no reason for anyone to get hurt. We can work this all out. That's what friends do. Yeah?'

He rubs at his forehead again, his eyes wide and manic as they fix on me. I know deep down that he wouldn't have killed Elena, and that it's ridiculous to even consider it, but right now, he looks so crazed that I'm questioning everything I know about him.

After all, he is the one who went for a weapon first.

No. He's just panicking and reacting to a tense situation like an animal would. It's the whole fight or flight instinct. By making himself look fierce, maybe he's hoping to frighten off the real killer. But there's nowhere any of us can go, and I'm terrified that one of the others will get hurt accidentally if they attempt to overpower him.

But of course that still begs the question: who *did* kill Elena? What if it wasn't Joaquín? I know I didn't do it, and I don't want to believe Fergus has it in him to be premeditated, so who does that leave?

What am I thinking? Could one of these one-time friends have harmed her? To what end?

It's bonkers, so I focus my attention on Fergus instead. He needs to put that knife down. If one of the others did dispatch Elena, they won't hesitate to hurt Fergus as well.

I slowly stand, and raise my arms in the air to show I'm not a threat. I keep my palms pointed in Fergus's direction, but he still takes an involuntary step backwards.

'I know you're scared,' I tell him softly, keeping my voice as calm as the adrenaline will allow. 'We're all scared, okay? But you need to put the knife away, Fergus. Please? We need to talk about what's happened, and determine a plan of action as a group. Waving a knife about isn't helping anybody.'

I wish I could read what's going on in his head. Assuming I'm right and he didn't kill Elena, then this bold move is an act of desperation. I know he's worried about Simone, and maybe, if he'd managed to get hold of her this morning, he wouldn't be reacting in this way. I need him to know that I'm on his side, and that the only reason I want him to drop the blade is for everyone's safety.

I take a tentative step forward, but Fergus notices and swipes his knife arm down in an arc – as a warning. I retreat until my legs crash into the bench, and I nearly stumble.

'Okay, okay,' I tell him, 'I'll stay back, but you need to listen to me, Fergus.'

He swipes the knife again as a warning shot for the rest. 'No, I don't. Not any more. You lot are always the same: you think you're better than me. I get it: you're smarter, you all graduated at the first attempt, have better-paid jobs. But I'm not stupid. You hear me? I have street smarts, and that's why I'm going to find out which one of you is screwing with us, and I *will* stop you.'

He's shuffling from one foot to the other, and his eyes are bloodshot. Is he even in control of his actions? I recall Simone telling me he'd been under stress since being threatened with redundancy. Have I made a huge mistake here? Could Fergus have actually snapped and drowned Elena, and is now trying to cover his tracks?

'Was it you?' he shouts, pointing the knife at me. 'You were the first one up this morning. How do we know you didn't wake early, kill Elena and then stash her body in the cage?'

'The hatch was already open when I got up,' I tell him. 'I swear. I think I was woken by a noise of some kind, but I didn't know what, but I now think it might have been the shark cage being lowered.'

'I heard a thump sound too,' Sophie says, raising a trembling hand into the air. 'I came straight out and saw Pete tidying up the mess. I thought he'd dropped a bottle or something.'

Fergus redirects the knife at Sophie.

'Pete was nowhere near the cockpit when I came out here,' she continues, 'so he couldn't have been lowering the cage at that time.'

I appreciate Sophie trying to come to my defence, but she could have left off the last three words. Just because I wasn't lowering the cage when she emerged from her cabin doesn't mean I didn't do it before.

The knife is pointing back at me again, as if it's a boom microphone and we're the audience in some demented chat show.

'What were you cleaning up out here?' Fergus asks. 'Blood?'

'No, just bottles and crisps. The sack is still in the galley. You can check it.'

'But why were *you* cleaning up? It was all of our mess.'

I shrug. 'I was just trying to help out, that's all.' The words sound lame as they tumble from my mouth. 'I had no reason to kill Elena,' I add, even though that means throwing the others under the bus.

Fergus turns the knife on Rhys and Harry, who gasp simultaneously. 'You two were fighting over her, so maybe one of you did it.'

'Uh, I was asleep when all this was going on,' Rhys says. 'I liked her, and we spent the night together... How can you think I could be so... heartless?'

I know better, I want to say.

'So, you're saying it was Harry?' Fergus says, leaping to the next conclusion.

'Me?' Harry screams. 'Don't drag me into this bullshit. I was sound asleep until Pete and Soph came knocking on my door.'

He stares at the two of us for corroboration. I nod vigorously, but Fergus has a point: of all of us, Harry had what was closest to a motive for wanting Elena dead. She chose Rhys over him.

What am I saying? Harry is my best friend – and the best man, for goodness' sake. How can I even be considering this?

Fergus is still pointing the blade at Harry, and I feel Sophie lunge past me in Fergus's direction. It all happens in slow motion. Fergus doesn't see the move until Sophie is on him, and as he attempts to swing his arm around in warning, it's already too late, and Sophie has barged his free arm. But the knife is not yet secured, so I dart forwards, thrusting my back between Sophie and Fergus's swinging arm.

I yelp as the blade bites into my upper arm.

Fergus immediately releases his grip on the handle, tumbling to the deck with Sophie on top of him. Harry is first off the bench, coming to my aid, pulling off his T-shirt, and wrapping it around the deep laceration.

'You're going to be okay,' he tells me, and I listen because, as an emergency room nurse, he must have seen hundreds, if not thousands, of knife wounds.

'Oh, shit, I'm so sorry. I never meant...' Fergus grumbles as Rhys and Christophe help him back to the bench, while Sophie goes in search of a First Aid box.

The cut is deep, and I'm in agony, but there's nothing I can do about it, so when Sophie drops three pills into my hand, I swallow them back without asking what they are. She hands me a fresh bottle of lager to wash them down with, and again I don't hesitate.

'Bucket of shite! I think this is going to need a stitch,' Harry says as he examines the wound. 'Is there a needle and thread in the First Aid kit?'

Sophie examines the contents, then shakes her head. 'Basic bandages and plasters only.'

Harry spins to look at the others on the bench. 'Is there any chance any of you have a needle and thread?'

I'm about to laugh at the absurdity of the question when Rhys's hand shoots up. 'I saw a sewing kit in the V-berth yesterday.'

Harry nods for him to go and fetch it. For a moment, all attention is on me while Sophie and Harry do what they can to stem the flow of blood. Nobody is talking about the body in the shark cage or what it means, but as I look back to the bench, I catch Christophe staring at me, and there is guilt in those eyes.

14

TEN YEARS AGO

'Bonjour, bonjour, bonjour,' I hear Harry singing as he enters my room. Dressed in a navy striped top, with his light brown curls tucked into a red beret, he looks like a typical tourist in France.

He halts when he sees me in my jeans and hoodie. 'What's going on? You're not ready yet?'

I switch off the radio and point at the small case beside the radiator. 'I'm packed and ready to go, but I have to drop my assignment in to my criminology professor first. I only have one seminar today, and then I'll be back.'

He doesn't hide his disappointment. 'But I bought Camembert and baguettes for lunch. I thought we could warm up for our trip.'

'You can save me some. I won't be more than an hour.'

He pouts dramatically, before breaking into a grin. 'I cannot wait to sample the best of what France has to offer. Christophe reckons he knows which areas to avoid, but I don't think we should allow him to dictate the entire trip.'

He winks and I shake my head with mock disapproval.

'You do realise the train doesn't leave London until seven

tonight, right?' I say, glancing at my watch. 'It isn't even midday yet.'

'Yeah, I know, of course, but I don't have any classes today, and I thought the two of us could hang out pretending to be French. It's been years since I took my French GCSE, but I reckon I still remember the basics.'

The weekend trip to Paris was Harry's idea, just the two of us, but as soon as we started talking about it, Christophe appointed himself our guide, and then the rest of the house invited themselves, so now the six of us will be crossing together. Well, eight actually, as I also invited Carly, and she insisted I bring my sister, who's been down in the dumps since she broke up with her boyfriend. I've warned Harry not to make any moves as she's only just turned eighteen and I'm not having anyone take advantage of her on my watch.

I'm really looking forward to a few days in another country, gorging on wine and cheese. It's the least I deserve for the amount of work I've put into this assignment over the last week. I've barely seen Carly because she's been on the late shift and I've either been glued to my laptop or in the library. But it's done, and all I need to do is hand it in, then I am free to indulge.

'Is it true French women don't shave their armpits?'

I stare back at him. 'How on earth would I know?'

'I'm sure I heard that somewhere before, and that's hot, no?'

I don't have time for this.

'We can converse in French for the rest of the day once I'm back,' I promise.

He nods in a disgruntled way, and I usher him out of my room.

'Okay, okay, may the sun shine warm upon your face.'

This is one of many turns of phrase I've heard him use since we met. I think this one means he hopes things go smoothly. For the first time in ages, I feel like everything is going my way.

* * *

The walk to the campus is blustery, but I make it in five minutes by jogging along the footpath. I'm genuinely in good spirits as I head into the building, and for once, if Professor 'just call me Ed' Chambers wants to deploy his Spanish Inquisition tactics, I'm ready for them. I'm actually the first into class, which has never happened before, but Ed won't know how keen I was because everyone else arrives by the time he shows up.

Never mind. I'm not going to worry about it, because in a few hours I will be Paris-bound.

He doesn't ask any of us about our assignments, instead focusing on a verdict from the High Court that was pronounced this week. The clock on the wall ticks slowly as I will the time to pass so I can bid the class, 'Au revoir.'

My notepad is already in my bag as soon as the bell sounds, but it's only when Ed asks us to leave our assignments on the corner of his desk that I even think about it. I pull my satchel up onto the table and open the flap, thrusting my hands inside.

Wait, what?

I open the bag wider.

No, this isn't right. Where the hell is my assignment?

I pull out my notepad, running my fingers through the pages in case it has become trapped somehow, but it isn't there either.

This cannot be happening!

It was definitely in there last night. I printed it off and stapled the pages together, and put it inside the satchel. I remember doing it. I double-checked the bag before I went to sleep last night, and it was there. I didn't check my bag this morning because I was trying to hurry Harry out of my room, and anyway, I knew I'd checked last night.

'Is there a problem, Pete?' I hear Ed ask.

I look up. The rest of the students have left, and now it's just the two of us.

I hold my satchel upside down and shake it, but nothing else emerges. Could it have fallen out of my bag when I was rushing to get here? I don't see how because the bag was clipped together.

Where the hell is my assignment?

'Pete? You have completed your assignment, haven't you?'

I lower my bag. 'Yes, I have. I thought it was in my bag, but now it's not here, so it must have fallen out somewhere.'

He doesn't look amused. 'Well, I'm on campus until four today, and so long as I have it before I leave, there won't be any problems.'

'Thank you,' I say, standing and pulling the strap of the bag over my head and shoulder. 'I'll see if it fell out at home, and if not, I'll print it off again and get straight back here.'

I don't wait to hear if he's okay with this proposal as I leave the room, eyes fixed on the floor in case I spot it. I retrace my steps all the way back to the house without luck. Fergus and Woody are in the garden smoking a joint when I enter through the gate.

'Harry's looking for you,' Fergus tells me, exhaling a huge cloud in my direction, before passing the joint to Woody, who looks worse for wear.

'Thanks,' I say. 'You haven't seen any pages flapping about in the garden, have you?'

His brow furrows. 'Pages?'

'My criminology assignment. It was in my bag last night, and when I went to hand it in to my professor, it was gone. I came through the garden and I just wondered whether it had fallen out here.'

He still looks confused. 'Sorry, I've only been out here for five minutes. Woody, you seen anything?'

Woody blinks at me slowly, but doesn't respond. I'm not even sure he's heard the question. I'm starting to get fed up with the amount of time he's spending here. There's even a sleeping bag rolled up in the front room for those nights when he's too paralytic to make it back to his own house.

I don't wait for him to elaborate before hurrying to the patio door and letting myself in to the kitchen-diner. Christophe is by the sink, washing up.

How long has he been waiting for me to return for a ringside seat to my unfolding drama?

He nods in my direction. 'You fancy a cuppa? Kettle's just boiled.'

'Thanks, but no, I need to find my assignment and get back to campus.'

'You've lost your assignment? Maybe you left it in your room?'

Well, you'd know the answer to that if you've been snooping around in my stuff again, I want to say, but bite my tongue instead.

I know I've smelt his cologne in my room, and last week I noticed that my laundry bin had been moved to the opposite wall while I was out. It isn't strong enough evidence, though. What I need to do is catch him in the act before I start spreading unsubstantiated accusations. With his room in the loft, it's impossible to sneak up and try to get in there without him hearing me coming. I've tried his door when I know he's out, but it's always locked. I wish I could figure out how he's getting in and out undetected.

I head out of the kitchen just as Harry and Sophie are coming down the stairs, each carrying a half-empty bottle of wine.

'Here he is,' Harry sings, as he sees me coming through the door. 'Grab a glass and join us.'

'I can't,' I say, heading straight through, eyes scanning the floor as I stalk back to my room.

Harry follows behind. 'What's the matter?'

I unlock my door and hold it open for him to follow me in.

There's a part of me half-expecting to find my assignment in the middle of the floor or on my bed, but it's nowhere to be seen.

I close the door, and usher for Harry to follow me to the opposite side of the room; I don't want to be overheard by anyone listening outside the door.

'I went to hand in my assignment and it wasn't in my bag,' I whisper. 'It was *definitely* in there when I went to sleep last night, and now it's like it's vanished into thin air.'

'Maybe it fell out?'

I shake my head. 'I don't see how it could have. Besides, I've retraced my steps and it's nowhere to be seen.'

He gasps. 'Do you think someone on your course stole it to make you look bad?'

The thought hadn't crossed my mind, but I can't see that anyone would have. For all their one-upmanship, the students in the tutor group wouldn't resort to underhand tactics like that.

I shake my head. 'I think someone in this house took it.'

He covers his mouth with his hand. 'Wait, you think that I—'

'No, no, no, not you.' I pause, listening for any sound of movement outside my door. 'I think Christophe has been breaking into my room and going through my stuff.'

Harry's face crumples into a cynical frown.

'I know he stole Fergus's lucky cigarette lighter,' I tell him, 'and I've smelt his cologne in here. I can't prove he took it, but the assignment was in my bag on my desk when I went to sleep and now it's gone.'

'But why would he...?'

'I don't know,' I say, shaking my head, 'but now I have to reprint it and go back to hand it to my tutor, which is a pain in the arse, but it is what it is.'

I move across to my laptop, lift the lid, and switch it on.

'Christ on a bike! Do you think Christophe's been in my room as well?' Harry asks.

'I don't know.' I sigh. 'Have you noticed anything missing or in a different place to where you left it?'

He shakes his head. 'I don't think so.' He turns and glares at the door. 'Let's get him in here now. I'll hold him down and you threaten to punch him until he confesses.'

I don't want to give Christophe the benefit of letting him know I'm on to his little games. Instead, I go to my recent files, search for the assignment and click to open the file. My heart skips a beat when all I can see is a blank page. I close the file and reopen it in case my laptop is having a funny five minutes, but the blank page continues to stare back at me.

'What's wrong?' Harry says. 'You look like you've just seen a ghost.'

'It's gone,' I say, pointing at the screen. 'Where the hell has it gone? I wrote 5,000 words, plus footnotes and citations.'

Harry leans round me and looks at the screen. 'Don't panic. Word keeps previous versions of files, so if you have accidentally saved the wrong thing, we should be able to recover a previously saved version.'

I haven't accidentally saved over my assignment, I want to scream, but he's offering to help, so I bite my tongue again.

'Hmm... That's strange.'

'What is?'

He waggles the cursor over a folder on the screen. 'Well, usually, you can go to file properties and recover previous versions of files, but this one doesn't have any.'

'I've been working on this file every day for the last week. I've saved it every day.'

'Did you back it up? We could recover it that way instead.'

No, I didn't back it up yet! This cannot be happening.

I shake my head.

'It's like a new file was created and then saved using the same filename, thus wiping out the recoverable copies. But why would you...?' He stops and stares at me. 'Are you sure you wrote up your assignment?'

Oh, God, he thinks I'm losing my mind.

What if he's right?

'I know I wrote it. I spent bloody ages editing and perfecting it. I'm not crazy, Harry, I didn't imagine this.'

Why would Christophe do this?

I freeze as a new thought replaces it, and I hear Woody's voice loud in my ears: *All sorts of weird shit would happen when nobody else was around. Things would get moved in locked rooms, strange noises in the middle of the night, that kind of thing.*

Harry must see my eyes filling as he pulls me into a hug and slaps me across the back. 'Listen, it could just be a computer glitch, but you're not going to get it fixed now. What you need to do is go to your tutor and ask for an extension. There's a lass on my course who is a whiz with computers. I'll call her and ask her to take a look at your laptop while we're away, and hopefully she can find the file and you can hand it in when we're back next week.'

It sounds so easy, and with this plan in my head, I race back to campus, catching Ed just as he's going into one of the lecture theatres. I tell him about the computer issue, that I'm getting it investigated, and will hand in the assignment next week.

He runs his tongue beneath his top lip. 'No, Pete, that isn't good enough. You've had just as long as everybody else to do this work, and I'm not giving you an extension.'

My heart drops. 'Please, Ed, I worked so hard on this, I swear. Just a couple of days and you'll be blown away by what I've done.'

'Do you know how many times I've heard that excuse? It's the modern equivalent of the dog ate my homework. You get that assignment to me first thing Monday morning – and I mean eight o'clock – or you will fail this module and lose 10 per cent of your grade. Your choice.'

He doesn't wait for me to respond before heading inside the lecture hall. That's it, then: I can't go to Paris. I'm going to have to stay and work. Whatever I produce in forty-eight hours won't be nearly as good as the original, but I can't afford to fail this module.

Someone in that house did this to me, and I'm going to find out who.

15

PRESENT DAY

I know Fergus didn't mean to injure me, but my arm is in agony, despite Harry's attempts to use the needle and thread to stitch up the cut. Sophie managed to find some dressings in the First Aid box, so my arm is heavily bandaged and taped. The painkillers are doing little to numb my senses, so I am topping up with wine, but it's so hot out on the deck that I'm not sure how much longer we can just sit here like ducks.

The gentle sway of the yacht is also making me nauseous, despite the motion sickness pill I took last night. And I still can't get over how deathly quiet it is. Aside from the water lapping against the hull, there's no sound. Nobody has suggested putting on music, as none of us are in the mood to relax. If there wasn't a corpse floating in the water, things might be different. What's also alarming is the likelihood that Elena's body will eventually come to the attention of our predator neighbours.

We need to try to make contact with someone, or at least attempt to make it back to shore, but knowing there's a killer out there – Joaquín or someone on this boat – is making it difficult to focus.

I don't want to believe that one of these guys could have so cold-bloodedly offed Elena, but if it wasn't one of them, then the only alternative is that Joaquín is out there watching our every move. As ridiculous as it sounds in my head, the thought chills me to my core. Across the horizon in all directions, there is no sign of any other boats, and yet I can't shake the feeling I'm being watched.

Rhys has managed to calm Fergus, lifting the board from the hot tub and encouraging him to get in. I've never seen him look as manic as when he was wielding that knife at all of us. If Sophie and I hadn't attempted to disarm him, would he have followed through on his threat? I still remember the odd way he acted the night of the power cut, and I know I shouldn't underestimate him, despite what my sister tells me. He was quick to accuse me this morning, after all.

But what about the other suspects among us?

Sophie surfaced quite soon after me – could that be because she was already awake, having just put Elena in the shark cage? She didn't think twice about operating the handle to lower the cage. Is that because she'd observed Joaquín the night before or because she'd already used it that morning? She could have snuck back to her room and waited for the next person – me – to wake and then pretended she'd been woken.

I look next at Rhys. I know how underhand he has been in the past; how many secrets he managed to keep from the rest of us, while outwardly lying to our faces. Yes, he had his reasons, but how can I trust someone so manipulative? What if he waited until he and Elena were in the throes of passion before murdering her? Maybe that was why he lured her away in the first place. We were all fast asleep after their grunting and moaning finished, so he would have been free to make his move without fear of being disturbed. We only have his word that Elena left some time before three.

Then there's Christophe. Little kleptomaniac Christophe, who assures us that he's sought professional help for his mental health, but what if it's manifesting itself in other ways now? He said he first started taking things when he was seventeen, and it became uncontrollable. That was why he stole Fergus's lucky lighter back when we were living together. He claimed he wasn't trying to hurt him, but was envious of the way Fergus relied on it, using the lighter as if it were a calming wand, improving his self-confidence with a flick and a spark.

Christophe started seeing a professional therapist and retrained to become a mental health professional himself after graduating. He now focuses on the condition and works with patients to help control their urges to steal. It almost reads like a fairy-tale, but maybe it's all part of a narrative that he's chosen for us to believe.

'How's the arm?' Sophie asks, joining me on the bench.

'Fine.' I grimace.

'Good. I was just talking to Harry, and we can't stay here indefinitely. I mean we have enough supplies to last a few days, but we don't know if anyone is looking for us or not.'

'The yacht company will be expecting us back on Monday afternoon and we're due to fly home at midday, so I'm sure if we don't show up, they'll send a search party. They know where we are. Joaquín radioed in our coordinates.'

'Did he, though? Did any of us hear him do it?'

The question throws me, and I can't answer.

Sophie's eyebrows knit together. 'Even if he did, we've been adrift ever since, so there's no telling where we'll be come Monday. With the dinghy and outboard missing, I can only assume Joaquín killed Elena and beat his escape. And for all we know, he could have brought us out here intending for pirates to come and rob us.'

I immediately think of Captain Pugwash and want to laugh, but she isn't joking.

'Pirates still operate in open seas, Pete. I was reading an article about it before we came away. You saw the Tom Hanks film about pirates taking control of his ship, right?'

It seems such a far-fetched idea, but it's easier to stomach than the thought that a killer sits among us. It is clear Sophie trusts the rest of us enough to assume a third party is involved. What does it say about my own suspicions?

'What about sending up a flare?' I say suddenly, as the idea punctures my mind. 'The yacht must be equipped for emergencies.'

She shakes her head. 'I already checked and can't find any flares. And before you suggest it, there was also no sign of an emergency life raft either. All I can conclude is that the yacht was ill-equipped to begin with, or...'

The killer has got rid of both.

'I think we need to take action, Pete. We need to try and get this yacht sailing again.'

'Do you know how to sail a yacht?'

She shakes her head. 'No, but it can't be too dissimilar to a car, right? It's got an engine, so it's not like we have to manhandle sails. If we can get the engine started, we should be able to sail until we spot land.'

'But I thought the navigation equipment was damaged with the radio?'

'It is, but we know where the sun rose, which means that's east.' She points in one direction. 'If we sail roughly south-west, we should eventually spot land.'

'But we don't know how long we've been drifting, and if we

don't know our starting position, how can we be sure we're north of an island?'

'Harry remembers. The tour was heading north from the mainland.'

It's as sound a plan as any, and ultimately we're going to have to report Elena's death to the authorities. I just want to get back on dry land, and back to Carly.

'Okay, what can I do to help?' I ask, my spirits rising.

'What are you two talking about?' Christophe asks, dropping in beside me.

'Just trying to formulate a plan to get us out of here,' Sophie says. 'We're going to try and start the boat and sail in the direction of land.'

'Great! What are we waiting for?'

'We can't find the keys. Harry and I have searched the cabins and the V-berth, but there's no sign of them.'

My renewed optimism wanes. When Sophie talked about setting sail, I thought navigating the yacht would be the biggest challenge.

After the mention of searching the cabin, Rhys and Fergus are now looking over, so Sophie stands in order to address us all. 'We think that maybe Elena had the keys on her when she went into the water.'

I already know what she's going to say before she speaks.

'Which means... one of us is going to need to go into the cage and search for them.'

My stomach rolls at the memory of the shark smashing against the bars.

'Obviously, none of us is keen to go swimming with a corpse, so I think – in time-honoured tradition – we should draw lots for who goes down there.'

'I can't swim,' Rhys immediately declares, taking a puff on his inhaler.

'You don't need to be able to swim, as we'll attach the rope around whoever goes down.'

'Are you mad?' Fergus calls out. 'You're seriously expecting one of us to frisk her? No way. I want to retch just thinking about it.'

'I know it's unpleasant, but it's that or we continue to drift until we're shark bait.'

Sophie's bedside manner has never been great, but that's brutal even by her standards.

'We'll write "No" on five bits of paper and "Yes" on one. Whoever draws "Yes" goes in.'

'Pete shouldn't be included in this,' Harry pipes up. 'His wound shouldn't get wet.'

Rhys looks on enviously.

'No, I'm not an invalid,' I declare, feeling the warmth of the wine in my cheeks. 'We *all* draw lots or none of us do.'

I just have to hope my luck is in.

Sophie writes on the scraps of paper, folds each one twice, and drops them into a clean glass. She returns to the gathered group.

'At least, we should let Pete draw first so he gets the best odds,' Harry states.

I'm about to argue, but the others quickly agree, and so I form a claw with my thumb and index finger and pinch one of the pieces, securing it in a balled fist. The others then take it in turns to draw a lot, with Sophie taking the last.

'Now, we all open them together,' she says, counting us down.

Fergus breathes a sigh of relief, Rhys's eyes light up, Christophe shrugs nonchalantly, and Harry and Sophie look concerned.

I open mine and my shoulders drop. I hold the 'Yes' marker for the others to see.

'No, this is ridiculous,' Harry says. 'I'm not letting you go down there. I'll go in your place.'

I shake my head. 'We all understood the rules, and it is what it is. Can you see if there's any kind of wetsuit in the V-berth, to protect my arm?'

Sophie nods and heads down into the galley. Fergus, Rhys, and Christophe return to the hot tub, the guilt of not volunteering to switch places too much for them.

'At the very least, I should go down with you,' Harry says. 'You did the same for me last night.'

'Do you remember how cramped it was in there with the two of us? There's already an extra body down there. I'll be fine. I'll check her pockets and be out in a couple of minutes at most.'

Sophie returns, carrying a wetsuit. 'There was only one, and I reckon it was Elena's given the size, but it will keep the dressing dry.'

She helps me put it on, and proceeds to raise the cage from the water. Harry lifts the lid, and I drop into it. The body is no longer floating, so I strap goggles to my face, take a deep breath and plunge my head in. It's as cold as it was last night, but at least the wetsuit is helping to moderate my body temperature, and the alcohol is taking the edge off.

The body is right at the bottom of the cage, so I come up for another big breath before diving down. I try not to look at the deathly pallor of her face, concentrating on rummaging through the pockets of her shorts first. I find nothing. She's wearing the white short-sleeve uniform, and so I check the square pocket of the shirt, but that too is empty. I catch sight of her face in my periphery, and choke as I see Raymond Grosjean's lifeless body staring back at me.

16

TEN YEARS AGO

The upright suitcase in the corner of the room serves as an unwelcome reminder of what I'm missing out on. Carly initially said she would stay behind, but there was no point in both of us foregoing the trip. I told her she'd only get under my feet, and that I'm better off ploughing through on my own. Harry suggested I could bring my laptop with me and do the work on the train, but I didn't want to spoil their fun by souring the mood.

I still have no idea who would do this to me. When I was telling Carly what had happened – how the printed assignment vanished into thin air, with the content of the digital copy also mysteriously erased – I genuinely started to question whether I'd imagined the whole thing. The look on her face suggested she was also concerned about my mental health, but I know I'm not making it up: that assignment was ready, and what's most frustrating is that I know it was well-written.

Professor 'just call me Ed' Chambers will know that it was rushed, and will mark accordingly. Sophie suggested just binning the whole thing off and going on the trip, and for five minutes I genuinely considered the suggestion, but I know I wouldn't enjoy myself with this hanging over my head. I wouldn't mind if I'd done something wrong, but somebody did this to me. The question is whether the act was aimed at causing me to fail the assignment, or to prevent me from going on the trip.

I try to push all thoughts of baguettes, croissants, and Camembert from my mind, and crack open another energy drink. I bought a multipack of them from the local shop, along with three large bags of crisps, and the largest bar of chocolate they sold. I need as much mental energy as I can ingest, though I know the come down is going to be fierce.

Carly has messaged a couple of times, but hasn't sent any pictures, which I guess is her way of attempting to not rub my nose in the fun I'm sure they're all having. As soon as they left on Friday night, I immediately started re-reading all my notes, trying to recall how I opened the assignment. I managed to get 500 words written, before realising this *was* how I started originally, before changing perspective, and subsequently had to start again.

I wanted to cry when I woke on Saturday and saw that it hadn't been a nightmare, and that I still had another 4,000 words to find. I ate the chocolate bar and sang along to an oldies station on the radio before determining there was nothing to be gained by feeling sorry for myself. A hot shower, and a jog to the shop to buy more energy drinks, and the fog finally started to lift from my mind.

By the end of Saturday, I had 4,000 words written – not all of them poor. Still not a patch on what I should have handed to Ed on Friday, but not as bad as I was fearing. Sleep didn't come well, though; presumably a result of all the caffeine and sugar I'd consumed. At three o'clock this morning, I actually crawled from my bed to my desk and added another thousand words before returning to sleep.

When I woke at eight, I re-read what I'd written in the night and promptly deleted it. Now, as I struggle to summarise my legal argument, I'm not even sure if this was the right topic to tackle to begin with. I felt so confident on Friday, but maybe I was just pulling the wool over my own eyes. Will Ed think this is any good, or will he make an example out of me?

I start at the sound of the front door slamming shut. The others aren't due back until eleven tonight, but has one of them returned early?

Very slowly, I push myself away from my desk, and tiptoe to my door, straining to hear a voice or any indication of who is in the corridor. I'm sure I didn't imagine the sound, but it is deathly quiet now. I glance back at my desk, and spot the packet of caffeine pills that I discovered in the medicine cabinet in the upstairs bathroom. The packet wasn't boxed up, so I had no way of checking for a use-by date. What if they weren't caffeine pills and I've inadvertently digested something psychotropic?

A deep cough sounds from just outside my door and a moment later, I hear the sound of a key being inserted into Fergus's door. I pull my own open to greet him, but my mouth drops when I come face to face with Raymond. His brittle, steel-grey, unkempt hair hangs down to the oversized black leather jacket, and his cheeks are red and puffy.

'Which one are you?' he croaks dismissively, his West Country accent gravelly, as he stands inside Fergus's open doorway.

'Um, Pete Routledge,' I reply uncertainly. 'Does Fergus know you're going into his room?'

He stares back at me, no shame about his actions. 'Drug search.'

My mouth drops open. 'Fergus doesn't take drugs,' I lie.

'Good. Then I won't find any in here then, will I?'

He doesn't wait for me to respond and steps further inside, allowing the heavy fire door to close. I remain rooted to the spot. I thought the point of us having locks on our doors was to protect our possessions. I had no clue Raymond had skeleton keys for each of our rooms. Nausea builds in the back of my throat at the thought of him violating my space.

He reappears a few moments later, and seems surprised to find I'm still in the corridor.

'You have no right to search our rooms,' I say firmly, half-tempted to phone Carly, but not wanting to waste her time.

'Actually, I do.' His deep Cornish brogue resonates. 'Check your tenancy agreement. One of the stipulations to you living in my house is that no illegal drugs are to be used on the premises. To that end, I am allowed to routinely perform checks of the property to ensure the stipulations are being met.'

He moves towards my door, but I block his path. 'There's no way you're going in my room without my permission. I want you to leave now, or I'll… I'll phone the police.'

He raises his eyebrows, clearly unimpressed by my threat. 'Be my guest. I'm not breaking any laws here. I'll continue upstairs.'

I want to stop him heading towards the stairs, but for all I know he might be telling the truth about the conditions in the tenancy agreement. I must admit I didn't read all of the small print before signing, and despite me asking her for it, Sophie has still not divulged the full details.

I hear him cross the landing and begin the ascent up to Christophe's room in the loft. The stairs creak as he climbs. I return to my own room, suddenly conscious of the packet of caffeine pills I left on my desk. Though not illegal, their presence might not be well received, particularly if he does find pot in Fergus's or Rhys's rooms. I push the packet into the rear pocket of my jeans and scan the room for anything else suspicious. I hate the thought of him returning to my room when I'm not here, so I'd rather he perform his search while I observe.

I stay there until I hear him heading down the main staircase, and proceed to open my door.

'If you must search my room, I'd rather be here to make sure nothing gets damaged,' I say.

The stench of his bad breath fills my nostrils as he squeezes his enormous jacket past me and sidles in.

'The others not invite you on their French trip?' he scoffs.

'I couldn't go as I have a deadline to hit.'

He glances at my laptop screen, and I quickly slam the lid shut.

'Can you open the drawers to your desk please, and remove any papers on the top?'

I do as instructed, and then proceed to open the drawers in the chest beneath the window. At least he has the decency not to run his hands through my underwear, encouraging me to do it instead. I doubt he showed any restraint rummaging in the others' drawers.

'That'll do for today,' he says, almost disappointed to be leaving empty-handed. His star players, Fergus and Rhys, must have got away with it.

I follow him to my door, and hold it open while he shuffles through.

'Soph never mentioned that you had keys for all the rooms,' I say.

He reaches into his pocket and extracts a keyring. 'All the locks are identical; I only need the one key.'

He smiles to himself when he sees the shock on my face. Is that how Christophe managed to get into Fergus's room so easily? And if that's the case, then he definitely could have got into my room and taken my assignment. My eyes widen as my imagination leaps from one conclusion to the next. If he came into my room while I was getting washed on Friday morning, he could have removed the assignment from my bag, returning to my room to wipe the file on my laptop after I'd gone to my seminar.

I don't know why he would want to cause me such trouble, but maybe it's because he knows I could drop him in it with Fergus. Either way, I have no physical evidence that he's been in my room, but I can definitely get some if I set up some kind of motion detector camera.

I will look into it later, before the others get back. Right now, I have an assignment to hand in. Ed told me to have it in his pigeonhole before eight tomorrow morning, but I daren't delay, especially after what happened on Friday. I print the file and staple the pages together, but keep hold of it in my hand as I head out the front door, taking the longer route to the campus.

It seems I'm not the only one who's handing in work late, as I run into Woody. He looks confused to see me until I explain about my missing assignment.

'I was going to say,' he explains, 'I thought you and the others were supposed to be in Paris. I was sure Fergus said it was *this* weekend.'

'Yeah, they're all there, including my girlfriend. I got stuck here working.'

'Oh, that really sucks!' He frowns with pity. 'I have to say, you must really trust your girlfriend to be away with your housemates.'

My brows knit together. 'Carly wouldn't cheat on me, and I don't believe any of my friends would go behind my back either.'

Woody quickly apologises. 'I just meant I'm not sure I'd be so willing to let my girlfriend go away with one of her exes – particularly not somewhere as romantic as Paris.'

My frown deepens. 'One of her exes?'

He doesn't hear my question. 'I warned Rhys it wouldn't be

easy moving in with the new boyfriend of someone he'd been out with, but you're clearly more patient and diplomatic than me.'

I don't hear any more of what he says, as blood rushes to my ears. Rhys and Carly had a relationship, and neither of them told me? Were they in love? Was it a bad break-up? No wonder they were both awkward when I introduced them at the housewarming party. And now they're together in Paris, and I'm not. Maybe I was wrong to assume it was Christophe messing with me.

17
PRESENT DAY

I nearly choke as I continue to stare at Raymond Grosjean's face in the shark cage. I know it can't be him, and that the body in the white uniform is too feminine to belong to our former landlord. My lungs strain as I fight to reach the surface, inhaling deeply the moment I break through the water.

I look back down into the murky sea, and Elena's lifeless eyes stare back up at me.

'Did you find the keys?' Harry calls down to me from behind the safety rope.

I shake my head, and hold my hand out, which he duly grabs, helping me up and out of the cage. 'I couldn't find the keys,' I relay to the group. 'I checked all of her pockets, but nothing.'

'The killer probably threw them overboard, or took them with them,' Rhys says with a listless shrug.

'Well, that settles it then,' Harry says, straightening his shoulders in defiance. 'We're going to have to swim for it.'

'Dinnae be an eejit!' Fergus coughs. 'What about the sharks? There's no way I'm getting in the water knowing they're out there.'

'We don't have another choice,' Harry fires back.

'But it's all right for you: you're a good swimmer. I'd drown before I get anywhere, and Rhys canny swim.'

Fergus has made no secret of the fact he isn't a great swimmer, but given there's no sign of land in any direction, I don't believe any of us is really up for the challenge that lies ahead.

'It doesn't have to be all of us,' Sophie says, moving to the opposite side of the yacht. 'I don't mind braving it. Once I get to shore or find another boat, I can get them to come back for you all.'

'Why do you get to go?' Harry asks. 'I'm as good a swimmer as you, if not better.'

'I swim most mornings, so I beg to differ.'

'This is ridiculous,' I say, my breath finally catching up with me. 'You don't know which way land is, nor how far it is. Plus we won't know if you've made it if we don't hear back from you. It's a crazy idea.'

'I disagree,' Harry says. 'There's bound to be another boat nearby. All I've got to do is reach it.'

'Yeah, I mean the killer's boat is probably somewhere nearby too,' Rhys says, his words dripping with sarcasm. 'Why don't you see if he'll give you a lift back to shore?'

This arguing continues for several minutes as everyone's frustrations and anxiety boil to the surface. The truth is that someone has brought this upon us, and I now can't stop seeing Raymond Grosjean's face. Did we bring this on ourselves for what we did?

I sit on the bench, the heat unbearable as the black of the wetsuit attracts the sun's rays. I fiddle with the zip, but am unable to peel it off my shoulders because of the shooting pain beneath the strapping around my arm. Fergus spots me struggling and comes across, taking control of the material, and helping manoeuvre it off my arm.

'We're going to die out here, aren't we?' he says quietly, and I see now how much this experience is affecting him.

'We're not going to die out here. You have to keep the faith. They will come looking for us when we don't dock on Monday. Trust me. And don't forget, Carly and Simone know where we are, and they may have already contacted someone, because they can't get hold of us.'

He tries to smile through his fear, but it isn't convincing.

There has to be something else we can do. Sitting tight when Elena's killer could be nearby – or amongst us now – waiting for us to let down our defences doesn't feel sensible, but neither does braving the water in the *hope* of finding help.

'Why don't we just hotwire the yacht?' I hear Christophe's voice carry over the din.

The others haven't heard him, so I shush them and invite him to repeat what he just said.

'Well, it's got an engine, right?'

It's not the craziest suggestion, though from the blank looks on the faces of the rest of the group, I'm not sure we have the skills to undertake such a feat. Of course, if we had access to the internet, we might be able to figure it out, but then again, if we had internet access, we wouldn't need to figure it out in the first place.

'Has anyone here ever hotwired a car?' I ask, not ready to dismiss the suggestion out of hand. Given Christophe's history of theft, I let my eyes fall on him automatically, expecting a positive response.

Nobody nods.

'I think I saw my cousin do it once,' Sophie offers quietly. 'He fiddled with some wires beneath the steering wheel when he couldn't find his car keys, but this was aeons ago and an ancient car. I don't know that it's as easy with modern cars, let alone with boat engines.'

I stand and slowly climb up to the cockpit, where I study the dials on the dashboard and the white leather steering wheel. Even if we could get the engine started, I'm not sure which of the switches and buttons would need pressing to get us moving. Sophie joins me a moment later, checking beneath the steering column for any kind of access panel. She finds a hinged catch and the plate comes off in her hands.

'Well, I've found the fuses,' she says, scrutinising the interior of the small access point. 'Not entirely sure if that's a help or a hindrance.'

She stands and begins to search for other panels.

'What are you looking for?' I ask. 'Maybe I can help?'

'Trying to see if there's any kind of logbook or instruction manual. You know, like you get with the car and can consult when weird lights flash up on the control panel? If there was one of those, then maybe it would shed some light on how to start it without keys.'

We scour the area, but there's nothing here.

'Maybe the captain kept it in the V-berth?' I suggest.

Sophie drops out of the cockpit and disappears through the galley hatch. I decide to follow her down because I'd rather feel like I'm doing something. She's already located a manual by the time I make it down there. She's sitting on one of the beds, thumbing through it.

'Where do you think the engine is?' I ask, and she points at the floor beneath my feet, where I now notice a rectangular access point.

Presumably it can be raised to allow access to the engine and motors.

'Do you reckon you can figure out how to do it?'

She glances up from the book, but the look she gives doesn't instil confidence. 'I'll do my best. Can you go and see if you can quieten the others down? I can't hear myself think with all that arguing.'

I head back out to the deck, where Harry is now trying to put on the wetsuit I used to go into the cage. Fergus, Christophe and Rhys are all trying to talk him out of what he's about to do.

'It's the hottest part of the day, man,' Rhys is saying. 'You won't last ten minutes in the water. Seriously, you can't go through with this.'

'I'm not some kid, I can look after myself,' Harry snaps back. 'I'm not going to just sit around and let some psycho come for us.' He fixes me with a hard stare as he says this.

'It's suicide,' Fergus chimes in.

'Soph thinks she can figure out how to get the engine started,' I lie, as I don't want to watch my best friend drown or get eaten. 'Plus, you've been drinking, so you're not exactly in peak physical condition. Give Soph time to try and figure out the manual, and if she hasn't managed to start it by morning, then we'll reassess our options.'

Harry zips up the wetsuit, mind already made up, but then I spot something on the horizon, and my blood runs cold. Shielding my eyes from the glare of the sun, I double-check before alerting the others.

I point at the dorsal fin poking out of the water.

I'm relieved when Harry nods and begins to remove the wetsuit.

'We can't stay out here,' I warn them. Rhys wasn't wrong about the heat. Just standing on the deck feels like a sauna. 'I think we should each go to our cabins, and cool down. All the doors have internal locks, so everyone should be safe.'

I'm about to lead the way when I see Fergus staring out to sea, his skin as pale as milk. I open my mouth to ask what he's looking at when I see the white trouser-covered leg and shoe bobbing like a buoy on the surface of the water. There's no sign of the rest of the body, but I'm in little doubt who it belongs to.

18

TEN YEARS AGO

The betrayal boils in my gut like nothing I've ever experienced. This is beyond anger: this is venomous rage. Carly and Rhys have both been lying to me. The woman I was falling in love with, and the housemate I thought I could trust not to stab me in the back. I'm not saying I would have been blasé about it had they admitted the truth – maybe it would have taken a few days to get over – but that's better than barefaced deceit.

I want to kill him.

They knew it was going to be awkward the night of the house-warming and neither had the decency to warn me. I knew that Carly had had other partners before me. She's two years older and employed in the real world; it would have been unusual if she hadn't had any boyfriends or sexual partners before me. And whilst we've acknowledged we both bring baggage into the relationship, at least she's unlikely to run into mine at the breakfast table.

My skin crawls at the thought of the two of them together. Her hands around his neck, pulling him towards her. His hands massaging her breasts in that way that always sends a jolt of electricity the length of her body. Her writhing at his touch, and his lips caressing her skin until his face is buried between her legs.

I knock back the vodka and quickly refill the glass.

When Woody told me about their relationship, it was like my whole world began to fade before my eyes. The evening sky seemed to darken beneath the weight of the cloud hanging over me. I don't remember walking home, but here I am, and the vodka bottle now stands empty on the kitchen table.

It's still several hours until they'll be home, but I'm determined I'm going to have it out with them both the second I see them. I won't be able to sleep until I know whether their affair has continued. Or maybe this weekend was Rhys's opportunity to win her back. That has to be why he would steal my assignment and delete the file on my laptop. He knew how hard I'd been working on it, and he'd have known I wouldn't be able to just not complete it. I've told all of the others how much every last percentage point is needed if I'm to graduate with a strong enough degree to get into law school next year. I have no evidence, but he has the strongest motive for wanting to see me suffer and miss the trip.

I take another swig of the vodka as I picture him putting his moves on her. Carly and I were to be sharing a suite, so nothing could have stopped Rhys from sneaking out of the bedroom he's sharing with Christophe and into Carly's bed. Most women would struggle to resist Rhys's charms if he came knocking, semi-clothed, in the middle of the night. I imagine her struggling with her conscience, and then buying the lie that I'll never find out because they're away and nobody will know.

A wave of nausea tears through my body, and I stumble up the stairs towards the bathroom, barely making it before my body heaves, but I belch audibly, rather than retch. It's so loud that I actually burst into laughter.

Maybe they'll come clean when I confront them. Maybe the

guilt of sleeping together in Paris will be too much for Carly and she'll come here and break up with me. Maybe she'll admit that she never stopped carrying a torch for Rhys, and now they've decided to give things a second try.

I'm not sure I'll be able to continue living under the same roof as Rhys. I can't afford to move out, but maybe he'll do the decent thing for once and pack his bags. I'm sure we could find a new housemate under the circumstances, or even just split his rent between the five of us.

I could text Harry and try to get a heads-up on what happened in France. He's always had my back, and if he suspects anything has been going on between them, he won't keep it from me. *Dicks before chicks* has always been his motto, and I don't doubt his loyalty. I desperately wish he was here so I could vent openly, rather than bottling up all these thoughts and feelings.

But what if they don't come clean? What if they refute Woody's claims, and Rhys denies stealing my assignment?

I wish I had something concrete to prove I'm right. When Raymond was here earlier, he didn't mention finding anything in any of the rooms, let alone my assignment. Maybe if I'd accompanied him on his raid, I might have spotted it in Rhys's room.

I freeze, remembering what Raymond said about the keys and the rooms: *all the locks are identical; I only need the one key.*

I can search Rhys's room myself. I fish into my pocket and pull out my own key. I have no qualms about going into his room as he trespassed first, and I'm only looking to claim back what is rightfully mine. If I find my original assignment I can get it to Ed before he reads the new version. I thrust the key into the lock, part of me doubting Raymond's claim, but it slots in easier than it does my door, and clicks as the lock is flicked back.

I'm in.

The room really is a carbon copy of mine, save for the

bedding. His is red and white strips to reflect his obsession with Manchester United, whilst mine is a simple blue-patterned cover I picked up in IKEA.

His bed and desk are on opposite sides of the room to where they are in mine, so actually the layout is more like a reflection than a carbon copy. His laptop – he has a top-of-the-range MacBook which his parents bought him – sits idle on the desk, beside a pile of books from his course. There's no obvious sign of the printed assignment, so I proceed to rifle through the drawers of his desk, and then the chest of drawers.

I don't realise until I'm done that there's a distinct smell of cologne in this room; one I've smelled before. He must use the same brand as Christophe, which means maybe I've been wrong to assume about more than one thing.

I lurch as I imagine Rhys coming on to Carly, and only the bed breaks my fall. Jesus, what if they've slept together in this bed?

I want to pull off the bedding and throw it out the window. I want to take a canister of petrol and douse every inch of the room before striking a match.

* * *

I start at the sound of the front door opening, and immediately realise I have fallen asleep on Rhys's floor. In my vodka-haze, I don't even remember lying down. If Rhys or the others catch me in here, it will undermine my accusation that he or Christophe (I haven't totally ruled him out yet) have been in my room and that one of them stole my assignment.

I push myself up from the rug, with no memory of drifting to sleep. But as I straighten, my head feels as though someone has just slammed a wrecking ball into it. The room spins, and it's all I can do not to crash to the ground. Bile bubbles in the back of my throat. I need to get out of here before I throw up.

I stumble towards the door with no idea whether I've left everything where it was before I arrived. Will Rhys realise I've been in here? I don't have time to check. I pull the door closed as I hear excited, chattering voices in the hallway. Sophie is trying to shush them because my bedroom door is closed, and she thinks I might be asleep.

I can hear Christophe's and Rhys's voices growing louder as they approach the staircase. I don't have time to get back downstairs without being seen, so I dart into the bathroom, flicking on the light with my elbow, and then press my ear against the door until I hear them on the landing. I flush the toilet before exiting the bathroom, making sure to put on my best surprised face as our eyes meet.

'Oh, you're not asleep,' Christophe says, before calling out to the others downstairs. 'Pete's not asleep; he was in the bathroom.'

I can't look at Rhys as my heart is thundering in my chest. Earlier, I was ready to punch his lights out, but now that he's in front of me, and I can see how athletic he is in comparison to me, I don't have the bottle to go through with it.

'You all had a good time, I take it?' I say, as casually as my racing pulse will allow.

'Yeah, it was fine,' Christophe says dismissively. 'We bought you a souvenir. Harry has it downstairs.'

I take this as my cue to leave, watching Rhys in my periphery as he unlocks his door and heads inside. I'm relieved when he doesn't immediately turn back and accuse me of trespassing.

I find Sophie and Harry in the kitchen. They smile warmly when they see me.

'So, did you get it all done?' Sophie asks.

'Delivered it this afternoon,' I say, more triumphant than I'm feeling.

'Yay, well at least that's one less stress on your shoulders.'

'Is Carly not with you?' I ask.

'She's paying the taxi driver,' Sophie says, and sure enough, a moment later, Carly walks in through the door, carrying a large wheel of brie.

A gift because she missed me, or is she just feeling guilty?

When she leans in for a kiss, I duck into my room. I hold the door open so she can come in. She needs to answer the questions burning in my mind.

'Did you get your assignment completed?' she asks, calmer than I'm expecting.

But of course she doesn't know I've found out her dirty little secret. Yet.

'Yep, all done. Not as good as the original, but I tried my best.'

She rests the brie on my desk and the plastic wrapping crinkles. 'Good, well then that means I can stay over and we can make up for lost time.'

She rests her hands on my arms, and again attempts to kiss me, but I turn my head.

'What's going on?' she asks. 'Are you mad at me for some reason?'

I don't answer, but fix her with a hard stare. I won't make this easy for her.

'You're pissed because I went to Paris? I told you I'd stay, but you insisted I go.'

Still I bite my lip, waiting to see where her guilt leads her next.

'Are you going to answer me? Is that what you're angry about? We had fun, but everyone said it wasn't the same without you there. I really missed you.'

'Even though you had Rhys for company?' The words spill from my lips before I can stop myself.

'Rhys? Why would I care if Rhys was there?'

'I don't know, Carly, why don't you tell me? A trip to the most romantic city in the world with one of your exes – can't see anything wrong with that.'

I see the penny drop, and she closes her eyes in defeat.

'I can't believe you never told me the two of you were in a relationship.'

'It wasn't a relationship. He was just... I don't know... a one-night thing when I was drunk and should have known better.'

She stops and looks at me as if she's expecting this explanation to make everything okay again, but she's sorely mistaken.

She sighs heavily, her eyes dropping to the carpet. 'I was out with some friends celebrating completing my police probation. We started drinking in the afternoon, and by the time we reached the club, we were wasted. I didn't know he was a student, and I don't even remember pulling him, but I remember the regret the following morning when I snuck out of his room. I never have one-night stands.' Her eyes fix on mine. 'It was way before I met you, so it's not like I cheated or anything.'

When Woody had dropped the bombshell earlier, I'd assumed he meant they'd been an item, but I can't recall exactly how he described them.

'Either way, you should have told me.'

'You haven't told me the names of all the women you've slept with before, and that's okay. I'd rather not know. I thought we were on the same page with that?'

Both of us have raised our voices, but I no longer care if the rest of the house hears. In fact, I *want* Rhys to hear us.

'It's not the same when you've actually slept with one of my housemates, and then colluded to keep it quiet.'

'Colluded? With who?'

'Oh, please, don't tell me the two of you didn't agree to keep this from me.'

I'm going out on a limb here, but the guilt in her eyes is thunderous.

'Get out of my room!' I shout, pointing at the door. 'You lied to me, and I don't know how I feel about you any more.'

She takes my pointing hand, and brings it in to her chest. 'Well, I know exactly how I feel about you, Pete. In fact, when I was in Paris, I bought you something to show you exactly how I feel.'

It will be so crude if she suddenly drops to one knee and proposes. We've only been together for a few months, and right now, I don't even want to breathe the same air as her.

She reaches into her pocket, but remains on both feet. She extracts a small jewellery box, which she prises open. Inside is a tiny padlock with an inscription on it.

'I was gutted when you said you weren't going to come, because I had this plan to stand with you on the Pont Des Arts Bridge and leave our own love lock there. Because what I've realised, Pete, is that I am in love with you. You're the first thing I think of every morning, and the last thing on my mind when I go to sleep.'

Her first use of the word love forms a lump in my throat. This is breaking my heart because, until a few hours ago, this was exactly how I felt about her, but that was before I found out she's been lying to me for weeks.

'I am sorry I didn't tell you about Rhys. I had no idea he was even living here until that housewarming party, but by then, it already felt too late to mention it. I told him in no uncertain terms that night not to mention it. He said it was in both of our best interests not to breathe a word. I'm sorry. I didn't mean to lie to you, but I didn't want a meaningless one-night stand in my past to upset what we have going here. I'm crazy about you, Pete, and I would never do anything to deliberately hurt you.'

My vision blurs as my eyes fill, but I can't forgive and forget just because she's told me she loves me for the first time. I'm worth more than that.

'You need to go,' I tell her firmly. 'I can't be around you right now.'

It pains me to see the despair in her eyes as she snaps the jewellery box closed, but she doesn't argue, grabbing her bag from where she dumped it near the door, and leaving without another word. I don't regret showing her the door, but I am worried I might one day regret not hearing her out. Only time will tell.

And as much as I want to now go and have it out with Rhys, I'm a drunk mess and will only embarrass myself. No, revenge is a dish best served cold.

19

PRESENT DAY

It's the sandal attached to the floating limb that makes me certain that wherever Joaquín is, he's minus a leg. Although it isn't close enough for us to drag in, the bloody chomp mark makes it clear how the severance occurred.

Did he accidentally fall in after forcing Elena into the cage?

I don't want to think about an alternative reason for his mysterious disappearance. He could still be out there in the dinghy somewhere, nursing his injury, but my gut tells me it's more likely he's been eaten.

The latch on the cabin door seems so flimsy as I slide it across, but at least I'm alone and safe. For now, at least. The cabin isn't as cool as I'd expected when I'd suggested we migrate indoors. I'd give anything to have the ceiling fan from our bedroom back home. The starboard-side window is a couple of feet square, but doesn't open, so I'm restricted to fanning myself with a magazine Harry left in here when we first boarded yesterday. I avoid looking at the images of bare-chested women on the front.

My heart sinks as I think about Carly at the festival, probably wondering why I'm not replying to any of her messages and why she can't get hold of me. She's never been a worrier about things she can't control – too pragmatic for that – so she's probably just assuming we're having far too much fun for me to even think about her. If only I could get a message to her. Hopefully she is keeping a close eye on Simone and offering similar reassurance.

It was Carly who first taught me the serenity prayer that I recite whenever I feel my own anxiety manifesting.

Grant me the serenity to accept the things I cannot change, the courage to change the things I can, and the wisdom to know the difference.

It doesn't hurt to keep it at the forefront of my mind. I can't change the fact that Elena is dead, nor the fact that I have no clue who actually killed her.

Sophie has taken responsibility for trying to get the engine started, and deep down, I want to trust she is doing her best.

I suddenly recall something I overheard Joaquín say. He was telling Harry about a flotation ball attached to the yacht's keys. So if they did go overboard, the keys wouldn't sink and could be retrieved. Well, I certainly haven't seen them floating near the boat, but then we've been adrift for so long they could be anywhere. It's just as likely that Joaquín had them with him when the shark struck.

Or could the flotation ball have come off the keyring? Is it worth us using the remaining air tank to swim down and check just in case? I park the idea in the back of my mind. With the risk of predator sharks nearby, it's too dangerous unless we know where they are.

It's been a hell of a day, and I just want to wake up from this nightmare. I'm physically and mentally drained, and the walls of my vision feel as though they're going to collapse in on me again. I lie down on the bed and focus on my breathing: inhaling deeply through my nose, holding it for five seconds, then exhaling through my mouth, and holding for another five seconds. I think of the voice of the instructor on my meditation app, telling me to feel where the breath goes in my body and willing my fears and anxieties to go away.

Grant me the serenity to accept the things I cannot change, the courage to change the things I can, and the wisdom to know the difference.

My eyes snap open. The router.

The last time I was lying in this position was when I woke up and realised I couldn't hear the engines. I checked my phone and there was no Wi-Fi signal. Sophie and I were looking for the router when we realised that Elena was missing, but we never actually located it when Christophe climbed through the window into the V-berth. Maybe if I could find the router, there might be a way to reset it, and... I don't know... find a device to connect to? I don't remember seeing Elena with a phone, but surely she must have had one. And if not a phone, then an iPad or tablet of some sort? We all agreed we wouldn't bring ours so we couldn't slip into the trap of working while away – wasn't that Christophe's idea? – but that doesn't mean Elena didn't have something. Would her killer be calculated enough to steal Elena's personal devices as well as our phones?

And even if her killer did think about it, would they have thought to check for a satellite phone? Surely a company like this wouldn't solely rely on the yacht's radio communication system? There must be a back-up.

I push myself into a sitting position, my anxiety settling as I focus on my new mission. I take a deep breath and push myself to my feet, but then I freeze.

Someone is in the corridor.

The carpeted floorboards creak as a figure moves along them slowly, trying not to be heard. We all agreed we would stay in our rooms until the intense heat died down, but there's something about the careful placement of feet that's setting off alarm bells in my head. I can't picture anything but the killer preparing to move on to their next victim. I can't just stand here and allow one of my friends to be murdered, or worse: myself.

I'm not armed, though, and whoever is out there might be. I turn my head, scanning the room for anything I can use to defend myself, but I didn't come prepared for such a confrontation. Frustration builds as I pick up the small umbrella I packed. It will have to do.

Pressing my ear to the door, I listen again for the sound of creaking floorboards, trying to determine whereabouts in the corridor they are, but the footsteps are fainter now, towards the galley. With a deep breath, I carefully slide back the latch and glide the door open.

Christophe stops at the far end of the corridor, his eyes wide with panic, like a rabbit caught in headlights. Sunlight peeking through the galley hatch glints off the enormous knife in his hand. I recognise it as one from the wooden block in the galley.

Is this it? The moment my life will be snuffed out? And by Christophe, of all people. What is motivating him to be coming for us like this?

He takes a step forward, tightening his grip on the handle, pointing it in my direction. He eyes the umbrella in my hand, and we both know that I am no match for him. The corridor is so narrow that I have no means of getting past him without getting cut again, and it's a dead end behind me.

'Christophe has a knife!' I yell. 'He's trying to kill me.'

He starts at the sudden break in the silence, and his eyes widen. Four cabin doors slide open almost immediately.

Christophe takes one look at all the eyes staring back at him and races through the galley and up onto deck, almost tumbling into the uncovered hot tub. He stops and spins on his heel just in time, waving the knife uncertainly at all of us as we gather around him in a semi-circle.

Harry is the first to speak. 'Put the knife down, Christophe.'

Christophe looks at the knife in his trembling hand, and then glares back at me, shaking his head.

'Did he attack you?' Sophie asks me.

'No. I heard him moving about in the corridor and came out to investigate, and that's when I saw him. I guess he was planning on coming for one of us.'

Sophie looks over to him. 'What are you doing with the knife, Christophe?'

His eyes are wide with panic. 'I thought I should get something for protection.'

To be fair, that probably would have been the first lie I would have come up with if I'd been caught red-handed too. I can't believe my first instinct about Christophe was right. That morning, when we were all gathered on deck, trying to figure out why Elena would have abandoned us, he must have snuck through the window access into the V-berth and swiped the phones from our rooms. Presumably he threw them overboard and sauntered back to the stern as if nothing was afoot.

The real question, though, is why he would kill Elena, and whether he was planning to hurt the rest of us. Could that mean he also killed Joaquín?

'I was the one who caught *Pete* in the corridor,' Christophe says defiantly, his eyes pleading with the others to believe him. 'Why don't you ask him where he was going?'

I feel Rhys and Fergus take a tentative step away from me.

'Don't try and turn this around on me,' I scoff. 'Why don't you tell us why you killed Elena?'

'I-I didn't,' he says, tears now rolling down his cheeks.

'What was the plan? Kill us all and feed us to the sharks, like you did with Joaquín? How were you planning on getting back to the shore?'

'I... I...' But he can't complete the lie.

He's out of time and out of luck.

'If you really didn't kill Elena, then you need to put down the knife, Christophe,' Sophie says, her voice always the one of reason.

Christophe looks at the shining blade, the glint paralysing all of us into inaction. Even if he were to lunge towards us all, there's no way he can succeed without one of the five of us overpowering him. I can see his eyes darting from person to person, considering his options. He takes a step forward, and for a moment, I think he's actually planning to go for us all, but then he places the knife on the deck, and kicks it behind him, as if fearing that one of us might be the real killer, and will pick it up and use it on him.

He continues forwards, his head in his hands, audibly sobbing, but I can't tell whether the tears are genuine or just for show.

'What do we do with him now?' Harry asks. 'It's not like there's a jail cell on board.'

'The V-berth,' Sophie says, putting a tentative arm around Christophe's shoulders and leading him down the steps into the galley. 'It's the only room we can lock from the outside.'

'What about the window access?' I question.

'We'll block it off from the top, so he won't be able to escape.'

I don't even know if that's possible, but it's better than any plan I've got. Rhys, Fergus and I stand guard at the door, carefully watching Christophe while Harry and Sophie do their best to barricade the window over his head. Presumably there's some kind of locking mechanism for that too, otherwise any Tom, Dick, or Harry could break in to the yacht when it's moored.

I don't feel safe, knowing that one of my friends could be capable of murdering Elena and Joaquín in cold blood, but what troubles me most is: what if the real killer is still at large?

20

TEN YEARS AGO

The mood in the house has been decidedly sour since everyone returned from Paris. After Carly left on Sunday night, Harry was the only one brave enough to come and check if I was okay.

I didn't ask, because I don't want to think badly of him, but if Woody knew about Rhys sleeping with Carly, then surely Harry must have known too, which means the rest of the house could also have known. Harry had met Carly several times before the new term and house hunt, so I want to give him the benefit of the doubt.

I was anticipating an awkward meeting with Rhys, but Fergus told me he's gone home to visit his parents for a few days. Too scared to face me, I suppose. Fergus was adamant that this trip home has been planned for weeks, but the timing is fishy. And I'm not sure I blame him for wanting to put space between us.

'She didn't technically do anything wrong, though,' Fergus says now, as we sit in the living room, each with a can of lager. 'I know she could have told you about their one-night stand, but it's not like she went behind your back.'

'He has a point, you know,' Woody chimes in from the edge of the other sofa, one arm propped on the folded sleeping bag.

I want to ask Christophe if he knew too, but what's the point? If he did, he'll probably deny it, and ultimately it won't make coming to terms with the problem any easier. I'm sure this situation can't be doing his anxiety any good. It certainly isn't helping mine.

I know Fergus is only trying to help me see it from Rhys's side, and to be fair, he's right: Carly didn't cheat on me with Rhys. But it doesn't make the heartache any easier to bear.

'Rhys still should have told me,' I say defiantly, because he's not totally blameless.

Carly has phoned and left umpteen messages, apologising and begging me not to throw away what we've got, and each message breaks my heart a little more. It's the manner of the deceit that angers me most. Had she told me the night of the housewarming, or even in the days that followed, I could have come to terms with it, but it's the fact two months passed since then, and she still didn't say a word.

Likewise, I'd have respected Rhys more had he taken me to one side and informed me. They chose to keep their one-night stand a secret from me, and it makes me question what other things she is keeping quiet. How can we build a loving relationship if I can no longer trust her?

'I'm not saying Rhys couldn't have handled things better,' Fergus continues, 'but it would be a shame to lose a friendship over something like this.'

I'm not sure Rhys particularly cherished our friendship, so is it really such a loss? He generally keeps himself to himself. He's closer to Christophe and Fergus than me. That said, we're tied into this tenancy agreement until June next year, and it's not like I won't be bumping into him in the intervening seven months.

Woody mutters his agreement. 'Of course, if you do decide to move out, I'd be happy to step in and take on your part of the lease.'

I'm sure he thinks he's being well-meaning, but it sounds so cold. I don't want to be the bigger person and forgive and forget, but I know I will eventually cave for the sake of the others. But I don't have to let up. I want to have a proper conversation with Rhys to hear what he has to say for himself, and then to make him understand how hurt I've been by his and Carly's actions.

I also want to figure out once and for all if it was Rhys who stole my assignment. I know now how easy it is to slip into another's room, and haven't yet revealed this to the others. I need to choose the best time and way. I also want to know from Sophie whether I'm allowed to change the lock on my door. I found a video on YouTube that explained how easy it is to do, but I still haven't seen the list of Raymond's stipulations and don't want to step out of line, and for the others to bear the brunt.

'Are either of you fellas up for takeaway tonight?' Woody says. 'I have a real craving for Szechuan chicken.'

He snatches up one of the glossy takeaway leaflets from the table as if he owns the place, and offers it out.

Fergus takes it from him, and studies it eagerly. 'I shouldn't waste money on takeaway, but I must admit I'm tempted. Do they do crispy beef in sweet chilli sauce? Aye, here it is.'

I haven't eaten a proper meal since I started writing my assignment last week, and I'd be better off going to the supermarket and buying some vegetables to cook, but I just don't have the motivation. It would be hard to stay home tonight and eat healthily with the smell of Chinese takeaway wafting through the house. Fergus offers the leaflet in my direction, and I take it from him.

'I'll text Christophe, Rhys and Harry and see if they want in,' Woody says almost too casually.

'Rhys is visiting his parents,' Fergus states.

Woody shakes his head. 'He was, but I spoke to him earlier and he's on his way back. In fact, he shouldn't be much longer.'

A cold shadow passes over me. I haven't yet prepared myself for what I want to say to him, and I feel a tightness across my chest. I suddenly want to flee this house and never return. But it's too late, as we all hear the front door slam shut, and the distinct aroma of his body spray carries on the gust of air.

I'm sitting behind the door when he pops his head in, but I'm not brave enough to look up, willing him to leave the room without noticing me. What I'd do for an invisibility cloak right now.

'Hey, Rhys, you're back just in time,' Woody says. 'We're choosing what we want from the Chinese. You in?'

There's a pause and I can feel his stare burning into the top of my head, but I don't look up.

'Sure, let me dump my stuff in my room and I'll be back.'

I wait until I hear him reach the top of the staircase before I leave the room and duck into mine. I need time before I'm ready to talk to him, and I need to plan what I want to say.

My phone is flashing on my desk, and when I pick it up, I see a message from Carly saying she's going to come over tonight, and that she isn't going to give up on fixing our relationship.

Does she know Rhys is now back? Is that the real reason she wants to come over? Are they in cahoots and planning some kind of intervention?

My heartrate is accelerating, and I know what's going to come if I can't let go of this stress. Maybe I should just go for a walk; a breath of fresh air could do wonders, but I know the anxiety will be back the moment I am close to returning, knowing that Rhys is inside, and probably trying to poison the others against me

I flinch at the sound of a guttural roar, which is quickly

followed by thunderous steps charging down the stairs. Rhys is already stomping towards my door as I pull it open to find out what the cacophony is all about.

I don't see his fist until it connects with my cheek and I stumble backwards into my room, trying to plant my feet.

'That your idea of a joke, is it?' Spit curdles at the corner of Rhys's mouth.

'What the fuck is wrong with you?' I demand, nursing the sharp pain in the lower half of my jaw.

'What's going on?' Woody asks, emerging from the living room, Fergus close behind.

'Pete has put a dead rat in my bed,' Rhys says, moving closer to me, and I'm so relieved when Fergus tugs him away.

'I have no idea what he's talking about,' I shout back.

Woody and Fergus are already staring at me, suspicion on their faces.

Rhys struggles against Fergus's grip. 'I went up to my room, and saw that the bedsheet was still a mess from when I left, and as I was making the bed, I saw a dead rat staring back at me.'

'Bullshit!' I shout, but avoid getting too close to him. He's clearly riled, but I'm not having him accuse me of something I didn't do without evidence to back it up. 'Show us.'

At this point, I'm half-expecting him to come clean and reveal his bluff, but instead he marches back towards the stairs, urging Woody and Fergus to follow him up. I tag on behind in case the three of them are colluding, but as I step into Rhys's room, sure enough, in the middle of the double bed, beside the pillows, is a dead rat, maybe six inches long.

'I can't believe you'd do something so gross,' Woody says, turning to glare at me.

I laugh at the suggestion. 'This has absolutely nothing to do with me. For starters, where would I get a dead rat from? And how would I have got it into Rhys's room with the door locked?'

I'm relieved I haven't yet told them what I learned about the keys to our rooms.

'My door was open when I came up here,' Rhys claims, 'so I must have not shut it properly before I left.'

I don't know if this is true and have no way of proving it one way or another.

'That still doesn't mean I was the one to put it in here,' I shout back. 'Not that you don't deserve it, but I wouldn't go anywhere near a rat – alive or dead.' I shudder.

'I'm going to have to get new bedding,' Rhys snarls.

'The least you could do is help him get rid of the rat,' Woody suggests, but I turn and leave instead.

The dead rodent has nothing to do with me, but I can't help smiling as I descend the stairs. I can't think of a more fitting retaliation: rats sleep with rats. Still, it does beg the question of who did put it in there. Woody seemed desperate to shift the blame and Christophe didn't even emerge from his room despite the noise, but what would they gain from trying to drive more of a wedge between Rhys and me?

21

PRESENT DAY

With Christophe locked up in the V-berth, a modicum of calm has returned to the group, and we are endeavouring to make the most of the yacht's luxury. Sophie has had her head buried in the engine manual, and even has the floorboard up, trying to figure out exactly which wires go to the starter motor, and which to the battery. I've warned her not to attempt anything without checking it with one of us first, as the last thing we need is her electrocuting herself or blowing us up.

Despite Harry's best attempts to lighten the atmosphere, having listed the party games he's prepared, Christophe remains the proverbial elephant in the room. I know that whenever there's been a lull in conversation, I've been replaying my every interaction with him, trying to see how I could have missed any potential homicidal tendencies. Maybe the kleptomania manifestation was secretly masking other issues, which have come to the fore now he's taken action to curb the urge to steal. The one person who'd be best to answer that is the psychologist on board, but given they're one and the same person, I'm certain he'd not give us a straight answer. Besides, he's probably learned techniques, as part of his training, which allow him to mask his real intentions.

We did briefly lose touch after university, with me moving to London to study at law school, and Christophe returning to Paris to reunite with his parents. It always seemed inevitable that Sophie and Harry would make the effort to keep in touch with me, and after Carly and I got back together, it didn't surprise me that Rhys kept his distance. According to his Facebook profile, he's now working as an estate agent with his own web design business on the side. Fergus tells me he really matured after graduation, but apart from exchanging birthday and Christmas cards, we've had virtually no contact. I wasn't surprised when Harry warned me Rhys had agreed to attend the weekend, and although I was going to decline, Simone begged me not to.

I've tried not to think about the pain Rhys and Carly caused when the truth came out all those years ago, but I can't help feeling a little jaded whenever our eyes meet. From what Sophie tells me, Rhys is now settled in a relationship with a vet, and they have talked about getting married and starting a family – but if that's true, he wouldn't have slept with Elena.

Sophie really is the glue that holds all of us together. She phones once a month without fail, and shares news of what the others have been up to, even when I don't ask. Although she has her hands full with her own issues, she still seems to yearn for our shared past, a sentiment I can't buy into after what I did.

I'd love to know if any of them ever wake screaming in the night, seeing Raymond's bloody and bruised corpse haunting them. I daren't ask the question, though, as maybe his visits are reserved for the person responsible for his death.

Could Christophe's vendetta have anything to do with that? We all agreed – no, *vowed* – that we wouldn't speak of that night again, and for a few years, I almost managed to convince myself that it didn't happen. Unfortunately, the past always has a habit of creeping up when I least expect it.

None of us had much of an appetite for dinner, but we certainly packed away enough wine and vodka to help us forget our predicament. It's dark when we declare it a night and all depart for our cabins. Sophie took food and drink to Christophe earlier, and as he hears us coming, he demands the chance to use the toilet. We can't deprive him of his human rights, whether he is or isn't the killer. Sophie moves to the door, key in hand.

'Whoa,' Harry says, reaching for her arm. 'What are you doing?'

'I'm letting him out.'

'Are you crazy? What if he's planning to attack us, or escape?'

'Harry's right,' I say, nodding. 'We need to remember that he armed himself before. I know he's our friend – or at least he was – but he may also be a killer. Let's just make sure we're ready for anything.'

Harry takes the key from Sophie and proceeds to the door, when I suddenly have a panic and open the bathroom door, scouring the area for any weapons Christophe could have concealed. I can't find anything, and give Harry a thumbs up to continue.

Christophe emerges, eyeing each of us suspiciously. If he is telling the truth about why he grabbed the knife from the kitchen, then he'll be just as wary of the rest of us, but I can't allow my mind to focus on that.

Christophe moves unsteadily along the corridor until he reaches the bathroom, and then pulls to close the door, but I hold it fast.

'Uh-uh, you can pee with the door open.'

It's a breach of his privacy, but it's the only way I can be certain that this isn't just a ruse. He shakes his head despondently, before lowering his shorts. The others stare at their feet, but I keep my eyes locked on the back of Christophe's head. I've fallen for his lies before, and I'm not about to repeat the mistake.

His movements are slow and calculated, but he eventually finishes, washes his hands, and exits the room.

'You're all making a huge mistake,' he says, eyeing us individually. 'I didn't kill Elena and Joaquín, and that means the real killer is still at large. Locking me up isn't going to protect you if that person means you harm.'

He's had hours on his own, and that's the best he's come up with? Stating the obvious isn't going to change our minds. If indeed one of the people here killed Elena and Joaquín, then we've improved the odds of guessing who by consigning Christophe to the V-berth.

He returns to the room without complaint, but scowls as he says good night. The last thing I see is him sniffing the armpits of the green polo shirt he's had on since we boarded. My breathing doesn't return to normal until the door is locked.

'I'm not being funny, but he kind of has a point,' Rhys says. 'We don't know for certain who killed Elena, and I for one don't feel safe with just a door between me and the killer.'

'What are you suggesting?' I ask.

He shrugs and points at the galley. 'Maybe we should each get something to arm ourselves with... Just in case.'

And therein lies a dilemma: is it safer to go to bed unprotected, or knowing the killer is now likely armed?

Sophie doesn't wait to check on anyone's feelings, and heads through the dinette and into the galley. She extracts the five various-sized knives from the block and offers them out to each of us. Rhys immediately reaches for the large chef's knife Christophe was brandishing earlier, Fergus takes the carving knife, Harry the bread knife, leaving Sophie and I to toss-up between the paring knife and utility knife. She shrugs at me, allowing me to choose. I opt for the larger, although I can't picture myself using it, even if one of the others did manage to get into my room.

We're not savages; this is crazy.

'Right, I suggest we all get our heads down,' Sophie says. 'Lock your rooms, and don't open them for anyone. If you feel like you're in danger, scream bloody blue murder and the rest of us will come running.'

She fixes me with a firm stare.

We proceed into our rooms without another word. The sound of five latches being engaged fills the empty silence.

Once inside, I turn the utility knife over in my hand. I'm not even sure it's that sharp, but the pointy tip should inflict some damage if called upon. I thrust it out a couple of times to get a feel for the weight and balance of it in my hand.

Should I be reading anything into the choice of blades the others made? Did Rhys go for the chef's knife because he's already used it, to make Elena compliant, or because he's terrified and thinks it serves as the greatest deterrent? Did Harry choose the bread knife because he's trying to lull us all into a false sense of security? That pitiful thing would be the most inept in a knife fight. Or could Sophie have given me the choice between the blades because secretly she already has a different weapon hidden somewhere?

I feel nausea building in my stomach, and desperately wish I could call Carly. She's always such a good sounding board when I'm preparing a case for trial. She asks me the questions I don't want to face, and helps me to wade through the minutiae. If she was here now, I'm sure she'd have already figured out who killed Elena. If only I could call her.

I inwardly curse as I realise again that I failed to check the V-berth for Elena's personal devices or a satellite phone. I have to assume that Christophe's searched the room while he's been in there, which means if he did find something, he'll most likely be keeping such devices hidden. Or if he didn't kill Elena, then maybe he'll be smart enough to contact someone to come and get us.

I freeze at the creak of the floorboard directly behind me. It's followed by a gentle tapping at my door.

'Pete, are you still awake?' I hear Fergus whisper.

I gulp, but can't speak.

'I don't want you to open the door,' he continues in hushed tones. 'I don't mean you any harm, but I didn't want to go to sleep without telling you how sorry I am about what happened earlier. My mam always used to tell me to never go to sleep on an argument or when angry. I didn't mean to cut your arm, and I am really sorry for what happened. I dinnae want you thinking it was intentional. We're family and I mean you no harm. Simone would go ballistic if she knew what happened.'

I know I'm being overly cautious, but turn so that I'm facing the door, holding out the knife in case he's somehow figured out a way of unlocking it from the outside, and this apology is an attempt to trick me.

I pinch the latch between finger and thumb, and hold it firmly. 'You need to go to bed now, Fergus.'

'Not until you accept my apology. If something were to happen to either one of us during the night… I'd never forgive myself for not making peace with you.'

'Okay, Fergus, I forgive you. Now please go to bed.'

'You do? Thanks, mate. Us against the rest of them, right?'

A banging against the door to the V-berth draws our attention.

'*Putain!* Why are you lot so fucking stupid?' Christophe yells at the top of his voice. 'I *didn't* kill Elena and Joaquín. The real murderer is still among you.'

22

TEN YEARS AGO

It's still early, and when Harry and I arrive at the Student Union bar, it only has a dozen or so people inside. We order a bucket of bottles and grab a booth as far from the main stage as possible. Thursday night at the SU bar is karaoke night, and by the time it starts in a couple of hours, the human-sized speakers will be blasting out all manner of cheesy pop songs and we won't be able to hear one another speak.

We've come here because there's something I need to ask Harry, and I don't want to be overheard by any of the others at our house. Also, the drinks aren't expensive, and I felt like I might need a couple for Dutch courage.

Following my heated argument with Carly ten or so days ago, I didn't think the atmosphere in the house could get any worse, but I underestimated how toxic things would become once Rhys returned from visiting his parents. The arguments have caused a real divide in the house, and I'm bloody sick of it. Harry has been as loyal as ever, but I know it can't be easy for him, given he and Rhys are on the same course. Similarly, Fergus doesn't want to side with Rhys over me, but they're part of the same lacrosse team, so he has little choice. Woody has convinced Christophe and Rhys that I was the one who placed the dead rat in Rhys's bed, and I still haven't determined if it was one of them or one of the others. I have no doubt now that someone is deliberately causing difficulties in the house.

I lift two bottles out of the bucket, twist off the caps, and hand one to Harry. We both grimace at the first sip, because like most of the alcohol sold here, the lager is cheap and imported.

'Cheers,' Harry says, raising his bottle and then clinking it against mine. 'So what was it you wanted to talk about?'

'The atmosphere at home.'

'Well, it's shit, obviously.'

I love how Harry is so direct.

'Do you think it's my fault?'

He slams his bottle down and the table wobbles. 'State o' you! Christ, no! Listen, as far as I'm concerned, you've done nothing wrong. Rhys is a slimy dick who should just apologise and then things can get back to how they were.'

I am still in love with Carly, and I miss her so much. But every time I think about picking up the phone and calling her, I remember how sick I felt when Woody told me what she did. If I can't forget what happened, how can I ever forgive her? How can I take her at her word if I can't trust her?

'Have you heard from Carly?' Harry asks.

'She's still phoning every day, but I think she must be starting to take the hint, as the messages are lessening. Either that or she's busy at work.'

'And you've not decided to let bygones be bygones yet?'

'How can I? She kept it from me for so long. How can I trust her?'

Harry shakes his head. 'Are you really that much of an eejit? I know you're my best friend, but if I don't say it, nobody will: Carly is not the bitch you make her out to be. She's smart, she's funny, she's better than you're ever going to get elsewhere, and you're clearly still in love with her. If you don't pull your finger out of your arse, she's going to find herself a bigger fish – sooner rather than later – and by fish, obviously I mean *dick*.' He feigns disgust. 'I've seen you coming out of the bathroom, and it's not much to write home about.'

Despite the brutality of the words, I can't help but chuckle, as I know Harry is just trying to cheer me up.

'If she's so wonderful, why don't you go out with her then?'

I mean it playfully, but something crosses his face, as if he's just received an electric shock. It's brief and subtle, and maybe it's just surprise at the question, but there's definitely something there. Has he actually considered making a move, or is it his own guilty conscience because he *did* know about them before we moved in?

'She's nuts about you too, and I hate that you're deliberately ruining your life over something that feels worse than it really is. So she hooked up with Rhys for one night. Big deal! I've slept my way through half the female student population, and I forget the faces of most I've shagged. It's what people do at university. You have your whole life to fall in love and settle down. If you're not going to give Carly a second chance, then it's time to put your equipment to better use.' He sits back and allows his gaze to work the room. 'Any of the beauties here take your fancy? I don't mind being your wingman. What about those two?'

He nods at two students who are chatting and laughing on stools by the bar. I don't recognise either, which probably means they're first years. Both are very pretty, but neither of them is Carly, and I don't want to act until I've worked out what to do about her.

One of them looks up and catches us staring, and I have to

lower my eyes. Harry continues to smile, tilting his bottle in her direction. I dart my eyes back and catch her whispering something to her friend. Her friend looks over next, before they both cover their mouths and lean closer, as if laughing at some big secret.

Harry is on his feet before I can stop him, and glides across the bar until he's beside them. To me, his chat up lines are cringe, and I have no intention of joining him. I do watch though, in awe of his ability to be so at ease when speaking to total strangers. I'm far too introverted for that.

But something isn't right. Neither of the girls are falling for his usual charm, and unless I'm very much mistaken, things are getting heated. The first girl looks angry as she speaks, and then I can see Harry waving his arms and reacting.

I leap out of my seat and hurry across the bar, reaching them just in time to hear Harry yelling a profanity. I grab his flailing arms and drag him away, offering an apology to the two girls, who promptly leave their seats.

'What the hell was that about?' I ask once we're seated back at the table.

'Stupid bitch!' Harry simmers, putting the bottle back to his lips and taking a long drink.

'Have you finally met someone immune to your fatal charms?' I tease, but he doesn't share in the joke. 'Seriously, what happened?'

In the back of my head, I'm wondering whether he's slept with her before, forgotten her face, and she took exception to this fact.

He finishes his bottle and extracts a new one from the bucket. 'She said she wouldn't be seen dead with someone who transmits STIs so openly. Stupid bitch. I happen to be very careful when it comes to safe sex. I always wear a condom.'

'Just forget about her, mate.'

'I can't. When I told her she was mistaken, she said she knew who I was and what I get up to, like I'm on some "Wanted: Dead or Alive" poster. I told her it was a case of mistaken identity. She said I have...' he leans in closer and whispers, '...genital herpes.' He sits back and throws the lid from his bottle towards the bucket. 'I mean, as if? Someone has been spreading shit about me on campus.'

I don't know what to say, so attempt to change the subject instead. 'I think we should consider moving out of the house.'

His brow furrows. 'Moving where, exactly?'

At least he didn't shoot me down straight away.

I shrug. 'I haven't started looking yet,' I lie, 'but I'm sure we could find a house share in another student property, or maybe a two-bed apartment nearby. We could be properly independent young adults.'

His eyes narrow. 'Are things really that bad?'

I nod. 'I bumped into Rhys on the stairs this morning, and you could have cut the atmosphere with a knife. Although it was clear I was going to the bathroom to shower, he made a show of dashing after me, and checking that his door was shut. He's convinced I put that dead rat in his bed, and nothing will persuade him otherwise. The whole house is in two camps, and yet I've done *nothing* wrong. He was the one who lied about sleeping with Carly, and I'm being made to feel guilty for it.'

'If anything, it's even more reason for you and Carly to get back together, and then to have lots and lots of deafening sex. You want to get revenge on Rhys, that's the best way. His room is directly above yours, so he'll hear every moan of pleasure.'

My face spreads into a huge grin. I don't want to admit how much I've missed the feel of Carly's body pressed against mine.

There's another girl standing beside the bar, and I swear she's looking directly at us. I smile, but quickly shake my head so she knows we're not looking to hook up.

'Speaking of super noisy sex,' Harry says, 'have you heard Sophie going at it some days?'

I shake my head. 'I didn't realise she was seeing anyone. She hasn't mentioned it.'

'Nor to me, but I came back early the other day, and I could hear what sounded like shouting and banging. At first, I thought she was being attacked by someone, but then I heard a man groaning, and her screaming for him to "fuck her harder". I stayed down in the kitchen because the walls aren't exactly thick. Anyway, eventually they quietened down, and in the minutes that followed, two men come down the stairs separately. Woody *and* our creepy landlord. I don't know which came from Sophie's room.'

My mouth drops so hard my chin practically hits the table. 'You think Sophie is shagging Raymond? Oh, come on.'

He raises his eyebrows. 'Which seems more likely? Fergus's Neanderthal friend, or the man Soph seduced the night of the housewarming?'

I knew she'd gone with Raymond the night of the party, but I hadn't realised it had become a regular thing. But what's the alternative? Woody is in a better age bracket, but I thought he had a girlfriend already. Sophie could do so much better than either of them.

'Soph eventually appeared, dressed in a robe, and went into the back garden for a cigarette. When she came back in, it looked like she'd been crying. And I swear I could see what looked like a red hand-shaped mark around her throat. She asked how long I'd been home, and I covered and said only a few minutes, and she asked me not to tell anyone about what I'd heard.'

'I'm not surprised she doesn't want to broadcast it.'

'You can't tell her I told you. Okay?'

'Scout's honour,' I say with a mock salute.

The girl at the bar is still looking over, and when Harry catches her eye and smiles, she marches over to our table. Harry is just opening his mouth to say hello when she slaps him hard across the cheek.

'You son of a bitch!' she spits, slamming something down on the table.

'Hey, hey,' Harry shrieks, cowering slightly, his hand covering the red mark spreading across his cheek, 'what the hell is wrong with you?'

'How could you do that to me?'

Harry looks as confused as I am. 'I've no idea who you are.'

This only angers her more, and I can see she is restraining herself from going for him again. 'We slept together two weeks ago. You should have warned me you had an STI.'

Harry stares back at her in disbelief, though there is finally a moment of recognition in his eyes. 'I don't have an STI, I swear to you. I don't know who told you that I did, but—'

She lifts her hand from the table, and I now see she's holding an A5-sized piece of paper. On it is a picture of Harry's face, name, and phone number, along with the words:

Don't trust this guy: he's got pubic lice.

'Where the hell did you get this from?' I demand, looking around for any copies pinned up anywhere. 'Harry, I really think you need to look at this.'

Harry twists his head, his eyes widening with every word. 'This is bullshit,' he shouts. 'Who gave this to you?'

There are twice as many people in the bar as when we arrived, and at least half of them are holding the leaflet. I need to get

Harry out of here. Snatching up the piece of paper, I pull him from his seat, but nearly knock into the girl, and have to release him to stop myself from falling. Like an escaped puppy, Harry tears off into the crowd, snatching leaflets from anyone holding them, but is stopped when he comes face to face with a guy with arms as wide as tree trunks who takes exception. He takes a swing at Harry, who's quick enough to duck, but then throws out a fist of his own, instantly wincing when it connects with the guy's jaw.

I push myself towards them, and manage to pull Harry away before he gets flattened, but I take a blow to the arm in the process. I heave Harry towards the exit, despite his protestations.

'We need to get out of here before someone phones campus security,' I shout at him, and he finally stops struggling, staring at the leaflets in his hands. One mentions herpes, another chlamydia; a third says Harry has gonorrhoea.

'I'm going to find the rat who did this to me, and I'm going to kill them,' he says as we make our way down the footpath towards the gate to our garden, passing the dark and menacing forest the footpath borders.

I understand his anger, but what I don't tell him – what I don't want to admit – is that I recognise the image on the leaflet because I'm the one who took it on my phone. The only way this image could have got out is if someone went through my stuff.

23

PRESENT DAY

I wake and instinctively reach for my phone on the nightstand, forgetting that it disappeared yesterday morning. How has it only been two days since we boarded? What was supposed to be a weekend filled with sun, sea, and hangovers has turned into a living nightmare that feels as though it will never end.

There is light beneath my blind, so if I had to guess, I'd say it's somewhere between six and eight. I must have managed some level of sleep during the night, but it certainly wasn't very much. I couldn't stop myself listening out for movement in the corridor: the creak of a floorboard; the sound of a door latch sliding open. I'd wake realising I'd allowed myself to drop off, and would then lie there listening; waiting for Christophe to escape the V-berth, or for the real killer to reveal themselves.

Christophe did finally stop shouting and proclaiming his innocence, and he has yet to start up again this morning, so hopefully we can get through the day without further incident. I can't hear any chatter or movement yet, so I can only assume the others are still barricaded in their rooms. I'm going to have to get up and grab a bottle of water. My throat is so dry and the early embers of a hangover are peeking out at the edges of my subconscious mind.

I remain where I am for now. Depending how deep a sleep I fell into, I might have missed the killer emerging from their room, and they could be waiting silently beyond my door. If it wasn't for my full bladder, I might stay here all day.

There's also part of me that doesn't want to be the first to emerge from their cabin because of the accusations Christophe flung my way yesterday. If another bad thing has happened and I'm found to be the first moving about, I know at least one of them will put two and two together, and then it might be me who gets locked up in the V-berth.

This is madness! I can't believe that Christophe – a guy I lived with for almost a year – could be capable of murder. I've shared jokes and secrets with him, and he never gave me a vibe of having murderous urges. Kleptomania aside, he is a normal thirty-one-year-old guy: flawed like the rest of us. If he's capable of drowning Elena, then all of us are.

I fight the urge to picture that night in the woods, reminding myself that that situation was totally different to this one. Elena was killed in cold blood; Raymond had it coming to him.

I try to close my eyes and urge sleep to wipe away these troubling thoughts, but my full bladder isn't going to let me. Pushing back the thin bedsheet, I stand, suddenly panicked when I can't find the utility knife I hid under the spare pillow, until I find it on the floor beside my feet.

Moving to the door, I consider my appearance in the mirror. My face looks gaunt, the rings beneath my eyes dark and red, my hair a dishevelled mess. Yesterday it bothered me how the others would regard my appearance. What a difference twenty-four hours makes when you're adrift.

Pressing my ear to the door, I strain to hear the tiniest sound, but there's nothing but silence. I tighten my fingers around the handle of the utility knife and prepare to thrust it out, as I slowly slide back the latch and then the door. My heart skips a beat as I wait for someone to charge in, wielding their own blade, but nobody does. The door to Christophe's cabin remains open, as he didn't use it last night, and I'm relieved to see the key is still in the lock of the V-berth, which means he didn't try to escape.

I shuffle along the carpet, keeping an ear out as I pass Harry's and Fergus's rooms on my left, and Sophie's and Rhys's on the right. The door to the bathroom is open, and I slip in, quickly sliding it closed and locking it, before dropping onto the seat.

I need a drink and food in my stomach to soak up last night's alcohol before I consider freshening up. Flushing the toilet, I wait for the tank to refill and the noise to pass before once more pressing my ear to the door and listening for the tell-tale sounds of movement in the corridor.

Gripping the utility knife, I unlatch and slide open the door, checking in both directions, before moving through the dinette to the galley. The hatch to the deck is already open, so I grab a bottle of water from the fridge and climb the steps.

I find Sophie on the cushioned bench, the yacht's engine manual in her hands.

'Morning,' she says, eyeing the knife in my hand. 'Hoping you're not planning to kill me. I put the paring knife back in the block in the galley.'

'That's very brave,' I say, trying to recall whether I noticed the handle sticking out of the block.

Sophie shrugs, shielding her eyes from the sun which is rising behind me. 'I figured if it's my time to go then so be it. I don't want to live in fear any more.' She pauses. 'Besides, I reckon I could take your skinny arse without too much effort.' She grins, and I find myself relaxing for the first time in hours.

She's right. All this suspicion between us is not helpful to figuring a way back home. As I stare out at the horizon, I can't tell how far we've drifted in the last twenty-four hours – when all you can see is blue water in all directions, it's impossible to get your bearings.

'That seat next to you taken?' I ask playfully, and she pats the cushion. I sit beside her. 'You figured out how to hotwire this beast yet?'

'Well, I think I've worked out what the battery should look like and where it should be, but I'll need some help in figuring exactly which wires are coming from the ignition slot.'

'And then what?'

'Then I run the cable against the battery and we hope for the best.'

I don't like the uncertainty of her tone. 'You can't put your life at risk, Soph.'

'I'll be putting all our lives at risk if I don't at least try.'

'You do realise Harry is still going to want to swim for the shore this morning?'

'Yeah, I know.' She sighs, clearly as frustrated about the situation as me. 'But he's a grown man, capable of independent thought. And you know how stubborn he can be.'

I actually consider Harry's determined nature a quality rather than a flaw.

'We won't be able to stop him going,' Sophie continues, folding the corner of the page she was reading, before closing the manual, 'so let's not stand in his way. Hopefully I'll get the engine fired up, and we can collect him on our way back to shore. Everybody wins.'

I hope she's right.

'You fancy some breakfast? I'm famished.'

She nods, and we stand, head through the hatch and into the

galley where we find Fergus, the blood drained from his face, his eyes glazed as if lost in another time.

'What is it?' I ask. 'What's wrong?'

He glances back over his shoulder towards the corridor. 'I... went to see if Christophe needed to use the bathroom, but when I unlocked the door... the V-berth... it was empty.'

I don't listen for more, pushing past him and racing along the corridor. The door to the V-berth is wide open, the key still in the lock, but Fergus is right: the room is empty. Either Christophe's vanished into thin air, or the ceiling window wasn't as well blocked as we all thought.

I move further into the cabin, crawling across the bed and staring up at the window access in the ceiling. A thin breeze blows through the gap where it is no longer latched. I thrust both arms up, pushing the glass pane with my fingers, before straightening and climbing through the window. Clearly, he managed to escape while we were all sleeping, but where the hell is he now? I look out to the horizon, searching for any break in the water where there might be a swimmer, but the sea is as smooth as glass.

I hurry around the edge of the boat, back to the stern, where Sophie is poking her head through the galley door.

'We need to find him,' I say, failing to keep the terror from my voice. 'Wake the others, check *every* room. Collect your knife.'

She nods and tears off towards Rhys and Harry's cabins, banging on their doors and urging them to wake up. My room is closest to the V-berth and I never heard Christophe getting through the ceiling window, so what else have I missed?

I circle back around to the bow, heading along the starboard side instead, and that's when I see it. The safety rope above the cabins is cut and hanging down below the waterline. I wait until I see Sophie back on deck, before I wave for her to join me.

I keep my finger pressed to my lips to ensure her silence and point down at the rope in the water, then mime someone pinching their nose, holding their breath. That must be what he's doing: hiding in the one place we won't check. I indicate for Sophie to help me grab the end of the rope which is still attached to the small post, and then, with me counting to three under my breath, we yank the rope up. It's harder than either of us are anticipating. We try again, and this time something does break through the water.

But neither of us is expecting to see Christophe's foot. The rope appears to be caught around his ankle, and as we continue to pull it out of the water, I think we both simultaneously realise that Christophe hasn't been holding his breath down there. He doesn't kick or struggle as we pull his lifeless body up.

But I'm the first to yell when I see the lack of head on his shoulders.

It's all I can do to lean over the side and retch my stomach lining into the water.

'Jesus Christ!' Sophie exclaims.

I pull my head back over, and force myself to look at the green T-shirt Christophe was wearing last night.

There are obvious bite marks in the tissue near his collarbone, suggesting his head is now in the stomach of one of our razor-toothed neighbours. Nobody deserves to die like that. The skin around his fingers and arms is shrivelled, suggesting he's been in the water for a fair while.

'We need to tell the others,' Sophie says, forcing herself back to her feet and scampering back towards the stern.

I remain where I am, frozen by the realisation that I've just lost one of my oldest friends. I need to put the fear behind me, though. His body is still half hanging over the edge of the boat where the safety rope is broken. I grip hold of his arm, and pull him up onto the roof of the V-berth, but then I freeze as my eyes catch sight of the words scratched into the hull:

YOU KNEW THE STIPULATIONS
WHEN YOU MOVED IN.
GAME OVER.

24

TEN YEARS AGO

Despite my reservations, Harry doesn't want to move out, and has insisted on us building bridges with the others. He's not even eager to seek out the culprit responsible for depositing the libellous leaflets at the SU bar. We've not discussed it, but my money's on Rhys or Christophe, given their odour in my room. I have no physical proof, though.

'It is what it is,' were Harry's final words on it.

I've tried to convince him otherwise, but Harry insists that the leaflets were just a storm in a teacup. It certainly doesn't appear to have impacted his sex life, judging by the fleet of hook-ups I've seen leaving his room every morning since.

'The house is so close to the campus,' he reminds me now as he fixes himself a round of cheese on toast.

I'm at the kitchen table, scanning the range of takeaway leaflets that have accumulated since we moved in. It was Sophie's idea that we arrange a sit-down meal for 'clear the air' talks. She suggested Harry and I cook something, but neither of us have the culinary skill or patience, and so it's going to be a toss-up between pizza, Indian, or Thai.

My stomach grumbles at the smell of the toast. 'I'm convinced we're going to too much effort here,' I tell him. 'We could just as easily have cornered them in the living room with some beers.'

'Soph said she wants them to see we're making an effort to let bygones be bygones. Otherwise, there's no telling how out of control this will get.'

I wish I knew how or when they accessed my room to steal the image from my laptop – because I know there's no way they could have got it directly from my phone – maybe they found it when the assignment was deleted from the laptop's hard drive.

'We're taking the moral high ground here, and when they realise we're offering an olive branch, I'm hoping they'll feel too guilty to continue acting the maggot.'

Almost costing me 10 per cent of my criminology grade was more than a game: it was spiteful. As was leaving a dead rat in Rhys's bed. I haven't asked Harry if he had anything to do with that, but I can't think of anyone else in the house who would gain from adding to the animosity between Rhys and me.

Carly's face appears on my phone's screen. I haven't seen her in three weeks, but we are now talking; trying to rebuild what we had. I'm not prepared to rush it. It's going to take time, and she tells me she understands and will be patient.

'Answer it,' Harry commands, popping a slice of Cheddar into his mouth.

He waves me away, and I answer the call in my room. 'Hey, Carly, sorry, I was chatting to Harry. How was work?'

'Yeah, yeah, fine. Had to chase a shoplifter down the high street. Nearly lost her at one point, but got her in the end. Only fifteen, but she has previous for pinching clothes from Primark. Maybe this time her social worker will talk some sense into her.'

I can hear the frustration in her tone. When we first got together, she told me she applied to the police because she wanted to make a difference, but now she struggles with the reality that some people just don't want to be helped.

'Have you got plans for dinner?' she asks.

'Yeah, Harry and I are buying the rest of the house takeaway. It's a sort of peace offering.'

She goes quiet, acknowledging her part in the fissure that has torn the residents apart. She's already apologised a hundred times, and I think I've moved past the angry phase, and it's now about moving forwards.

Baby steps.

I haven't told her about the rat in Rhys's bed, nor the defamatory leaflets. Maybe Harry's right and it's best just to leave everything in the past.

'I have a couple of days off at the weekend,' Carly says, 'and wondered if we could maybe get away from the city for a couple of nights?'

She's trying so hard, and I can't keep rejecting her efforts. 'Where did you have in mind?'

'Bruges? We could catch the train from London. I hear it's very picturesque this time of year.'

She knows I've always wanted to visit Belgium, but the trip to Paris I missed out on put a major dent in my savings fund.

'My treat,' she adds quickly, as if reading my mind. 'I've found a great last-minute deal online, and if you say yes, then I can book with a click of the button.'

'I can't let you pay to take me to Belgium, Carly.'

'Yes, you can. It's the least I can do after you missed out on our trip to Paris. I'll make a deal with you: I'll book transport and accommodation, and you can get dinner. Say yes. Please?'

Maybe a couple of days away from the house would benefit us both. I don't know how Rhys and Christophe will react to tonight's peace offering. They don't know that Harry and I are extending the olive branch, but Sophie said she would get them back here by seven. They could take one look at us and refuse, but I'm hoping us making the first move will ease tensions.

'Well?' Carly asks.

'Yes, okay, go on. Book it.'

'Thank God,' she exhales, 'because I accidentally clicked it a few seconds ago and it's non-refundable. We leave Friday morning, back Sunday night. Is that going to be okay with your lectures and stuff?'

I take a deep breath. 'Yes. Looking forward to it already.'

'Good. You should probably pack warm—'

I don't get to hear the rest of what Carly is saying as the smoke alarm outside my door explodes to life, and I have to cover my ears.

'What's that noise?' I vaguely hear her say.

'Smoke alarm. Harry must have burned something. I'd better go.'

I don't hear her agree before disconnecting the call. I wrench open my door, and hurry to the kitchen where smoke is billowing from the grill. There's no sign of Harry, so I open the patio doors and fan the clouds towards them.

'Oh, shit, sorry,' Harry yells as he races down the stairs. 'I literally nipped upstairs to grab my phone. Ah, shit, my lunch is feckin' ruined.'

'Perhaps if we open the front door too, it will help,' I suggest, and head back through the hallway to the door, where I prop it open with my foot. After a couple of minutes, the smoke alarm resets itself, and calm returns to the house.

I return to my room and type a message to Carly, telling her she doesn't need to call the fire brigade.

I stop typing when something overhead catches my eye.

How come the smoke alarm in my room didn't sound when I

opened the door? There was enough smoke, but it didn't make a peep. In fact, come to think of it, why would I need a smoke alarm in my room when clearly the one in the hallway is loud enough and sensitive enough to wake the whole bloody house?

I stare at the small white box on my ceiling. Maybe it isn't working properly. If the battery was dead or missing, it should chirp at me.

I pull out the chair from beneath my desk and position it directly below the alarm, before clambering up. I'm appalled at the amount of cobwebs I can now see hanging from the ceiling, but I can sort those later. Digging my nails into the side of the box, I fiddle and adjust until the lid pops open, and then I study the innards of the device. It doesn't look as I would have expected, and there's no obvious sign of a battery compartment.

'Harry, can you come here a second?' I shout to him.

He appears a moment later and gives me a puzzled look as he sees me on the chair. 'Jesus, you're not planning on topping yourself, are you? It was only burned toast.'

I ignore his lame attempt at humour. 'Can you have a look at this for me, and tell me what it looks like to you?' I jump down, and he climbs onto the chair.

'What am I supposed to be looking at?'

'Well, I assumed it was a smoke alarm at first, but it didn't go off just now, and it doesn't look right. If I didn't know better, I'd say that's some kind of security camera.'

He looks a little closer. 'I'd say you're probably right... Wait, does that mean the box on my ceiling isn't a smoke alarm either?'

I shrug my shoulders and charge after him as he races up the stairs to his room. He mounts the chair and extracts the lid. It's a carbon copy of what's in my room, and I'm almost certain that the shiny black cylinder is a lens.

He frowns at me. 'Why on earth are there security cameras in our rooms?'

I can't answer his question but the thought sends a shiver throughout my body. 'Worse still, who has been watching the feed?'

I picture the times Carly and I have been intimate in my room, unaware that somebody could be watching. Anger flares behind my eyes.

'Do you think Raymond put the cameras up there?' I ask.

'It would explain how he knew about the housewarming that night.'

It would also explain how he knew we were all supposed to be in Paris that weekend when he came round for his supposed drug search. I choose not to reveal that titbit to my friend.

'Ah, Jesus, what a pervert!' Harry says, appalled, before jumping down. 'He's been watching us getting changed, and...' His hand shoots to his mouth. 'How long has he been watching us, the dirty bastard?'

This isn't right. He – assuming Raymond is the one behind the cameras – has been watching us. It's the ultimate violation of our privacy.

I leave Harry's room and head downstairs, trying to determine what to do next. Should I phone the police and report this abuse? Should I tell Carly? Today was supposed to be about burying the past, but now I just feel nauseous. I need to let the others know, and we need to get rid of the cameras as soon as possible.

I start at a noise from the kitchen, an interruption to my thoughts.

'Something smells... burnt,' I hear Sophie say.

'I didn't realise you were home.'

'Just got back,' she says, wincing as she moves to the grill pan and examines the two charred slices.

'Are you all right? You look... uncomfortable.'

She grimaces as she makes her way to the table, and props herself on the end. 'Bloody idiot that I am, I fell down some stairs on campus.'

I move to her side and look for any obvious cuts and bruises. 'Yeesh, are you okay?'

She puts out an arm to keep me getting too close. 'Yeah, I'll be fine. My ego and ribs are badly bruised, but nothing a couple of days' rest won't cure.'

I'm about to mention our discovery of the cameras, but a voice in the back of my head tells me that she already knows.

'The smoke alarms in our rooms,' I say instead, casually. 'Do you know how often we're supposed to test them? Or when the battery was last changed?'

She gulps audibly and looks away.

'You know they're not smoke alarms, don't you?'

She nods slowly, wincing in the process. 'Yes, okay, you're right: they're not smoke alarms, but you don't need to worry. They were part of Raymond's stipulations, but I've already taken care of it. They're not switched on. If they were recording, then there would be a little red LED that you'd be able to see through the lid. You've nothing to worry about.'

'That's easy for you to say. How do we know he doesn't switch them on when we don't realise?'

'Raymond is a lot of things, but he showed me how the set-up works. He used them for a couple of days when we first moved in, but as soon as I realised what he was doing, I told him to stop. I promise you, Pete, they're redundant. Trust me.'

She pushes herself up with a gasp, and I offer to help her to her room, but she refuses my hand, and tells me she's going to go and take a shower. As she moves into the hallway, I can't help but notice the fading yellow bruises on the back of her neck. They must be a few days old, so couldn't have been caused by today's apparent fall. I recall what Harry said about her noisy sex life with either Woody or Raymond, and I can't help wondering whether she really did fall, or whether she's in over her head with one of those creeps.

25

PRESENT DAY

It can't be. It *can't* be. It. Can't. Be.

I run my fingers over the jagged edges of the words etched into the hull, and all I can see is the ghost of one man hovering nearby. A man who made my skin crawl. A man who made our lives a living hell. A man we buried in the ground in the dead of night more than ten years ago.

I slap my cheek hard, trying to shock my body into action. I slap the other cheek, and then repeat the process, waiting for the words to disappear. Have I had a full mental breakdown? Is that what this is? The words aren't actually there, but my subconscious is making me see them because I've been feeling so guilty about what played out a decade ago. I slap my cheek again, but the words don't go anywhere.

'What the feck is that?'

I jump at Harry's voice over my shoulder. He's staring down at Christophe's body, and as I look up at his face, I can see the blood has drained from his cheeks. Fergus is next to appear at the bow, coming around the other side of the yacht, with Sophie following. There's no way I can hide the message and pretend it isn't there.

Then Rhys appears and it is all Fergus can do to keep him back.

'What the hell is this?' he yells, screwing up his eyes up, his cheeks flaming. 'What the hell have you done to him?'

Sophie moves forward to help Fergus contain the rage. 'We found him like this. Just now.'

But Rhys isn't buying it, and continues to push and pull to escape Fergus's clutches. 'No, this is *his* fault. Pete's the one who accused Christophe, and now look what's happened!'

He's squirming, desperate to get to his slain friend, but I can see how hard it is for him to look at where the flesh is bloody and torn.

From what Sophie's told me, the two of them remained good friends after we all graduated and have been on a couple of lads' holidays together since – not telling the rest of us. It's only natural, I suppose, when university friends move away, they're bound to lose contact. Life moves on; things can't stay the same forever.

'I think I'm going to be sick,' Harry says, burying his head in his hands.

I know how he feels, but my body is still paralysed with fear. Do the others realise the implication of those words?

You knew the stipulations when you moved in. Game over.

'We can't just leave him there,' Sophie says, her pragmatism kicking in. 'The sun is already up and it'll be scorching out here soon enough. The body will cook.'

The thought of burning flesh filling the air makes my stomach flip, but I resist the urge to retch again.

'Where can we put him?' I ask, forcing my eyes to meet Sophie's.

It's not like we have a large enough fridge or freezer to preserve the body. And even if we moved him to his cabin, it won't be long before decomposition sets in, and that will bring its own treasure chest of problems.

'We'll have to put him in the shark cage with Elena,' she says calmly. 'There's nowhere else.'

How on earth are we going to be able to explain to the authorities that two people have been killed during this trip, assuming we ever make it back to shore? It was supposed to be a break away from the stress of everyday life, and a chance to reconnect over happier memories. How could it have gone so wrong?

Rhys breaks free of Fergus's grip and drops to his knees beside the corpse, almost as if he's searching for proof that the body in Christophe's green shirt is someone else. I don't realise until it's too late, but he spots the words etched into the hull.

'What the fuck is this? Who wrote this? Was this you?'

He's glaring at me, but I shake my head and take a step back. Fergus and Sophie lean over the side of the boat. My eyes drift to the horizon again, scouring for any glimpse of something to make this all make sense.

'This is so fucked up!' Sophie spits. 'Raymond Grosjean is dead.'

'Of course he is,' Fergus echoes. 'This is just some prick playing games.'

'But what if it isn't?' Harry counters. 'Think about it: who else would want to torment us in this way? The reference to "stipulations" is a huge clue.'

'Because Raymond Grosjean has been dead for ten years, and we all buried him in the ground,' Sophie snaps. 'Or have you managed to forget that little episode?'

'Hey, screw you,' Harry snaps back. 'I've just lost an old friend and I want to know who the fuck killed him. You were the one who was so pally with our landlord, perhaps there's more you haven't told us about?'

'Pete will tell you: he's dead. He was there when it happened. Come on, Pete, tell them that we checked his pulse. He was definitely dead.'

I can feel four pairs of eyes burning a hole in the top of my head, but when I speak, my voice is croaky. 'She's right. He was dead. Wasn't he?'

Harry picks up on my own uncertainty. 'What if he wasn't? What if we just *thought* he was dead when we buried him? What if he woke and managed to claw himself out of that feckin' hole and has been plotting against us for the last decade?'

'This isn't some bullshit episode of *Murder, She Wrote*,' Sophie shouts. 'People don't spend ten years biding their time and plotting revenge on others. This is real life, and unless one of you can explain how Raymond could board our vessel, kill at will, and then vanish again without a sighting or a sound, then I'm all ears.'

She has a point. There's been nothing but ocean on the horizon since we woke and found Elena missing yesterday morning. How has it only been twenty-four hours?

'Maybe it's his ghost come back to haunt us,' Harry fires back, but he's clutching at straws. 'Or maybe he bought himself a small boat to live from. For all we know, he's out on the water somewhere, and comes and goes when we're below deck. Come on, Pete, you remember what a creepy fecker he was. Wouldn't it be just like him to be screwing with us now?'

Harry's desperate to find answers, but it stirs another thought in my mind. My head spins around to look at him. 'Wait, what company did you book this through?'

'What? I don't know. I hardly think that's relevant right now, do you?'

'What if Raymond has something to do with the company?'

'Raymond is *dead*,' Sophie screams out. Her own part in his demise must be playing on her mind, as mine is with me.

'Okay, well, maybe not Raymond,' I reason, 'but someone who was close to him? Did he have any siblings that you remember, Soph?'

'He was an only child, I think. He had no children. It was just him and his mother alone in that house until she died.'

For some reason, I instantly recall Woody suggesting the late Mr Grosjean's spirit was haunting the property, though we disproved that theory long ago.

But what other answer is there? There's no way Joaquín could have known about our time at university, and the only people alive who know how much Raymond taunted us are on this yacht right now, and they all seem as shocked about what's happened to Christophe as I am.

Sophie and I had assumed he'd managed to get free of the window in the ceiling of the V-berth, but now that I'm thinking about it, doesn't it make more sense that someone helped him escape? Surely, if he'd seen Raymond's ghostly face, he'd have screamed for the rest of us to come to his aid? But if it was someone on this ship that he trusted, would he have been more willing to go along with it?

I look at each of them in turn, hoping to spot a guilty face amongst them, but I'm becoming delirious. The warm air and dehydration are getting the better of me. If we don't get off the deck soon, we'll all be in trouble.

The yacht shakes as Harry spins and stomps to the stern. Sophie, Rhys and I hurry after him.

'What are you doing?' I ask, as he races down the hatch and into the dinette.

I watch as he grabs the remaining air tank and checks the dial. Satisfied, he hauls it up, along with a set of goggles and the wetsuit I wore yesterday.

'You can't go,' I warn him as he climbs back up to the deck.

'We have no other choice,' he tells me firmly, putting the air tank on the floor, and pulling the wetsuit up and over his arms. 'Besides, look!'

He's pointing at something over my shoulder, but when I turn to look, the sun's reflection on the water leaves me squinting. Shielding my eyes, I'm not sure what he's referring to, but then I spot it: the tiniest sliver of something just above the water.

Land.

It must be several miles away, and as strong a swimmer as Harry may think he is, it will take a Herculean effort.

'You'll never make it,' Sophie says, surveying the distance. 'The best thing we can do is focus our efforts on getting the yacht there. Either by trying to hotwire the engine, or finding something we can use as oars, or fashioning a sail of some sort.'

'You focus on that. I'm swimming to shore and getting us help.'

There's a look of determination in Harry's eyes that I've not seen before, and I instantly recognise that he's holding something back from us. I saw that look once before when I felt he was covering for the Carly–Rhys revelation.

I grab his arms. 'What aren't you telling us?'

His head dips. 'I wasn't *entirely* honest about how I booked this trip.' His cheeks redden. 'I won the trip. Your sister dragged me and Fergus to so many bloody wedding fayres, and I entered every competition I saw to try and win free stuff for them. And then, right when I was starting to plan this weekend, I received an email out of the blue. It was from some travel company, saying I'd won this excursion, and all I had to do was choose the dates and arrange flights. That's when I contacted you all.'

I swallow down the feeling of dread. 'What travel company?'

'I looked them up, and the website looked legitimate; nothing out of the ordinary. Then when we got to the dock and Joaquín and Elena were waiting for us, I didn't think any more about it.'

We were lured here with the promise of paradise, though it's anything but. I now understand his urge to get off this yacht, even if it does mean taking his chances with the sharks.

I look to Sophie. 'Are you sure Raymond never mentioned a sibling?'

She opens her mouth to speak, but sighs instead. 'Not that I remember. You know what my relationship with him was like: we didn't talk a lot. He was always quite mysterious about his family life. Remember the cameras in the smoke alarms?' She turns and heads up to the cockpit. 'We need to get Christophe in the cage, and then I'm going to do whatever it takes to get this paperweight to move towards land.'

'And I'm not hanging around waiting for whoever it is to come back,' Harry adds, moving to the port side. 'I'll send someone back for you,' he says, offering me a reassuring nod.

I pull him into a hug, in case this is the last time I'll see him. 'Take care of yourself.'

He grins with false bravado. 'Ah, don't worry about me. If those sharks mess with me, they won't know what's hit them. Look, whatever happens, I will come back for you. Brothers for life, right?'

My vision blurs and I nod. 'For life.'

He glances up to where Sophie is raising the shark cage. 'If you do get this bastard started, please don't mow me down when you're passing by, yeah?'

He doesn't wait for her response, and climbs over the safety rope, lowering himself into the chilly water, and then he glides away. I don't like that he's going to be out there on his own, and he didn't even think to take a weapon with him in case of a shark attack. The sea looks so blue and inviting, but there's just so much of it, and it's hard to see where the water stops and the sky starts.

I'm staring at a blue void, and it's swallowing up the one person I care about as much as Carly.

The whirring motor breaks the deathly silence, and the shark cage begins to rise out of the water. Sophie climbs down from the cockpit and asks me to help carry Christophe to it. I agree because Fergus and Rhys have vanished to their cabins. I can't help wondering how many more of my friends are going to end up in the cage before this nightmare ends.

26

TEN YEARS AGO

I'm exhausted when I make it in through the door. I can't believe so many shoppers were still filling trollies so late on Christmas Eve. It's not like Christmas Day isn't the same date every year, so why wait until only hours before to be stocking up on turkey, vegetables and potatoes? I wasn't even supposed to be working today, but the offer of triple pay was too good to turn down.

All I want is a hot shower and a drink to let the stresses of the day wash away. But I was late leaving the store, which now means I'm going to have to order a taxi to get me to the train station. I could just as easily phone Mum and ask her to come and get me, but I don't want to take the piss asking her to come down from the Cotswolds. It was hard enough explaining to her why I was choosing to stay here to do overtime when I could have been relaxing with her and her new family.

As I lean into the door, there's a small part of me tempted to phone and say the train's been cancelled and I'll have to try to make it home in the morning, but I'm not prepared for the histrionics this would likely cause. Plus, it would be weird being in this large house on my own. The silence is eerie, with the others having already packed up and gone. Fergus left as soon as his final lecture was done last Friday, then Rhys and Christophe left a couple of days after, followed by Sophie, though Harry stayed until this morning to keep me company. He's used the time to put some work into his dissertation, and I know I really should have been doing the same, rather than working ten-hour shifts at the supermarket.

Carly's doing overtime as well, though I'm sure if I asked her to drive me to Mum's, she would, but then I'd feel compelled to introduce them, and given we're only just starting to get back on track, it feels a bit soon to be welcoming her into the family home. I've promised myself that if things are still going strong at Easter, I will take her to meet Mum and my stepsiblings.

I unlock the door to my room and head inside. The thought of being squashed on a train carriage, while manhandling my suitcase, doesn't appeal in the slightest, so I've given myself half an hour to shower and change into something clean. I've been in these clothes since eight, and even I have to acknowledge how bad they smell.

Even though the house is empty, I wait until I'm locked in the bathroom before I strip off. I don't trust Raymond not to put in a surprise visit, on the assumption that we've all vacated the house already. Stepping into the shower, the warm spray begins to ease the tension in my back and shoulders. It's been a challenging few months one way or another, and I really hope that the New Year brings with it less stress and hassle.

I dry myself and then tie the towel around my waist. I've just opened the door, when I hear the front door slam shut.

I freeze.

'Hello?' I call out, embarrassed by the fear in my voice.

There's no response.

I'm sure I didn't imagine it. Is it possible one of the others returned because they forgot something?

'Hello?' I call out again, waiting to hear Harry or Sophie shout back, but they don't.

What if it's the ghost of Raymond's father?

I practically laugh out loud at the thought. That's not to say that what I heard wasn't Raymond performing one of his unannounced searches. I don't like the thought of him leering at me like this, and given what I think he's been doing to Sophie, I'd dare him to try anything funny with me. In fact, with Sophie now away, this would be a good time to have a word with him and tell him a few home truths.

I move to the top step. 'Hello? Raymond?'

I strain to hear the sound of further movement, or breathing coming from anywhere downstairs, but the house is as silent as when I got home. Fear of the unknown always brings with it a burst of adrenaline, and so I thrust my shoulders back and point my chin high as I head down the stairs, ready to confront Raymond, or whoever it is who's returned. I'm conscious of the fact that it could just as easily be an intruder. There have been warnings around campus of a spate of burglaries at student houses, and if someone has been watching the house and saw everyone packing up, maybe they think it's a prime target.

The hallway is empty. The doors to mine and Fergus's rooms are closed, but the door to the living room is ajar. Tiptoeing backwards, I move into the kitchen and locate a chef's knife from the cutlery drawer – just for my own peace of mind – and hold it out in front of me as I creep back through the house, bypassing my room and nudging the door to the living room open with my toe.

It's empty. No sign of anyone lurking, waiting to attack.

I let out a sigh of relief, and double back to my room. I dress quickly in jeans and a thick hoodie, and grab my suitcase from the bed. The sooner I get out of here, the better. I can't ignore my gut telling me that Raymond is lurking nearby. I shudder at the memory of him rifling through my things inside this very room.

I bundle on my coat, and wheel my case into the hallway, before locking my bedroom door. I still have the knife in my hand, and I know I can't take it with me to Mum's, so I head back into the kitchen to return it to the drawer. I stop still when I see the trail of small blue pellets leading to the wooden door down to the cellar. They resemble sweets at first, but as I creep closer, there's a repulsive odour that suggests these are something toxic.

Raymond is the only person with a key to the cellar door, but I try the handle regardless, and start when the door opens. I quickly close it and move back to the kitchen door. Whatever is down there is none of my business, and the taxi I ordered should be here any minute.

Yet I don't move. Curiosity gets the better of me, and despite myself, I return to the cellar door and pull it open. The smell of the pesticide is much stronger as I step into the dark hole, fumbling my fingers against the damp brickwork in search of a light switch. There's a warm breeze drifting from the void, and then my fingers strike gold and the endless pit beneath the steps illuminates, and I see just how far it stretches. It's the length and breadth of the house, a space wide enough to hold a swimming pool with room to spare. In one corner is a huge desk, with monitors attached to the wall, like you'd expect to see at NASA rather than in the basement of a student house.

In the opposite corner, there's a king-sized bed, a refrigerator and a small bathroom. It's like an open-plan bungalow, and what's worse is it appears someone has been living here. Given Raymond is the only person with access, instinct tells me it's him. A shiver runs the length of my spine.

I should be going outside to meet my taxi, but I can't stop

myself continuing down the stairs, propping the door open with a chair before I begin my descent. The stairs are wooden, but remain silent as I tread on each step. When I reach the ground, I find the walls have been insulated and treated with something that looks like it might help to disguise any sound from down here. The floor is covered in laminate floorboards and feels cushioned as I tread further into the room. The only thing the space is lacking is windows, but the ceiling lights are strong enough to give the impression of daylight.

How long has Raymond been living here, and how has he been so free to come and go without any of us noticing?

This is crazy: from what Sophie said, Raymond has a flat somewhere across the city, so why would he need to live in our basement? My stomach turns, and I glance back over my shoulder in case he suddenly returns and catches me down here.

I move across to the bank of desks, and nudge the mouse. All six of the screens blink to life, and my mouth drops open when I see black and white bird's-eye views of each of our bedrooms. Sophie promised that she'd made him switch off the cameras, but he was lying – or she was. He can see everything from this desk.

I spot a pile of more blue pellets down near where the computer bank is plugged into the wall, and remember what drove me down here in the first place. A dead rat lies just beside the pellets, and I instantly picture the rat Rhys discovered in his bed. I feel physically sick.

I hurry from the room, up the stairs, barely making it to the kitchen before I heave into the sink. When we moved in, Sophie described Raymond as odd, but this goes way beyond that. What frightens me most is how much of this she's aware of, which makes me wonder what else she might be keeping from the rest of us.

27

PRESENT DAY

I stare out at the water until Harry is nothing but a speck, and the glare from the sun's reflected rays becomes too much for my eyes. I can't see any fins on the horizon, but it's going to take a couple of hours of nonstop swimming for him to get to the shoreline. Hopefully he'll find some buoys along the way where he can rest up.

It's possible we've now drifted far enough that we're out of the shark zone, but given we don't know where that zone starts and ends, nor how far we've drifted, it's impossible to predict. I raise my eyes skywards and offer a silent prayer that Harry makes it, for his sake as much as ours.

I follow Sophie around the port side, where the safety rope is still intact, until we reach Christophe's headless body.

'How are you doing with all this?' I ask her.

'The fact that one of our friends is dead, the day after we discovered Elena? All I want to do is drown my sorrows. Usually, in this situation, I'd phone my sponsor and he'd talk me back from the ledge.'

I hadn't really considered how hard Sophie must be taking all of this. The others tend to wear their hearts on their sleeves –

Rhys and Fergus especially – but Sophie never lets her true feelings show. She's been a closed book since the day we met at that infernal house. When I think back to everything she kept from us – what Raymond had been doing for months – I don't think I could have kept that bottled up.

'Is there anything I can do to help?' I ask now, guilt overriding my other emotions.

She strains a smile. 'I'll be fine. Let's just get Christophe into the cage, and then I can try and get us sailing.'

She moves to Christophe's legs and wraps her hands around his ankles. I keep my eyes away from where his head should be, and try to push my hands under his armpits. There's a rancid smell already starting to emanate from the body, and it's only going to grow stronger the longer we leave him in the sun.

'On three,' Sophie says, though I wish she'd said to go on one.

We both lift Christophe and proceed around the starboard side, moving slowly, as there is water along the edge where we lifted the body out of the water. One slip and the three of us could be flailing in the cool sea.

We continue to move, and when we reach the open cage, Sophie crouches and lowers Christophe's feet back into the water.

It feels so callous to be disposing of him in this way, but there really isn't any other option. If and when we do manage to get back to shore, an autopsy of the remains should hopefully reveal what really happened to him. That's if we do ever make it back to dry land.

Sophie helps me lower the rest of Christophe into the water, and he soon sinks beneath the surface, allowing Sophie to close and lock the lid. She climbs back up to the cockpit and engages the motor to lower the cage back into the water. Out of sight, out of mind.

'Have you eaten anything yet?' she asks, as she climbs back

onto the deck. 'We should probably try and keep our strength up in case we need to swim for shore later.'

I don't ask, but I sense she's not counting on Harry making it back either.

'I haven't eaten – no appetite.'

'We need something to give us a steady release of energy. Complex carbohydrates. Do you think you could cook some pasta for us all?'

I nod. 'I'll do my best.' I pause. 'What about Rhys and Fergus?'

'What about them?'

'Rhys can't swim, and Fergus isn't much better. To be honest, I don't think I could make it back to shore from here, and I'm fairly proficient.'

'Well, keep your fingers crossed that it doesn't come to that.'

She turns to move away, but I pull her back. 'And if it does?'

She raises her eyebrows. 'Then we cross that bridge when we come to it. I don't want to leave anyone behind, but we can't live on this yacht indefinitely. At some point, we're going to have to try to escape.'

I want to tell her that there's no way I'm leaving anyone to die on this yacht, but she shakes away my hand and continues down into the galley. I look out to sea, trying to work out whether we're drifting closer to, or further away from, the sliver of land, but it's impossible to tell. There's no sign of Harry at all now, and I just have to hope he's still going strong. I could have volunteered to go with him, but there's only one wetsuit, and with my bandaged wound, it would be too big a risk me trying to keep up. There's no telling what paddling will do to the stitches, and if the wound reopened, it would attract sharks.

I can't imagine the future without Harry there. We don't see each other as often as I'd like – work pressures – but I know he's always at the end of the phone if I need to talk. I always intended to ask Harry to be best man at my own wedding one day – even though Fergus pipped me to it. I know Carly loves him as much as I do, but in allowing him to get into the water, I've put that in jeopardy now. I should have forced him to stay, but he probably wouldn't have listened.

I'm about to head down the galley steps when I see Rhys coming through the hatch. He doesn't say anything, but I can see his eyes are red raw, and his cheeks puffy. He's been crying.

'Are you all right? Can I get you anything?'

He shakes his head, and walks across to the cushioned bench, dropping onto it with a huff.

'Have you seen Fergus? I was going to cook some pasta in a bit. Do you think—?'

'Fergus is sleeping,' he interrupts. 'He was so angry about Christophe and still about not being able to get hold of Simone, but I managed to calm him down.'

I can't picture Rhys consoling anyone, but then I probably know him least well of the whole group. We never really hit it off. Looking back on it, the secret he was keeping about Carly probably drove a wedge between us long before I found out.

'Okay, well, I'll make enough for him and plate it up anyway.'

'Do whatever you want. You always do, you do.'

I glare at him. 'Excuse me?'

He rolls his eyes. 'What? Truth hurt, does it?'

'Listen, I know you're upset about Christophe, but there's no need to—'

'My God, just shut the fuck up, will you? Why have you always got to make yourself the victim? I'm not being funny, but why can't you just accept that you screwed up, and Christophe lost his life as a result?'

'Wait, I screwed up?'

'Yeah, you were the one who accused him of killing Elena and, as always, the others believed you over anyone else, and you got your way.'

'Christophe threatened me with a knife.'

'Did he? Or did you just see what you wanted to see? You were the same back when we lived together. Always looking down on the two of us because we didn't come from middle-class backgrounds like you and Harry.'

The urge to shout back and point out that Christophe's upbringing was more privileged than my own is so strong, but that's what he wants me to do, so I bite my tongue. 'I only said what I saw. He armed himself in the middle of the night. What normal person does that?'

'Someone who's fucking terrified, that's who! You manipulated the others into locking him in that prison, and then you waited and struck. The others can't see what a psycho you are, Pete, but I'm onto you.'

I bite down harder. 'I had nothing to do with Christophe being killed.'

'What it is, is either you're the killer and you lured him out before acting, or you left him at the mercy of the real killer; either way, you've got blood on your hands, boyo.'

'How dare you?' I snap. 'If you hate me so much, why the hell did you agree to come away on this weekend?'

'Christophe and I only came because Fergus begged us to. He's so desperate to please Simone, and that's the only reason you're here, because she asked that he include you. We were prepared to put the past behind us and be here for Fergus. We suspected you'd make this weekend all about you and your perfect life with Carly. But I never thought you'd turn on us like this.'

'That's not what happened, Rhys.'

'Bullshit! Do you have any idea how much the rest of us struggled all those years ago? We buried Raymond Grosjean in the ground, and then you moved on like it never happened. Buggered off to law school in London and never looked back. Going through something like that should affect a person psychologically, or at least it should any normal person. But not King Pete. While the rest of us were struggling to deal with the aftermath, you're living your best life, you are. How is that fair?'

I've never heard Rhys so vocal and bitter, but is it just him that feels this way, or is he right and the others detest me just as much? He's wrong to think I'm living some picture-perfect life. I still have nightmares about that night; about what *I* did. I have ploughed all my anxiety into helping the state punish those who have broken the law, trying to deliver justice to the victims who deserve it. I'm far from perfect, but I'm trying to be better every day.

He pauses as the anguish strains his vocal cords. 'He was my best friend.'

'Shut up, Rhys,' Sophie shouts, having mounted the galley steps. I have to look away when I see the open bottle of wine in her hand.

'Oh, and here comes nursemaid Sophie to the rescue once again. Always trying to fix everyone else's problems, but never looking at her own internal struggles. That's why you're here, isn't it? To make sure the guy you've been in love with for more than ten years is okay.' He stares straight at me as he says this.

Sophie doesn't respond, instead taking a long swig from the bottle. 'Is this what you want to see, Rhys? I'm more than aware of my own problems, and if you tried to fix your own, then you wouldn't need me to step in and save the day.'

I move across to Sophie, and try to take the bottle from her, but she snatches it away and takes another long swig.

'Sophie, please, not like this,' I say. 'Let me help you.'

'He's right, you know. I much prefer fixing everyone else, rather than focusing on myself.' She's already slurring. 'That's why I allowed Raymond to be that way with me. I felt like the mother hen of the house, protecting you all from what he was really like. And how many of you thanked me for that? Not a single one of you. And that's why I choose to drink away those painful memories. So screw the both of you! I'm getting drunk, and there's fuck all you can do about it.'

She heads back to the hatch, almost stumbling down it. I want to go after her, to stop her throwing away her hard work, but something holds me back. Is Rhys right, and she's been holding a torch for me for all these years?

And what about her relationship with Raymond? It was complex, but could it have developed more than any of us realised? Could she be suffering with some twisted version of Stockholm syndrome, and that's why we remain adrift and alone on this yacht?

28

TEN YEARS AGO

I deliberately returned to the house earlier than expected with the intention of changing the lock on my door, but once I got back, I decided on a different plan of action. I currently have no evidence that either Raymond or Christophe (or Rhys for that matter) have been in my room when I'm not here, and changing my lock without such evidence screams of paranoia.

Instead, if I set up surveillance cameras of my own, I'll get the proof I need.

So, having placed a piece of black insulating tape over the lens in the smoke detector on the ceiling, I now disperse the battery-powered security cameras I purchased online while I was away. They are all motion-detection models: one is hidden in the eye of a teddy bear on my bed, facing the door to my room; one is hidden in the ornament on my chest of drawers; and one is hidden in the fake can of Diet Coke on my desk. Between them, all angles of my room are covered. And neither Rhys, Christophe nor Raymond will have any idea they're in here, just waiting to capture their trespassing.

I'm only home for two days before I capture the first motion. It happened while I was out at work.

I load up my laptop and download the footage from each of the memory sticks in the cameras. I'm not surprised to learn visuals have been recorded on each. I check Teddy-cam first, and witness a scrawny figure in an oversized leather jacket enter my room shortly after I left just before ten this morning. Unfortunately, the camera isn't well enough positioned to capture Raymond's face, but I'm certain the figure is him, a suspicion confirmed when I observe the footage captured by Ornament-cam on my chest of drawers.

I capture a still of Raymond's face as he closes my bedroom door. He's wearing dark jeans, a plaid shirt and what appears to be a white vest beneath. Interestingly, he's wearing socks, and not shoes, suggesting he's either removed them before entering, or wasn't wearing any to begin with. Maybe I should set up a camera in the kitchen, pointed at the cellar door so I can capture his movement from that part of the house too.

Coke-cam captures Raymond's passage across my room to the chest of drawers, where he stands for a moment, admiring the new ornament, before opening my top drawer and running his hands through my things. I shudder as he grabs several pairs of underpants, lifts them out and stretches them against his groin as if he's actually trying to determine whether they would fit him. There is something deeply disturbing about this man.

I capture a still of the act. Thank goodness I got new underwear for Christmas – that handful will be going straight in the bin.

I continue to watch as he presses the underpants to his face and begins to fiddle with the zip of his trousers. My stomach rolls and I'm relieved when his head suddenly snaps round as if he's heard a noise outside the room. He quickly returns the underpants to the drawer and closes it behind him.

I have it: the evidence I need to prove Raymond has been going beyond the tenant–landlord agreement. There's only one thing left for me to do. I pick up the phone and dial Carly's number.

She comes over straight away, and I talk her through everything I've witnessed, including the fact that all the doors can be unlocked with the same key. She listens, takes notes, and allows me to finish before offering her opinion.

'What do you want me to do?' she asks.

'I want you to arrest him for trespassing,' I say matter-of-factly.

She nods and secures the hat on her head. I hadn't realised how pretty she looks in her uniform, and even though she finished her shift an hour ago, she is still wearing it; the consummate professional.

'Do you know where he is now?' she asks.

I shake my head. It's not possible to see which direction he went once he left my room. For all I know, he's as likely to have left the property as he is to be back in the basement.

Carly kisses my cheek, promising she will sort out Raymond, and then I watch her leave.

* * *

I don't hear back from Carly until the following morning. She arrives in jeans and a shirt, and when I open the front door, rubbing the sleep out of my eyes, she tells me to get dressed and that she is taking me for brunch at a restaurant in the countryside.

It's all very mysterious, and when I try to ask her what happened with Raymond, she tells me she will let me know once we reach our destination. There is a calm certainty about her manner which fills me with confidence that our troubles with Raymond are now long behind us.

The pub restaurant is set away from the main road and has a welcoming feel to it, even from the car park. The building is fitted in a mock-Tudor style, with picnic tables sitting aloft decking, and a roaring fire inside the main entrance. There are families seated in booths and at tables, and at first, I'm worried that they won't have room for the two of us, but then Carly confirms her name to the maître d' and we are escorted to a reserved table with a view out onto the lake that the grounds border. There are two ducks and a host of ducklings splashing at the edge of the water, and I genuinely feel much calmer with this serene view.

We order two full English breakfasts, with Carly and me quietly agreeing we'll swap my sausages for her bacon when the food appears. Our food arrives, and we both tuck in, the conversation more stilted now. The bacon is smoked and crispy, and the yolk on the fried egg is runny enough that I can dip the rashers into it. I wait until we've both finished before broaching the subject of Raymond, not wishing to spoil the mood.

'I had a quiet word with him at the police station,' she says, 'and warned him about his future behaviour.'

I wait for her to elaborate, but she just sits there, smiling.

'What does that mean? Did you arrest him or not?'

Her brow knits together. 'I can only arrest him if he's broken the law.'

'He broke into my room and rifled through my underwear. You saw the video.'

'He maintains that he entered your bedroom to perform a routine drugs search. He produced a written contract that each of you signed stipulating that you agreed to the performance of such activity. I can't believe none of you – and you a law student as well – didn't read the tenancy agreement properly before signing it.'

'But surely he has to give us some kind of notice before he turns up?' I think back to the FAQ leaflet the Student Union handed out at the start of second year. 'Like twenty-four hours, or something?'

'Not after you all signed a waiver that states otherwise. Legally, he can turn up and gain entry whenever he wants.'

Why didn't Sophie warn us of this?

'But you saw what he did: touching my underwear is a violation of my privacy.'

'Yes, and that's what I warned him about. He has promised he won't do it again.'

I feel like I've been punched in the gut. 'Is that it? What about the camera I told you about in the smoke alarm?'

'He says they are a security measure for when the property is vacant. Squatting can be a real issue for landlords, and he has them for security only.'

'He has them bloody wired to a wall of monitors in his secret room in the basement! Go down there and see for yourself.'

'I'd need a warrant to go searching in the basement, and I have no justification for requesting one.'

I puff out my cheeks, struggling to maintain the serenity I felt when we first arrived. 'He's filming us down there, Carly. He probably has footage of the two of us having sex. Are you telling me you're okay with that?'

'No, but I haven't got any evidence of that. Had you taken some pictures, that *might* have helped, but even then, it's your word against his.'

'What about the fact he's hiding in the basement?'

Carly scoffs. 'He owns the house! He has just as much right to be there as you do.'

'You must be able to charge him with some kind of indecency order, or an ASBO or something for what I recorded.'

'Yeah, about that... Are there any signs or notices warning people that you're recording them in your room?'

'What? No, of course there bloody aren't.'

'Then, actually, you're the one breaking the law. You need to delete the video footage, or Raymond will have grounds to seek civil restitution.'

'What about him recording me?'

'Again, it's stipulated in the contract you all signed that cameras are in each of the rooms, but will only be switched on when the property is empty.'

Although I haven't seen evidence that he's been recording us, I am certain he would have been.

'If you could get down to the basement, and check the hard drive of the computer, you'll find evidence that he's been recording us.'

'And how am I supposed to do that, Pete? My having a quiet word in his ear was my way of doing you a favour. If my inspector found out I'd had an unofficial word with my boyfriend's landlord, he'd have my guts for garters. I've warned him, and that should be the end of it.'

I already sense it won't be, and that's before I see Sophie's name on my phone screen. I hold a finger up to silence Carly while I answer it.

'What did you do?' she hisses, as soon as the line connects.

'What do you mean? What's going on?'

'Raymond is here shouting the odds. Says we're in breach of his flaming stipulations and he has no time for little boys who go running to the police. He says he's going to tear up our agreement and we have to find somewhere new to live.'

I swallow hard. I've made matters worse, not better. 'I-I'm sorry, Sophie. I recorded him in my room, fiddling with my underwear, and Carly had a word with him.'

She sighs so heavily that the white noise is deafening, and I have to yank the phone from my ear.

'Okay, well, leave it with me. I'll see if I can convince him to change his mind.'

'Wait, no, don't do anything inappropriate. I can be back within the hour and then I'll... apologise to Raymond myself.'

'That won't make a difference. Don't worry about it, Pete. I understand why you told Carly, but I wish you'd told me instead. There are things you don't know about Raymond.' She groans. 'I don't have time to get into it now. Listen, do me a favour, and stay out of the way until tonight. I'll do what I can to get things resolved. And please, not another word to Carly, yeah?'

She hangs up, and I can't help picturing the consequences of what I've done: that monster leering at Sophie while she prostitutes herself for my error in judgement.

29

PRESENT DAY

I've left Rhys to stew on the deck while I fix some food – macaroni cheese from a packet – and try to talk Sophie out of throwing her sobriety even further away. She's consumed three quarters of the bottle of chardonnay, but I've fixed her a black coffee and am encouraging her to nibble on breadsticks. My stomach is grumbling at the smell of the cheesy pasta. Stirring the pan is helping to keep my mind from thinking about Christophe's body in the shark cage, and Harry swimming for all our lives.

'Brunch smells delicious,' Sophie says, reaching for another breadstick and biting off the end.

'None of this is your fault,' I tell her firmly, while continuing to stir. 'What happened to Raymond ten years ago... We all went into it with our eyes wide open.'

She cocks a single eyebrow. 'I was the one who chose to ignore the red flags, though. It's not like I didn't see it coming. Raymond wasn't the first monster who took advantage of me.' She pauses and stares at the bottle on the table, just out of her reach.

Sophie has never told us much about her upbringing, and I

accepted that there was probably a good reason why she chose not to openly share such details, and never wanted to pry. It feels like she now does want to get into it, but I'm not going to push; I want her to feel comfortable opening up to me.

'When I was seven, my parents decided to start fostering. They'd tried for years to conceive after I was born, but IVF failed. It was a bit weird having different children coming and going; some stayed for a night; others a few weeks. Then Nick came to live with us. He was fifteen and I think I was twelve. He was a bit of a troublemaker, and had been suspended from his last school, but the social workers spoke highly of him regardless; said he was very intelligent, and not being stretched seemed to be a possible cause for his rebellion.

'He moved in, and for the first few weeks, it was like inheriting a cooler older brother. He was handsome, and when he was enrolled at my secondary school, he soon became popular. The girls in his year fawned over him, and he loved the attention. I became cooler by association. Suddenly the girls who'd once snubbed me wanted to share make-up tips, and invited me to the park after school. I knew it was because they fancied Nick, and I was okay clinging on his coattails.

'He knuckled down at school, worked hard, and made an effort to make my parents' lives easier. To those looking in, his placement in our house was a godsend that went both ways. My parents even mooted the idea of formally adopting him, but given his age, it seemed more hassle than benefit to him.

'What nobody knew – to this day – is that when my parents were asleep, Nick would sneak along the corridor and come into my room. At first, I felt good that he'd chosen me over my host of new friends. We fooled around in bed, and he made me feel so much more mature, and it was exciting at first. He said I wasn't allowed to speak about it, or he'd stop and claim I was making it all up.'

I remove the pasta from the heat, and force myself to watch her, my gut tightening with every word. Suddenly all the booze and drug-taking are making sense. Why didn't I pay more attention?

'Things carried on that way for three years, until one day he upped and left without a by-your-leave. He was eighteen, and no longer the problem of social services. My parents were heartbroken, and I don't think things ever really went back to how they'd been for either of them. Mum would say Dad put too much pressure on Nick to go to university, and he'd say that she mollycoddled him too much. Nick stole thousands from them, but they never sought to press charges.

'I was fifteen and thought I was in love. He understood me like nobody else did, and it's only recently I've been able to reflect on how he manipulated me during those formative years. For so long, I blamed myself for him leaving, and things got so bad at home that I couldn't wait to escape to university. Once there, I masked the pain with alcohol and weed, but it always returned the next morning.'

She reaches for the bottle, but manages to stop herself.

'Soph, I had no idea,' I say, joining her at the table. 'When you told me about what Raymond was doing to you... I had no idea it wasn't your first time being abused.'

'How could you have known?' She angles her head towards me. 'But I knew you wanted to help, and that's why I trusted you. You were the first person who really listened to me when I spoke about Raymond's behaviour, and I never saw any judgement in your eyes. It's also why I... why I never told you how I felt about you. When you and Carly broke up, I almost came clean, but I always felt I had too much baggage, and didn't want to drag you under with it.'

I guess Rhys was right. I don't know what to say. I press my hand against hers, before dishing out the pasta into four bowls, and pushing one towards her.

'You should eat something.'

She picks up a fork, and shovels down a mouthful.

'There's something else I want you to know,' she adds, after she's swallowed. 'I didn't quit my job at the investment company two years ago. I... I was going through a rough patch, and ended up overdosing. It was a stressful time, but that feels like an excuse. I was doing lines of coke in the ladies' toilets, and when I woke up, I was in a hospital bed. The doctors warned me that I was on a downward spiral and the best thing for me would be a period of reflection in a crisis centre.'

I don't know how to respond. I had no clue she'd been struggling so badly.

'At first, I didn't want to listen – you know how stubborn I can be – but then I heard my boss was going to fire me for gross misconduct anyway, and rehabilitation seemed a better choice. I only agreed to it to avoid facing my colleagues, but once I got there, talking about my problems really helped. You must know: I never spoke about Raymond directly, nor what happened to him. I just spoke of an abusive ex, without naming him.'

Neither of us wants to consider the prospect that he escaped the grave we buried him in. In the cold light of day, I'm no longer surprised that Woody decided not to come away this weekend. Maybe he'll never know what a lucky escape he had.

Something stirs in the back of my mind, but it's just out of reach.

One of the cabin doors slides open, and I spot Fergus emerging from his cabin. He looks more forlorn than when I last saw him, and he joins us at the table, taking one of the bowls of pasta.

I can only hope he didn't overhear what we were discussing. I don't know what to say, and as an awkward silence descends, I search for anything to break it.

'Rhys is still up on deck,' I tell him. 'I left him to cool off.'

Fergus's brow furrows, but he doesn't say anything.

'When you've eaten, would you mind letting him know that I cooked some pasta for him too?'

Fergus nods, and tucks in. I wait to see if Sophie is going to continue speaking, but Fergus's arrival has cast a shadow on her openness, and I sense she won't be lowering her guard again any time soon.

'Can you hear that?' she asks, after several minutes.

I set down my fork, but can't hear anything out of the ordinary.

'Rhys is coughing,' she continues, sliding out of her chair. 'I'm sure he has his inhaler on him, but I'll go check he's okay.'

I finish my pasta and am about to reach for another breadstick when Sophie screams for us to come up on deck. Fergus leads the way, but halts abruptly as soon as he is out of the hatch. It's only when I manoeuvre him out of the way that I see the cause for alarm.

'We... we need to do something for him,' Sophie is screaming between sobs, her hands covering her mouth in shock.

Rhys is lying on his side and blood is flowing from his mouth and nose. It's like something out of a horror scene. His face is contorted in terror. His body is convulsing on the white plastic deck, and when he coughs, more blood erupts from his mouth. A pool is spreading across the deck, and it looks like he's already lost more than is healthy.

'Fergus, go and get some towels from the bathroom,' Sophie

says, taking control. 'Rhys, can you hear me? I need you to tell me what's going on. Did you eat or drink something?'

The only sign that he's still alive is the slow blink of his eyes, but he doesn't speak. As he looks over my shoulder, his eyes widen as if he's seen something, but when I turn, I see nothing but the bow.

'You said he might be having an asthma attack,' I remind her, knowing this is not the result of asthma, but uncertain what else to suggest.

Sophie ignores my suggestion, and steps around the rapidly expanding pool, trying to shift Rhys into the recovery position. He coughs again, and tiny droplets of red land on my toes.

Fergus returns with the towels, and Sophie uses one to mop the red puddle from around Rhys's head, and wipes his mouth and nose with the other. As soon as his face clears, more blood instantly appears from his nose and gums.

'Do either of you know if he suffers from any underlying medical conditions?' Sophie asks, her face paler than ever. 'Could he be on any anticoagulant medication?'

I look to Fergus, who is more likely to know, but he shakes his head. 'Not that he told me. Just the asthma.'

I spot the bloody inhaler gripped tightly in his hand, and point at it.

'My aunt was asthmatic; Ventolin shouldn't do something like this,' Sophie says with a dismissive shake of her head. 'He must have some kind of condition, or he's ingested something toxic.'

What she's saying is, somebody has done this to Rhys, and given the discovery of Christophe's body this morning, it's not an unreasonable conclusion to draw. But what kind of substance could produce such graphic blood loss?

Rhys gasps for air, staring directly at me, as if trying to point, but then he coughs out more blood and there's a gargling sound before his body slumps and stops moving altogether. His head sags to the side and his chest stops rising.

This can't be happening.

I reach for his wrist and check for a pulse, but there's nothing there. The whole deck is swimming in his blood, and I sense that, even if we managed to get his heart beating again, it's already too late to save him. Sophie must be thinking along the same lines, as she closes Rhys's eyelids.

I back away, not wanting the toxic blood to infect me. I remember seeing a film about the Ebola virus once, and the death scenes portrayed weren't dissimilar to what we've just witnessed, but that's a rare disease, and has to be passed by someone else who's infected in the first place.

Fergus has his head in his hands, but Sophie is pointing at Rhys's face. At first, I can't see what she's gasping at, but then I see the blue tinge to his lifeless tongue.

'P-poison,' Sophie stammers. 'I-I mean *rat* poison. Raymond used to use it to kill rats in the cellar. He was fascinated by death and pain. He tried to kill any rogue animals that wandered onto the property.'

I think about the metal noose I found in the garden the day we first viewed the house. Had I not come to its rescue, that kitten would have died.

'He told me once that certain rodent poisons can cause the tongue to change colour. Some contain anticoagulants as the means of killing the rodent. Oh, Jesus!'

I picture the pellets I found in the basement all those years before. It can't just be coincidence.

My gaze again falls on the bloody inhaler in his hand, and I snatch it up, pointing the mouthpiece towards the sea and depressing the small metal canister. A cloud of gas escapes, and I dare myself to sniff the air, instantly recognising the repulsive odour.

As impossible as it seems, this has Raymond's name all over it. We saw him die. We buried him in the ground. If he really is back from the dead, which of us is he coming for next?

30

TEN YEARS AGO

When I told Carly about Raymond's reaction to her quiet word, she told me not to go back.

'I can come with you and help pack up your stuff,' she says. 'You can move in with me until you finish your exams.'

'There's barely enough room for you at your flat, let alone two of us.'

'Then we'll find a bigger place. I'm not sure I want you living in his house any more. I'm worried you're going to do something you'll regret, like thump your landlord or something. Don't flush away your career before it's even started. Between us, I'm sure we could get somewhere reasonable. Besides, it's only for a few months before you head to London anyway.'

Not only is the lack of room an issue, but Carly's place is across town as well, making it a two-bus journey to the campus. I politely decline the offer, though I know I'll need to crash for a couple of nights.

All is quiet when I enter, and my room looks untouched. I'm even more determined now to change the lock on the door. It's a little after four, and my appetite is finally returning, so I head into the kitchen and switch on the kettle. There's bread in the breadbin and milk in the fridge, so someone must have nipped to the shop for supplies. That must be a good sign. At least Raymond hasn't demanded everyone move out immediately.

I drop two slices of bread into the toaster and fetch the milk and butter from the fridge. I hear a door open upstairs, followed by slow, delicate footsteps on the stairs. I smile when I see Sophie, a pink-coloured kimono wrapped tightly around her body.

'Hey,' I say, pulling a troubled face, 'I didn't think anyone was home. Is Raymond still… angry?'

She shakes her head and grimaces. 'I've sorted it.'

She moves unsteadily to the kitchen table and sits down.

'Are you… Are you okay?'

She doesn't meet my gaze.

'Soph, I asked if you were okay.'

She rubs her shoulders with a pained scowl. 'I'll be fine.'

I don't believe her, but decide not to press until I know what the future holds for the rest of us. 'I was going to make some tea. Do you want a cup?'

'No, but you could fetch the bottle of vodka from the top drawer of the freezer.'

I do as instructed, locating a clean glass from the cupboard, and placing both on the table in front of her. She winces as she lifts her arm and fails to unscrew the cap. I take the bottle from her, remove the lid and pour a measure. She winces again as she raises the glass to her lips and swallows the contents in one.

I pour her another measure, and then take a swig from the bottle. 'Okay, I can't take this. Are you going to tell me what Woody has been doing to you?'

She smiles thinly and drains the glass again.

'Soph, I know you've been… seeing Woody. Harry told me he heard loud moaning coming from your room, violent sounding, and it always seems like you're in agony after he's been here. Is he abusing you physically?'

She doesn't respond, but the answer in her tear-filled eyes is deafening.

'You can't let him get away with this, Soph. We need to report him to—'

'It... isn't Woody,' she interrupts, struggling to keep the flood-gates closed.

She lowers her hand from where it's been pinning the satin material over her neck, and I instantly see red abrasions covering her upper chest. The gasp escapes my throat before I can stop it. Deep down, I know this is the tip of the iceberg, and when she lowers her hands to the table, I move closer, and carefully lower the material so I can see the purple swelling around the back of her neck and shoulders.

'Oh, dear God, Sophie. Who did this to you?'

She pulls up the kimono gingerly, but doesn't answer.

'I'm calling the police,' I say, pulling out my phone.

'No,' she says, resting a hand over my mine. 'It was calling them that caused this in the first place.' She can't look at me. 'It was... Raymond. He... He was so angry that you spoke to Carly about him. He's... He's a proud man, and he was going to tear up our lease, unless...'

The words trail off, but her hands point at her injuries.

I move around so I'm facing her again. 'Raymond did this to you? There's no excuse for his behaviour. He needs reporting.'

She shakes her head, the pain almost too much for her to bear. 'It won't do any good, Pete. He was pent up and frustrated. He's... He's calmer now. He said we can stay and that's the end of it.'

She moves a hand up to her eye to wipe a solitary tear as it escapes and runs the length of her cheek. As it moves, it blots against the foundation beneath her eye, revealing the red beneath, and leaves a trail behind it. I press a finger beneath her chin and slowly twist her head, the light from the kitchen window reflecting off the swell of her cheek. She's clearly tried to cover the bruising, but now that I'm aware of it, it's impossible to miss.

When she lowers her arm back to the table, I can see bloody grazes around her wrist as well, as if some kind of restraint has scratched and clawed at the skin there. I don't want to think about what she has had to endure all because of me, but I can't keep burying my head in the sand and pretending it isn't going on.

'But you're also right, in a way, about Woody,' she continues. 'I have been seeing him, but it's only casual. You can't tell him anything about this. He's so protective that I worry what he'll do.'

'You're not going to be able to keep this from him.'

'I'll think of something.'

I've been so hung up on my own issues – Carly, my dissertation, the intruders in my room – that I had no clue that Sophie and Woody had become more than just a casual hook-up. That explains why he's here so often. I'd assumed he was still crashing on the sofa, but come to think of it, I can't remember the last time I spotted his sleeping bag rolled up on the living room floor.

Sophie pushes the tumbler towards me, and I pour another vodka into the glass. 'Raymond is very demanding and likes it rough,' she says quietly, the world's greatest understatement.

'Are we talking bondage?'

She nods. 'Some. It all started that night we had the house-warming party. I took him upstairs and asked him what it would take to forget that we'd broken the rules. I'd expected him to suggest a second dinner date or a bribe, but he was so angry. I ended up... giving him a hand job. I felt disgusted, but I saw it as a means to an end. He left, and nothing more was said.

'I happened to mention it to Rhys, and... I don't know... He must have let it slip somewhere because Raymond found out and he thought we'd been mocking him for it. I told him we hadn't, but this time, he wanted more. I didn't understand what at first, but when I moved my hand towards his crotch, he pushed it away, grabbed hold of my neck, and forced my head down.'

I'm overwhelmed with guilt.

'It's not like it was the first blow job I'd ever given, so again I chalked it up to experience and we moved on. Then Rhys had a cash-flow problem not long after, his direct debit payment bounced or reversed or something. Of course, Raymond came calling at my door, and this time, I slept with him. In fairness, he was gentle then, and as much as it appalled me, it bought Rhys the time he needed to settle the debt.

'Over time, whenever he considered one of us to have broken a rule – like when he found a bag of weed in Fergus's room – he would call on me and I would have to resolve the problem. It became a habit, and when I saw how much he seemed to enjoy the power he had over me, I would use it to my advantage.

'The first time he slapped me was after we got back from Paris and you had got weird with him searching the house. He told me in no uncertain terms to get you in line, and I told him to go and fuck himself. He was livid and lashed out. I should have told you all and we should have moved out, but everything was so difficult because of the falling-out between you and Rhys, and my problems seemed to shrink under that.'

I would wrap her in a hug if I didn't think she'd scream out in agony. 'Soph, surely you can see that enough is enough. This can't go on.'

She knocks back the vodka. 'He was so pissed off after being spoken to by Carly, the embarrassment, he said. He was fuming, and I told him it was a mistake and that I'd ask you to leave if that's what it took, but he didn't listen. Before I knew it, he'd grabbed me by the throat and pinned me to the wall. He kept punching me until I fell to the floor, and then he kicked me until I passed out. When I woke, he was gone, but... I think he had sex with me even though I wasn't conscious.'

I think I'm going to be sick. It takes all my willpower not to lose my shit when she's doing so well to hold hers together.

'He's physically abusive towards you and has sexually assaulted you. Soph, please, let me go to the police station with you. He can't be allowed to get away with this.'

Another tear escapes, and she quickly claws it away with her fingertips. 'You don't understand. I can't go to the police. They won't believe me.'

'Have you seen yourself? You are covered in bruises and cuts. They *will* believe you.'

'Raymond is too careful for all that. Yes, they'll see that I've been raped and beaten, but they won't be able to prove it was him that did it.'

'They'll search and find his DNA on you.'

'He'll argue it was consensual and that someone else beat me up. And they'll believe him.'

I shake my head. 'No, Soph. *You're* the victim here. They'll understand.'

'It's *you* who doesn't understand, Pete. I was raped during Freshers' Week two years ago.'

I hang my head because I don't know what to say. I can't begin to imagine what she's been through. That's the trouble with privilege: you can't see the inequality others suffer.

She knocks back another shot, and it seems to loosen her tongue. 'I was out with some girls from my halls, and we were all pretty drunk by the end of the night. We got separated and I woke in a bush in the middle of town with no memory of how I got there or what had happened. I stumbled home, and went to bed, and when I showered in the morning, I realised that somebody had raped me. I figured my drink must have been spiked, and I went straight to the police to report it. I couldn't remember who or what had happened at first, but then I had flashbacks to this guy – Martin – a friend of a friend who'd been dancing with us. I had this memory of the two of us kissing on the dancefloor, so I told the police that he must have been the one who raped me.

'They interviewed him, and we both made statements, and he couldn't account for his whereabouts, but was adamant that he wouldn't have assaulted me, and definitely didn't spike my drink.

'It was going to trial, but then a video emerged of him and another girl having sex in his room the same night, so the police dropped the charges. They threatened to prosecute me for time wasting, and it was sheer good fortune that they decided not to proceed. I didn't lie, though. *Someone* spiked my drink and raped me, I just don't know who. But now I have that hanging over my head, so it's my tainted word against Raymond's.'

My heart is pounding for her, and I'm desperate to tell her she's wrong, but the justice system in this country doesn't favour victims of assault. The prosecution rate is alarmingly low.

'What if I tell them I've witnessed his violence towards you?'

'Then you'd be lying, and given your choice of future profession, it wouldn't reflect well when you're proved a liar.'

'But there must be *something* we can do?'

She sighs quietly. 'There might be. If we could get evidence of what he's doing, then maybe – just maybe – there's a chance. You said you'd set up surveillance cameras in your bedroom, right?'

I nod slowly.

'Well, what if you set up some cameras in my room too? Then, when the shit hits the fan the next time... we can catch him in the act.'

31

PRESENT DAY

I keep expecting Rhys to suddenly leap up from the blood-soaked deck, wipe the red liquid from his face and reveal that this is all just some elaborate prank. None of the blood is real, and his convulsing and Fergus's ghostly pallor were all just a part of a well-rehearsed act. But Rhys doesn't rise, and the thin puddle continues to sway and flow in rhythm with the boat on the increasingly agitated sea.

The wind is whipping up around us – the onset of a storm? – and it's causing the yacht to tilt and bob with every ebb and flow. White spray splashes up with every dip and rise. One thing's for certain: we won't be able to stay up on deck if the wind gets much stronger.

'What are we going to do with Rhys's body?' I shout over the din to Sophie, who is pacing, and probably not aiding the shift of the boat.

'He'll have to go in the cage with the others.'

She is so matter of fact that it could be mistaken for heartlessness, but I know she's just trying to be practical.

'You two put him in the cage,' she says, 'while I try to find something to mop the deck with.'

She disappears down into the galley in search of tools.

I look to Fergus and raise my eyebrows, encouraging him to prepare himself for lifting the body, but he can't keep his eyes off his fallen friend.

He suddenly drops to his knees, and lays Rhys out flat onto his back, holding two fingers to his neck.

I try to pull him away. 'It's too late. I already checked for a pulse. He's gone.'

'No, I'm sure I can still feel a pulse. It's faint, but there's something there. Give me your hand.'

Without another word, he grabs my hand, and pulls me down to my knees, pressing my fingers against his skin.

'I can't feel a pulse, Fergus, I think you're imagining it.'

'No, no, it's there. I can feel it. He's still alive. We can't just throw him in the cage like some discarded bag of crisps. He'll drown and then we'll have killed him. Maybe if we can get him talking, he can tell us what happened?'

He's agitated, and I wish Sophie had sent me in search of the mop and bucket instead. I snatch my hand free, and attempt to stand, but another jerk of the boat has me crashing back to the floor, dangerously close to the puddle of blood, but I manage to keep my shoulder away as it slams into the wooden deck. I try again, this time parting my legs more, and scoop my hands under Fergus's armpits. I heave him up, but he fights all the way, trying to pull himself back to Rhys. As soon as Fergus is on his feet, I twist him round so he is facing me.

'He's gone, bro. There's nothing we can do for him.'

Sophie reappears, mop and bucket in hand, and a disappointed look on her face when she sees Rhys is where she left him.

'I'll get the cage up,' she says, pointing up at the cockpit.

The motor whirs as the mechanism engages and the cage begins to rise out of the water. Elena's body has floated to the top. Her long dark hair splays out, and her white face stares back at me through the metal bars. I can't have Fergus seeing her like this – he can't see what will also happen to Rhys's body – so I keep him facing away, as I manoeuvre the cage, unlock and raise the lid. I try to push Elena's face beneath the water with my foot, but it bobs with every attempt. Maybe we should have thought of tying them to the bottom of the cage so that this wouldn't have been a problem, but in truth, I never realised just how many bodies we'd be trying to hide in here. One thing's for sure: the cage isn't large enough to hold all of us.

'Don't look,' I tell Fergus forcefully. 'Okay? You take Rhys's feet, and I'll lift him by the arms. Best thing is for you to keep your eyes closed. Stay behind the safety rope and edge along as I pull, but stop when I do.'

He nods his understanding, and looks at Sophie, who's standing in the safety of the cockpit. Then he stoops and coils his fingers around Rhys's ankles. I don't have a choice but to step into the bloody puddle to get my hands under his arms, but we manage to lift him up. It takes a heave to get him on to the rim of the vessel, and Fergus closes his eyes as I instructed, while we edge along until my bottom grazes the lid of the cage. Then I position Rhys's torso on the lid and gently slide him down into the water.

Once his body is in, I slam the lid shut and reach down to lock it. I should warn Fergus to keep his eyes closed, but I'm too busy fiddling with the lock, and I hear him gasp and retch when he spots Elena's face just below the bars, as if she's trying to escape.

I straighten and try to get to him, but he's having none of it, hopping back onto the deck, which Sophie has just cleaned, and hurries down below, screaming that he's not putting up with this any more.

'Probably best to give him a minute,' Sophie suggests, as she continues to drain the blood into the bucket of soapy water. The bubbles have turned a hellish red colour. 'I think there's a storm brewing, which means we'll be sitting ducks if we can't get this yacht moving. As soon as I'm done with the clean-up, I'll attempt to bypass the ignition.'

'With all due respect, Soph, are you sure that's such a wise idea?'

She slows the mop to a stop. 'What choice do we have? The way I see things: either Raymond really is back from the dead – and I don't believe that for a second – or one of you is responsible for what happened to Elena, Christophe and now Rhys. I know I'm not a killer, so that just leaves the two of you. Frankly, I don't want to ride out a storm trapped below deck with either possibility coming to fruition.'

She's about to start mopping again, but I grab hold of the plastic handle. 'It wasn't all that long ago you had your head buried in a bottle of wine, so you'll forgive me questioning the steadiness of your hands before you start playing with electrified cables.'

She glowers under the weight of my expectant stare. 'Funny, but watching one of your closest friends bleed to death from the face has something of a sobering effect. I'm fine. I didn't drink too much. Back in the day, it used to take me two bottles before I even felt tipsy.' She thrusts out a hand, holding it flat at the bottom of my nose, as if to prove just how steady it is.

I start to see Sophie in a new light. I haven't had a drink all day, and after what we've just witnessed, not a single part of me would be that steady. Is there another reason she's not reacting to Rhys's bloody end as any normal person would?

I swipe her hand away. 'I need to check on Fergus. How long do you think you'll be before the blood is gone?'

She looks at what remains of the puddle. 'A few minutes.'

I head through the hatch and down the steps, into the galley. There's no sign of Fergus here or in the dinette, so I continue to the narrow corridor, and find him in his room, the first cabin to the right.

'Sophie's going to try and hotwire the yacht in a minute.'

'What? No, we can't leave. What if Harry swims back?'

It's been over an hour since Harry left, and I don't even know whether he could have made it to the shoreline in that time. I feel like we've drifted closer to the thread of land we saw this morning, but it's now indistinguishable from the dark cloud coming ever closer to our location. I don't want to consider the prospect that Harry won't make it to safety. I can't lose another friend. Not today.

'If he's swimming back, we'll be able to collect him on the way,' I say, in an attempt to pacify Fergus.

'But we might not see him unless he's on the same course as us. Please, Pete, we should just sit and wait for help to come.'

His confidence in Harry to make it and send aid is admirable, but the only reason he'd return is if he didn't find help. *If* he doesn't make it, we'll remain stranded out here at the killer's mercy.

Unless that's what he actually wants?

My brow furrows as I consider the man standing before me, and he fixes me with an equally quizzical look. With Harry gone, I have nobody I can discuss my suspicions with. There's so much going on, and I just don't know who I can or should trust. Fergus is about to marry my sister, but he wasn't always so reliable at university. Sophie, on the other hand, has been a good friend for so long, but what if the abuse she experienced for all of our sakes is now manifesting and forcing her to react?

I take an unsteady step backwards, casting my gaze towards the countertop in the galley, and notice the knife block: the large chef's knife and one of the smaller ones are missing. I didn't use either when preparing the pasta lunch, and it was definitely full when I last saw it. I glance back at Fergus, but his hands appear empty as he twists his fingers nervously.

I hear Sophie return with the mop and a now empty bucket; presumably she tipped the bloody water overboard, though I'm not sure that was such a smart move, given there may still be sharks lurking nearby.

'I need to lift up the floor so I can get at the engine,' she says, squeezing past me, along the hall to the V-berth. 'When I tell you, Pete, I want you to go up to the cockpit. I've managed to extract the ignition block, and you'll see two cables poking out of the bottom. When one of them moves, I want you to shout to Fergus which one it is, right or left. Fergus, I want you standing by the hatch, so you can then shout the message to me below deck. Got that?'

'We can't move the boat,' Fergus says, the most decisive he's been this entire trip. 'We need to give Harry time to find help.'

Sophie shakes her head. 'You – we *all* – need to accept that Harry's already dead.'

My head snaps round, and my vision blurs as I feel the penny drop. All this time, I've been clinging on to the hope that his cheeky grin will suddenly reappear from out of the water, but there's no faulting her logic.

'Even with a tank of air, there's no way he'd have enough to cover that distance. It must be a good two to three nautical miles back to that strip of shore, and we don't even know if that was the mainland, or Paradise Cove where we were supposed to be heading.' She takes a breath, and looks from Fergus to me. 'Harry's gone. And unless we want to join him, we need to get this yacht started.'

Fergus doesn't budge. 'There's three of us. Let's put it to the vote. I vote we stay. Sophie votes we go. Pete?'

I hate being put in the middle like this. I don't want to disappoint either of them, but if by some miracle Sophie does manage to hotwire the engine, I also don't want to think of Harry being stranded in the water and us not finding him.

I look at Fergus's pleading eyes, and then at Sophie. And then it hits me: if Raymond isn't behind all of this, then one of these two is. I can't breathe. I no longer know which of them to trust. I don't want to spend another second at the hands of a killer, so I fix Sophie with a hard stare. 'Are you sure you know what you're doing?'

'As certain as I'm ever going to be. It's this or we never get home.'

I nod. 'Then we try to get the engine started.'

I don't wait for Fergus to argue, climbing the steps out of the hatch and then up to the cockpit. I see where Sophie has managed to pull out the ignition block, and I see the two cables she's referring to. I focus on them, looking for any movement.

'Right,' I call out, when the first one jiggles, and I hear Fergus relay the message. 'Left,' I call out when I see the second cable twitch.

There's a sputtering sound, as if the yacht is waking from a deep slumber. And then there's the loudest explosion.

The whole yacht shakes as plumes of thick black smoke appear at the bow.

32

TEN YEARS AGO

It's been two weeks since we returned from the Christmas break and Sophie revealed the true extent of her relationship with Raymond. The physical bruises have healed, but I sense she's still tending to the psychological scars, judging by the number of empty bottles in the recycle bin. She's also been spending more and more time in Christophe's room, and there's only one reason I can think of for her to be up there.

I've shared my concerns, but she assures me she has everything under control, and despite my reservations, she's a grown woman in control of her own mind, and I do have a tendency to overanalyse situations.

The others have subsequently returned to the house, and it feels like a fresh start. Rhys has been seeing a girl from his course, and since the new term started, there's been no awkwardness or animosity between us. I still haven't wanted Carly to stay over since Paris – although there's now tape over the lens in the smoke alarm, I still don't know whether the device has a microphone as well.

I ordered additional cameras for Sophie's bedroom. They've

been set up, covering all angles. As and when Raymond shows his cracked face, the trap will be sprung. I'm not comfortable with Sophie using herself as bait, but she's leaving me little choice. Ultimately, if we want Raymond prosecuted for his brutality, we need evidence.

The cameras are hidden in an open and empty can of Stella Artois; in an ornamental waving cat – the kind I've often seen in our local Chinese takeaway; and in a picture frame that now holds a humorous postcard declaring 'Smile, you're on camera'. If I walked into Sophie's room looking for where the cameras were hidden, my eye would be drawn to all three spots, but without that foresight, they just look like poor taste souvenirs.

'You've checked the motion sensors are working?' Sophie asks, as I pack my rucksack with criminology textbooks.

'Checked and double-checked,' I reassure her. 'What time are you expecting him to come round?'

It's Thursday, and all of us are due to be out between midday and two. Fergus, Harry and Rhys have been on campus since nine, and I'm about to walk with Christophe who is starting his shift at one of the pubs near the campus.

'He's likely to come and do his routine room check just after twelve. He'll be angry when he can't unlock your door. He'll come knocking, and I'll casually pretend I didn't know you'd changed it. He'll be fuming, especially after you taped up the lens in the smoke detector.' She pauses, and looks down at the tremble in her hands, the first sign of nerves I've seen from her since she suggested this plan of action. 'He'll demand I make it up to him, and then...'

'I don't like this plan,' I tell her forthrightly. 'Why don't I pretend to go, and then sneak back? I could hide out in the garden, and if things get too rough, I can leap out and we can fight him off together.'

'I can handle this, Pete. You don't need to worry.'

But I *am* worried.

Sophie's plan only works if he does what he did last time, but what if he's angrier and goes too far? She doesn't seem prepared to consider the amount of danger she's voluntarily putting herself in. I'm terrified that I'll come back and find he's killed her. She was in such a bad state last time, and his violence has been escalating. It's only a matter of time before he does damage that can't be reversed. What if today's that day?

'Will you at least message me when he gets here? I don't want to leave you on your own for a second longer than necessary.'

She offers a non-committal grunt. 'Relax, everything is going to go to plan.'

'At least message me when he's gone, so I can get back here and we can get you and the footage to the police. We'll tell them you had no knowledge of the surveillance cameras I set up. It'll seem like less of a honey trap that way. They'll take photographs of your injuries, and paired with the video, it should be enough for them to arrest and hopefully prosecute him.'

Sophie offers me a thin smile, but it only heightens my own anxiety.

'Pete? You ready to go?' Christophe calls from the kitchen.

I want to shout back that I'm not ready and have decided to stay here, but Sophie is ushering me towards my door. Before I leave, I pull her into a tight hug – almost as if it might be the last time I'm going to see her. I watch as she slowly walks upstairs, and then I turn to Christophe.

'I'm going to be late,' he moans, unaware of what's about to unfold in this house.

I look back up the stairs at Sophie's door, and then make a choice. If I can't be here to help fight him off, then I need to do whatever I can to help her protect herself in case he does go too far.

'I forgot something,' I quickly say and hurry back to my room. 'You go on ahead, and I'll catch you up.'

He looks at his watch, but doesn't argue, stomping towards the patio door, and out into the garden. I quickly unlock my door, enter and go to the bottom drawer of my desk. I fish around until I find the bottle of extra strength sleeping pills I swiped from my mum's medicine cabinet over Christmas. I twist off the clicking cap and drop two into my hand. Two are usually enough to knock her out for the night, she tells me, but given Raymond's size, I pop out a third pill to be safe.

I lock my door and hurry back to the kitchen, where I crush the pills between two teaspoons, before tipping the contents into the open bottle of whiskey that Sophie has left on the table. It's Raymond's favourite brand, she said, and he always has a drink when he first arrives. I shake the bottle and watch the residue slowly dissolve into the caramel-coloured liquid. I stop and spin around when I feel someone watching me, but Sophie's door remains closed. Putting it down to paranoia, I place the bottle on the table, then hurry out into the garden, catching up with Christophe as he unlocks the gate out to the footpath.

* * *

Time on campus drags. I can't stop watching the clock. It's the longest two hours of my life. Sophie hasn't messaged to say Raymond arrived, nor has she messaged to say he's gone. It's possible he was a no-show, in which case all my nail chewing has been in vain. I want to message her, but if I'm to make out to the police we haven't entrapped Raymond, I need my phone's history clear.

She also wouldn't be able to contact me, I realise, if my worst fears have been realised and he's killed her. Or maybe he figured out what was going on and dragged her from the room so none of it is caught on film. I know worrying about things I can't control is a waste of energy, but my mind refuses to focus on anything else. Even when Professor Ed asks me a question to check I'm paying attention, I blag a response, apologetically adding that I've been under the weather. Whether he buys it or not, I simply don't care. Maybe I could message one of the others and see if they've heard from Sophie? No, that still won't look right.

As soon as the bell sounds, I'm the first one out of my seat. Books already in my bag, I charge out of the room, down the three flights of stairs, and out into a gale. The weatherman said to expect a storm this afternoon, with winds of up to fifteen miles an hour. As I battle through it, I can't help picturing Dorothy's house landing on the Wicked Witch in Oz.

There is already a tree down, blocking the main road near the cut way back to our garden, so I dart between queuing cars, and hurtle along the footpath, sheltered by the endless trees to my left and the high fences of the properties to my right. I burst through the gate, and hurry up the path, buffeted by the wind, and then dive through the patio doors. It's a huge relief to see Sophie sitting at the kitchen table, a glass of wine in her hand. Fergus and Woody are with her, but neither is speaking, and Fergus's skin is so pale – shock, maybe? There's no sign of the bottle of whiskey I left on the edge of the table.

Sophie is wearing the same pink-coloured kimono she was in before I left, and isn't shielding her neck or shoulders. I can't see any sign of obvious bruising on her face either. Maybe my suspicion that Raymond didn't show up was accurate.

'Everything okay?' I ask breathlessly, conscious that Fergus and Woody weren't privy to our plan, and that Woody didn't even know about Raymond's abuse.

None of them answer, and so I slide the satchel of books from my back and move further into the kitchen. It's only now I notice the cellar door is ajar, and I panic at the prospect that Raymond is still here, that Sophie's usual wiles have failed her for the first time. What if he's already torn up the lease, and we're now officially homeless?

There's an odd atmosphere, and I feel awkward as I wait for one of them to tell me what's going on.

'You're back early,' I say to Fergus, but he can't meet my gaze.

'Raymond came to the house,' Sophie says, her eyes transfixed on the cellar door, as she sips from her glass. 'Said he was doing one of his regular room searches, but needed to check on some rat traps in the basement.' She pauses, struggling to get the words out. 'When I came down, I found him like this.'

She doesn't elaborate, and I find myself drawn to the door. I gasp when I pull it open. The light is on, and he's lying at the foot of the stairs, eyes closed, a small red puddle around his head, like some kind of devilish halo.

'Oh, my God,' I say with genuine shock. 'Is he...?'

'Looks like it. Fergus, Woody and I were just discussing what we should do about it.'

My eyes widen when I see the empty bottle of whiskey still tightly gripped in his hand, and realise that this is my fault.

I killed Raymond.

33

PRESENT DAY

The horizon disappears from view as the thick black smoke rises into the air. I know instantly that Sophie's attempts to hotwire the yacht have failed, but more important now is that we get her back on deck.

'Can you see Sophie?' I shout down to Fergus who is statuesque at the hatchway. 'Is she okay?'

He temporarily disappears from sight as smoke billows out of the galley.

'Fergus?' I call out again. 'We need to get Soph out of there.'

He's either in a trance, or can't hear what I'm shouting, so I hurry down the steps and pull him away from the hatch, slapping his cheeks, until his eyes focus on my face.

'Are you okay? Are you hurt?'

His eyes dart left and right, but he eventually shakes his head, without speaking. I try to shake him out of this trance, but he's moving at a much slower rate, and no amount of cajoling is getting him to communicate. Is this what shock looks like? I didn't see the explosion, but I heard it and can see a ring of black around the edges of his face that suggests he might have been much closer to the fireball than I realised.

I don't have time to coax him out of this state, because I need to find out if Sophie is okay. Tightening my grip on his shoulders, I push him towards the bench, as far from the hatch as possible, and sit him down.

'I need you to stay here,' I say, leaning over, my own panic rising.

He looks back at me blankly.

'Fergus,' I try again. 'Please just stay on the seat. Don't move for any reason. Is that clear? Nod if you understand.'

His head bobs slightly.

It will have to do. I hold an arm in front of my face as I march back towards the hatch. It's virtually impossible to see into the galley as the smoke is too thick. The darkness beyond is interspersed with flashes of red, yellow and orange, as flames lick at the cabin doors in the corridor. There's no sign of Sophie, and I can't hear her calling out for help, which isn't a good sign.

I cup my hands and shout her name at the top of my voice, straining to hear any sound over the crackling of flames. Smoke billows around me, and I have to step to the side to catch my breath.

I'm going to have to do something to extinguish the fire. It isn't just about getting to Sophie now, it's about preservation of life. If the fire continues to spread, there'll be nothing left of the hull to keep us afloat until help arrives.

I remove my T-shirt and fashion it into an unconventional mask around my nose and mouth, leaving only my eyes exposed. It's four layers of the cotton material, which should help filter out some of the carcinogens in the smoke, but I won't have long. Taking a deep breath over the side of the boat, I can already see orange flames dancing at the porthole into Fergus's cabin.

I move back to the hatch, and step into the black hole, using my toes to feel for the rungs of the wooden staircase, and lowering myself into the galley. I keep my eyes shut, concerned that the smoke will sting and make them fill with water. I try to remember back to school lessons when they would advise us to stay low and get out by any means. There was never any advice about getting *into* a fire-filled home to rescue someone.

I drop to my knees, and open my eyes a fraction. I can see the vinyl floor of the galley, and the sink is just to my right. Could I fill a pot with water to douse the flames? I shake my head, recalling something else about not throwing water on an electrical fire. I don't know if it was Sophie's interfering with the battery that caused the explosion or something else, but I don't want to exacerbate it.

I can't see the raised floorboard that leads down to the engine block because the smoke is just too thick. I call out Sophie's name again, but she doesn't respond. I shout to tell her that I'm going to try to get to her and that she should try to make some noise to let me know where she is.

I don't hear anything over the crackle of flames, but I can no longer see the corridor. The galley and dinette are full of smoke as it struggles to escape the enclosed space. I open the cupboard beneath the sink, looking for anything I might be able to fill with water, when my hand brushes against something cold and metallic, I grab hold of it and pull it towards my face. I could punch the air: it's a red fire extinguisher. It's only about the size of a can of hair spray so it isn't going to be able to extinguish the fire, but if it can help me get closer to the hatch, it might just be enough to find Sophie.

It's a struggle to read the instructions as the smoke surrounds me. The instructions aren't in English, which doesn't help either, but I wrestle out the plastic pin, and grip my fingers around the black plastic jaws. It's so hard to breathe, despite the mask, but I take as deep a breath as I can, and stand, squeezing the jaws as I do and waving the red can through the black smoke. The space in front of me immediately clears, but that could just be the way I'm wafting my arm.

'Soph?' I croak, but there's still no sound of her calling back to me, or trying to indicate where she is.

I continue to wave and squeeze, but there's a sudden whoosh as the liquid splashes against the door to Fergus's cabin, and the immediate space in front of me transforms from black to orange. I feel the heat of the fireball's tongues as they lick at my face. It's all I can do to dive backwards and out of their reach. It's like the fire has been fed rather than suffocated. I try to read the instructions on the extinguisher again, but the words blur in front of me.

I sniff the end of the nozzle. I'd recognise the smell of petrol anywhere.

Why would someone fill an extinguisher with petrol?

For the same reason they'd fill a Ventolin canister with rat poison.

Is this all part of the killer's plan? He couldn't have foreseen that Sophie would try to hotwire the yacht, could he? I don't have time to consider the probability as the flames bite at the smooth concave ceiling above me. I crawl through the galley, keeping my covered face pressed against the floor, until I reach the steps up to the stern. I can't breathe. I will my tired muscles to keep going; if I can't inhale fresh air, I'm going to pass out down here and then I'll be no help to Sophie or Fergus. I'm all they've got.

I'm about to lose consciousness when I feel the cold air swirling around the deck. I manage to crawl until I can see the sky, and then I cough up the inhaled smoke. I can just make out Fergus at the far side of the stern, still statuesque. At least he's one less thing for me to worry about.

I can't leave Sophie below deck. She's probably passed out from smoke inhalation, but that doesn't mean she can't be saved. Access through the galley and dinette is a no-go because of the fire, but if I can get through the window into the V-berth, there might be a chance. I pull off the makeshift facemask, and wave it around in the gale that's buffeting the boat.

I cling to the safety rope as the yacht tips from side to side in the brewing storm, scaling the port side until I reach the bow. The smoke is escaping through the sides of the small window, and when I unlock it, and raise the hardened glass, my face is ambushed by a steady stream of black air. I refasten the mask around my face, and for a moment I'm sure I can hear someone calling my name. It has to be Sophie. I do my best to fan away the smoke, before crawling headfirst through the gap, landing on the soft mattress of the narrow bed. It's almost impossible to see anything, but as I slide off the mattress onto the carpet tiles on the floor, I can just make out the raised floorboard, which Sophie must be beneath. The flames seem to be focused at the far side of the corridor where the petrol ignited; that means there's a chance.

I crawl over the carpet, ignoring the burn and graze of fibres as they scratch at my uncovered arms, chest and legs. It feels like I'm scaling a mountain, and I struggle to breathe. I don't have the lung capacity to call out Sophie's name, and as I make it to the open hatch, I'm not ready for just how dark it is. I'm staring into a void. I do my best to thrust my hands into the space, feeling around for any sign of her, willing my fingers to brush against even a strand of her hair.

'Sophie?' I croak, my lungs burning with the effort, but I can't see or hear her calling to me.

I know I need to get out of here, but I ache all over. If I could just take a moment to rest and compose myself, I'd be able to continue the search. I can no longer tell if my eyes are open or closed. I just need a short rest.

There's a sudden bump, and it feels like I'm being lifted into the air – as if a spirit has come down to drag me to the final judgement. I don't put up a fight. If it's my sentence to spend an eternity in hell, then I only have myself to blame. I float out through the window in the roof of the V-berth, and feel rain splashing against my face as I rise out of the smoke.

But then I feel something hard against my back, and someone slapping my face, until I cough and retch up the smoke that has been swelling inside my lungs. When I look back, I'm surprised to find myself on the stern deck. Fergus is still sitting on the bench, staring out to sea, oblivious to the cacophony and disaster threatening our existence. But there is another figure leaning over me. His mouse-brown curls are dripping wet and plastered to his head, but when he grins at me, I'm close to tears.

'What the hell happened?' he asks, pushing the hair back over his head, breathless himself. 'Where's Rhys? Where's Soph?'

I can't answer, pulling Harry towards me and squeezing him tighter than ever. I never thought I'd see him again.

'I tried calling to you as you headed towards the bow, but I don't think you heard me,' he says. 'I found you passed out down there. Where are the others? Why is the yacht on fire?'

I still can't answer as the lump in my throat blocks the words. There's no way Sophie can have survived the explosion and subsequent fire. My eyes sting with tears.

'Where are Rhys and Sophie?'

My lips tremble, and I shake my head.

Harry surveys the wreckage. 'We need to do something. The boat's at an odd angle, which probably means we're taking on water. Unless we can plug the leak, then we're going down.'

I look back towards the bow, and he's right that it's definitely dipping; that must be why crawling from the V-berth felt like such an uphill struggle.

'We're going to have to do whatever we can to stay afloat until help arrives,' he says, trying to stay positive, but all I can think about is the sharks waiting for their supper.

34

TEN YEARS AGO

We should call an ambulance. And the police. Regardless of what hell he put Sophie through, this man is dead, and he should be treated with the dignity we would expect others to treat us with. I know all of these things, and yet I remain firmly rooted to the spot, staring down at Raymond's lifeless corpse.

I never meant for this to happen; that must count for something. I only wanted to make him less of a threat to Sophie, but if he lost his footing after drinking the whiskey, infused with the sleeping pills I crushed and tipped in, then I'm responsible for his death.

And yet.

There's no way of knowing if the sleeping pills impaired his ability to walk, and he could have just as easily tripped on the stairs sober. I'm culpable, but shouldn't he also take some of the responsibility? Why should I spend the next twenty to thirty years in a prison cell? I did a stupid thing for a worthy reason.

A thousand thoughts are racing through my mind, and the one that keeps leaping to the front is that none of this is real. I'm having a nightmare and any moment the alarm is going to sound and I'll awaken with a great relief.

I just have to wake up.

The walls of my vision are closing in, and I know deep down that this isn't a dream, that I've flushed away my future legal career. I stagger backwards, snatch up the open bottle of wine and take a long drink from the bottle. I swallow and regain some of my composure. I've never run from a fight before, and I'm not about to start now.

'We need to phone the police,' I say, unable to keep the tremor from my voice.

'Not yet,' Sophie says, a cold edge to her voice. 'I've messaged the others and told them to get back for a house meeting. There's something you all need to know before we do anything else.'

Fergus is staring at the open door. He hasn't moved; practically catatonic. Is this his response to stress?

The front door closes, and Rhys and Harry call out to us, their voices high-pitched and full of energy. They have no idea what they're about to walk into, and I envy them. What I'd give to go back two minutes – two hours, even.

'What's all the fuss about then?' Rhys asks, bounding in, but he pulls up when he spots me with the wine bottle in my hand.

'What's happened?' Harry demands, immediately sensing the atmosphere.

'Any sign of Christophe on your travels?' Sophie asks.

'I'm here,' he calls from over my shoulder, locking the patio doors behind him. 'What's so urgent that we all had to drop everything and get back?'

Sophie doesn't answer, quietly standing, and closing the door to the basement, before pressing past Harry, and continuing to the living room. We all follow.

'I need all of you to take a seat,' she tells us. 'I'll be back in a minute.'

She vanishes without another word, and Woody and I sit as instructed, neither of us able to look at each other. The others whisper around us. Sophie returns, carrying a laptop I don't recognise, and takes her place at the head of the table. She's also brought an unopened bottle of vodka from the freezer, and places it in the centre of the table. I fetch six glasses from the cabinet in the corner and hand them out. I can't stand drinking vodka unmixed, but the wine has done little to take the edge off my anxiety.

'Raymond is dead,' Sophie says in her matter-of-fact way. 'We will need to do something about that, but before we do, there are things you all need to hear.'

I stare at my fingers as they knit together involuntarily, but I can see the disbelief on Rhys's and Christophe's faces in my peripheral vision.

'What do you mean he's dead?' Harry is the first to ask.

'He's in the basement,' Woody replies, detached.

'How? When?'

'Good riddance!' Christophe shouts, grabbing the glass bottle by the neck. He unscrews the lid, and pours himself a shot. He knocks it back in one. 'Never did like that creepy prick. Does this mean we need to start looking for new digs? I assume that's why you've called this house meeting?'

I can't believe he can be so blasé at a time like this; does the sanctity of human life mean nothing to him?

'Is he definitely dead?' Harry asks. 'Have you checked for a pulse? Do you want me to go and check?'

'He slipped on the stairs and fell,' Sophie replies, still gripping the closed laptop. 'He whacked his head on the way down. There's a lot of blood.'

'But there might still be something we can do,' Harry continues. 'No disrespect, but maybe someone with a degree of medical training should check on him. Have you called for an ambulance?'

'No, I haven't. If we call for an ambulance, they will call the police.'

'And what's wrong with that?'

'The police will want to speak to each of us and we all have motive for wanting him dead.'

'I don't,' Rhys pipes up, pouring himself a shot.

Sophie lifts the lid on the laptop and runs her finger over the trackpad until she finds what she's looking for. She then turns it around so the screen's facing us. It shows a window of a paused video, a figure in an oversized leather jacket from behind. Even without seeing his face, I instantly know we're looking at Raymond, courtesy of one of the cameras in the smoke alarms. There's a double bed, window and chest of drawers in the background.

'This is Christophe's room,' Sophie continues, starting the video clip.

Raymond can be seen approaching the tall chest of drawers, and sliding open the top drawer, dipping both hands inside, and rummaging around, as he did in my room two weeks ago. There's a part of me relieved that I'm not the only one he chose to victimise in this way.

I look away when I see him lift a framed picture of Christophe's mum, before proceeding to unfasten his belt and trousers.

Christophe's mouth drops as he watches him begin to masturbate. 'What the actual...?'

'And Fergus, remember that fish you snuck in, the one that died? Raymond told me himself that he dropped one of his rat poison pellets in the bowl,' Sophie says. 'There's probably clips of him doing all sorts in all of our rooms at one time or another, but this is all I've managed to find on his computer. These videos were recorded in the last seven days. He's been tormenting us since we moved in; it explains why the rent was so cheap.'

Fergus runs a hand through his uncontrollable red hair, his gaze focused on the tablecloth. I sense now that Sophie may already have shared this with him before I returned, and that's why he's been so frozen since. I want to tell him not to worry about it, but my head's still spinning. Sophie's right that the paramedics will phone the police, but I'm not worried about the group's motives. A post-mortem examination of the body will undoubtedly find sleeping pills in his system, and even if I get rid of the bottle, how long will it be before they figure out I'm involved?

Harry fills all of the shot glasses, and hands them out.

'There's more,' Sophie says, closing the laptop.

I start when she stares directly at me. 'Raymond was the one who set the trap that kitten got stuck in.'

I picture the red welts where the barbs had punctured the poor animal's skin, knowing that it would surely have died if I hadn't freed it.

'Raymond also snuck into your room and stole your criminology assignment,' she adds.

I don't know why, but I immediately stare at Rhys and Christophe; maybe it is guilt at assuming either of them would have wanted to cause me such stress.

'And that dead rat you discovered in your bed,' she continues, turning to look at Rhys, 'it wasn't Pete. That was Raymond too. He took pleasure in making each of our lives more difficult, and then sat back and watched us turn on each other.'

I think about how stressful the whole situation of my missing assignment was. The look of disapproval from Professor Ed; questioning my own sanity; missing out on the trip to Paris with Carly and the others. The only time the paper was left unattended would have been when I was asleep the night before it was due. With Raymond having a key to my room, he must have snuck in and taken it from my bag without me realising, and then snuck back to delete the digital copy while I was having my arse handed to me by Professor Ed.

It makes my skin crawl, thinking about all the times Raymond was probably inside my room, even while I was asleep, and just for a moment, I'm glad he's dead.

Sophie looks at Harry next. 'Those leaflets you discovered in the SU bar stating you had STIs? That was Raymond too. He was a sick individual.'

Pushing the laptop to one side, she unlocks her phone and turns so we can all see. On the screen, Sophie is wearing the pink-coloured kimono she's still in, but this footage isn't from an overhead camera. From the angle, I'd guess it's the footage from the ornamental waving cat. Sophie is pressed against the wall, and Raymond is pinning her there with his hand around her throat. The bottle of whiskey standing near the camera is virtually empty, which means at this point he would already have ingested most of the crushed-up narcotic.

She starts the footage, and we watch as he punches her in the gut with his free hand, before forcing her to the floor, and kicking her repeatedly, but I can see how unsteady he is on his feet. Sophie stops the footage just as he's about to unfasten his trousers.

She reaches for Woody's hand, and I can see now he can't bring himself to look at the screen. 'If the police see these videos, we'll all be in the frame for murder,' she says evenly. 'This gives us motive. It won't matter that we're innocent.' She looks at me; five other pairs of eyes turn on me as well.

'It's true,' I say, staring back at my fingers. 'They'll push for manslaughter at the very least.'

'Can't we stop them finding any of these clips?' Woody asks.

'I found the laptop in the basement,' Sophie explains, 'but there's only a week's worth of footage on it. It's likely he has a second storage facility somewhere, but even if we checked his flat, we'd never know for certain that we'd got it all. I don't want to sway anybody's opinion, but I thought you should all know the facts before we make an informed choice.'

It's clear that she's in favour of not reporting the crime, but we can't leave his body in the basement indefinitely.

'This is bullshit,' Christophe blurts. 'This is nothing to do with me.'

'We weren't even here when he died,' Rhys echoes. 'Those videos only prove that Raymond is... *was* a scumbag. Doesn't prove any of us had anything to do with how he died.'

I can understand their refusal to accept any responsibility for what's happened. I too have an alibi for the time of death, but that doesn't mean the police won't consider conspiracy to murder. We'll be taking a huge chance if we do phone the police, and I have more to fear than the rest of them.

Sophie stands. 'I need to get changed. Take five minutes, and we'll talk again when I'm back.'

She leaves the room, but I hurry after her.

'What aren't you telling me?' I whisper.

She feigns surprise, but I stare her down. She eventually grabs my arm and pulls me towards the kitchen, closing the door.

'After Raymond... *raped* me today, he left me in my room, saying he was going down to check on his rat traps. I stayed where I was, hoping that the cameras had caught his actions, but then I heard him yell out. I hurried down the stairs, and that's when I found Woody standing where you are now.'

'Woody was already here?'

She nods. 'Apparently, he and Fergus came back together. I asked what happened, but he couldn't speak, just pointed at the door. I saw Raymond's body, but I can't be certain if he tripped, or... if one of them pushed him.'

35

PRESENT DAY

The yacht rises and falls as the dark sea buffets us in its merciless grasp. The once tropical and inviting water now reflects the dark greys of the threatening cloud overhead. I can't remember the last time I spotted the sun's golden rays, and it's hardly surprising that my skin is pocked with goose bumps despite the wild orange flames.

Harry demands answers.

'Sophie wanted to get the engine started,' I relay. 'She sent me to the cockpit. She was down in the engine block, and I had to shout out which cables she was pulling on. There was a… bright flash… Fergus was standing near the hatch. It seemed like the engine was sputtering to life, but then… Boom. So much smoke. Fire. I tried to get to her, but…' My words trail off as I resign myself to the fact that I've lost another dear friend.

'Well, thank goodness I managed to reach you and drag us both back on deck,' Harry says, glancing over to Fergus, who's so pale and motionless, he resembles a waxwork. 'Help is on the way.'

Harry is still wearing the wetsuit he left in, and the goggles are hanging around his neck, but there's no sign of the air tank. I've untied the smoky T-shirt that was covering my face, and put it back on. Fergus is in denim shorts and a T-shirt, which is doing little to protect him from the cold wind swirling around us. None of us are dressed for the storm, but sheltering below deck is no longer viable. In fact, all of our options are rapidly diminishing.

'Do you think it's possible that Sophie is still alive?' Harry asks. 'When you were below deck, did you see where she was?'

I shake my head. 'It was so dark and smoky. I called out to her, but there was no response.'

'And do you know whether she was more likely to be at the bow or stern end of the raised floorboard? I'm just thinking we should still try and mount a rescue mission for her. If we can get the fire under control, then we might be able to get to her.'

'The fire extinguisher contained accelerant,' I warn him, unable to stop my body shivering. 'Who is doing this to us?'

I picture Raymond's bloodied face at the foot of the stairs. Could we have made a mistake about him being dead? But who else could be targeting us in this way? Who else knows what happened that night, and that we'd all be out here so isolated?

My mouth drops open as I picture the only person who meets that criteria. 'It has to be Woody.'

I scan the horizon again, looking for any sign of a boat that Woody could be on, waiting to come for the three of us, but the waves are too large to really see much of anything. Even the sliver of land from earlier is almost indistinguishable.

I've never seen Harry looking so terrified. 'No! There's no feckin' way this has anything to do with Woody! Are you off your rocker? Why would he?'

'The night we found Raymond... Soph said when she came downstairs, Fergus and Woody... They were just standing there...

looking down at the body. She said she thought maybe one of them pushed him, and...'

It's been years since I've spoken to Woody, let alone seen him. After that night, he didn't hang out at the house again. I assumed he and Sophie had called it quits; the guilt too much for both of them. I know he stayed in touch with Fergus, but they can't have been close as he didn't ask Woody to be the best man.

I can't escape the feeling we're being watched. It's been with me since we boarded.

The yacht rises into the air as it catches on the wash of an enormous wave, and then we're falling just as quickly back to the water. It's clear that the bow is now dipping beneath the waves, and Harry is right: unless we take action, it won't be long until the hull is submerged. It's not a question of if, but *when* the yacht will sink.

We have to act now.

'We should use sea water to try and douse the flames,' I shout over the din of the storm. 'How long until help is on its way?'

'Soon,' says Harry. 'I swam for what felt like hours, and stopped when I made it to a buoy. There was an emergency radio locked inside it, and I contacted the lifeguard on shore. They were able to locate my coordinates, and told me to wait there. But I told them you were all in danger, and that they had to come and rescue us.' He looks down. 'There wasn't enough air in the tank to make it back here, so I ditched it. It was slowing my ability to swim. I was so relieved when I saw the yacht bobbing on the horizon. We're now closer to shore than when I left.

'I heard the explosion, and saw the rising smoke. If only I could have made it back sooner, I could have warned Sophie to stay clear of the engine. I knew it was risky playing around with something none of us understood.'

His *I told you so* speech isn't helpful, given our current predicament.

'Did they say how long they'll be? Do we have an ETA?' Fergus shouts to us, his shock finally starting to dissipate.

'They said it could take up to an hour,' Harry says, 'so the way I see it, we need to find some way to keep us afloat. The buoy I got to is maybe half a mile from here, but I'm estimating.' He looks at Fergus, who's made no secret of his inability to swim any great distance. 'We need to get below deck and see what we can fix or salvage. Are you going to be okay to go back down? Have you got your breath back?'

My breathing is still haggard, but I'm not about to wave a white flag, knowing that the three of us will be stronger when pulling together. The waves are rising so high that it will be almost impossible to see another boat approaching. If Woody has been idly waiting, now would be the perfect time for him to come for us.

'What about the shark cage?' Fergus sputters.

We both turn to look at him.

'It's heavy, right?' he clarifies. 'Maybe that's what's dragging us under. If we could disconnect it, it might buy us some additional buoyancy.'

Harry and I exchange looks. It's a valid point, but I'm not sure either of us is ready to let go of Rhys and Christophe – and Elena – so mercilessly. We've no idea how deep the seabed is, and whether someone will be able to recover the bodies if we cut them adrift.

'Fergus is right,' Harry says with a firm nod. 'Any idea how to disconnect the cage? I think I left my cable cutters in my other wetsuit.'

He looks straight at me, and his lips tremble, as he tries to hold back the chuckle, but I can't contain my snort of laughter. It says a lot for the human spirit that even in the greatest adversity, we're still able to find humour.

Fergus doesn't share in the moment, standing and moving past us. He climbs up to the cockpit and yanks on the handle that both Elena and Sophie used to raise the cage. Unsurprisingly, this time there is no whirring or shift of the cable. I can only assume that the explosion and fire have knocked out the yacht's electrical circuitry. I am surprised that Fergus knew exactly which handle to pull on, as I didn't think he'd been watching when Sophie used it.

'If there's no electric current any more, we can use water to put out the fire,' I say to Harry.

I scan the deck, looking for anything large enough we can fill, but all I locate is a glass jug we used for cocktails on the first night. It holds barely a litre of liquid, but it doesn't stop me leaning over the side of the boat and filling it to the brim. I move towards the hatch down to the galley, and throw the seawater towards the orange flames that have engulfed Rhys's cabin, across the hallway from Fergus's now-charred wall and bed.

The flame shrinks and sizzles, before returning with a vengeance. It's progress, though. If we can get enough water, we might be able to stop the fire, and if we can do that, we can get to Sophie. I call out her name again, and tell her we're coming. Harry takes the jug from me, and refills it at the starboard side, before offering it back to me. This time, I'm braver and climb down into the galley. It's more dangerous down here, but I can better target my attacks.

I pull the neck of my T-shirt over my mouth and nose, and stay on the starboard side of the galley and dinette. I'm able to climb through the hole in what was once the wall of Fergus's cabin. Surprisingly, the fire has yet to spread to Harry's cabin, so I step out into the corridor, almost falling through the hole where the floorboard is raised.

It's still so dark, with no light able to penetrate the thick smoke. I drop to my knees, setting the jug to one side, and peer into the hole, searching for Sophie. And as a wave lifts the whole yacht, there's a moment where I see a flash of red hair, and realise that Sophie is directly beneath the floor I'm lying across. Stretching out my arm, and tucking it beneath the floor, my fingertips brush hair. I shuffle closer to the edge and tuck my toes into what remains of the doorway of Fergus's cabin, and push my other arm through the darkness until I can touch both of Sophie's shoulders. I shake her, trying to call out, but my voice is barely a whisper.

She doesn't move, but I know I won't get a second chance at this, so I push myself further into the hole, tuck my fingers into the skin beneath her arms, and yank her up with all my might. Her foot must catch on something, because I can only just get her head above the edge of the floorboards. I lower her slightly and try again, but she's stuck firm.

'I need you to try and wriggle, Soph,' I splutter, but then the boat rises again and there's a flash of light that falls across her face, and I see the blood-red scarring across her right cheek. Her eyes are wide, and pupils dilated.

I realise she's been dead for some time.

It's a sucker punch, but I don't have time to think about it, as I notice the sound of gushing from below us. I release my grip on Sophie's arms and she drops into the void of darkness.

As the boat rises on another venomous wave, the flash of light shows exactly where the water is rushing in through the bulkhead. It looks as though a bomb has gone off, and even with the greatest will, there's no way we can block it and stop the inevitable submergence.

Regardless of Fergus's fear, we cannot stay aboard the yacht. It is beyond salvage. I tip the jug over the nearest orange tongues, but there's no point wasting any more time in trying to extinguish the fire. I keep as low as I can and make my way back through the hole in the cabin wall, finding a panicked Harry now in the galley, searching for me.

I point towards the hatch to the deck, and he helps me climb up. I rush to the stern, and pull down my shirt, willing fresh air to enter my lungs.

'S-Sophie's dead,' I stammer to Harry and Fergus. 'I s-saw her down there, and...' I can't finish and shake my head instead.

I can no longer see the tip of the bow above the raging water. It's like a giant whale swallowing us whole.

'We're going to have to get to that buoy,' I say. 'Can you remember the way?'

Harry opens his mouth to answer, but stops as something over my shoulder catches his eyes. I turn, and my mouth drops open when I see the glint of the chef's knife in Fergus's hand.

'You're not going anywhere.'

36

TEN YEARS AGO

Sophie looks calm and collected when she returns to the lounge-diner, whereas I feel anything but. The wind howls beyond the bay window, the curtains shut to block out the dark night sky. Branches of the tree in the front garden scratch at the window. Carly jokingly refers to us as a coven, but it doesn't feel like a joke right now.

Between them, Rhys and Christophe have polished off the bottle of vodka, while Harry and I have been discussing the ramifications of our options. Fergus and Woody have just sat there without a word, staring at one another. I can't help thinking about what Sophie said before she went upstairs to change: *I can't be certain if he tripped, or... if one of them pushed him.*

It seems too ridiculous to consider. Fergus is the last of us with a motive to want Raymond dead. I saw how much he respected and wanted to impress his coach. Although Sophie hasn't broadcasted the abuse she's received from Raymond, she's not been great at covering up either, so could he have just snapped? Did he see Raymond tottering and give him a helping hand?

Or did Woody work out what their coach had been doing, and

pushed him in an effort to protect Sophie? I don't want to think the worst of Fergus or Woody, and I hate myself even more being relieved at how that would put me in the clear. Regardless of the drugs in his system, it would mean I'm not responsible for what happened, and for my own sanity, I have to cling on to that possibility.

Sophie has changed into navy blue tracksuit bottoms and a thick graphite-coloured hoodie. With her red pixie haircut, she could pass for a boy in the darkness. Is that her intention? She reaches for the empty bottle, a disappointed scowl on her face. A hush falls over the room.

'Fellas, we have a decision to make,' she says, retaking her seat at the head of the table. 'Given our predicament, we need to take action. As far as I see it, we can either phone the police and report what's happened and take our chances, or...' She pauses, allowing our imaginations to fill in the blanks.

'None of us have done anything wrong,' Harry interjects. 'I vote we phone the police.'

He fires me a hard stare, willing me to concur. If he knew what the police would find in Raymond's blood tests, he wouldn't be asking.

'Let's go around the room,' Sophie replies, looking at the rest of us in turn. 'I vote we don't phone the police. Woody?'

It's an interesting ploy to ask Woody next, even though he's furthest away. I sense Sophie is trying to determine whether he was involved in Raymond's untimely fall. If Woody votes to report the crime, would that suggest he's innocent? Or just that his conscience is getting the better of him, and *that's* the reason he wants it reported. It's so hard to conclude.

'If we don't phone the police, what the hell are we going to do with the body?' Christophe bowls out, and Rhys eagerly nods, as if the same thought was also at the forefront of his mind.

Sophie shrugs. 'We get rid of it... somehow.'

This really is the key question we haven't considered. It's one thing to talk about hiding a body, but quite another to go through with it. I've read enough serial killer trial transcripts to know that it's almost impossible to do without leaving a trace. And none of us have the kind of connections where we could just phone someone to take care of it for us. Maybe if we had a bath of high-strength sulfuric acid; but it would take hours for the muscle and cartilage to dissolve, and a good couple of days for the bones to corrode. And then what would we do with the acid? And that's not knowing whether our bathtub wouldn't react to the acid itself. That scene from *Breaking Bad* where the bathtub dissolves flashes through my mind.

I know I'm not capable of sawing Raymond into smaller, manageable chunks. I hate the sight of blood at the best of times, and I can't imagine any of the others volunteering for such a gruesome act either.

'But how, though?' Christophe challenges.

'We can discuss that when the group has reached a consensus. Fergus?'

All eyes turn to the quietest one in the group. He's no longer concentrating on that spot on the tablecloth, but is instead looking down at his hands. 'We bury him.'

I'm shocked at his answer, but I don't know whether we should read anything into it or not.

'That's two votes for not reporting the accident. Rhys? Christophe? Pete?'

'I vote bury,' I say quickly, in an effort to subtly sway Rhys's and Christophe's choices.

Harry fires me a surprised and concerned look.

'Think about everything he's done to us,' I say, compelled to justify my decision. 'He was a twisted bastard who got what was coming to him. For me, it's a no-brainer.'

I slowly let out my breath, hoping none of them think too hard about why I'm trying to sway them.

'Screw it,' Rhys says loudly, tipping his head back to drain the contents of the nearly empty shot glass. 'I'm not being funny, but he was a dick and deserves to rot in the ground.'

Wow, are we really going to do this? Where are we going to find a Raymond-sized hole at this time of night, and how are we going to move him into it without anybody seeing?

'Christophe?' Sophie asks next.

'Oui, fuck it, I'm in. He belittled half of the lacrosse squad and for what? Let's bury the prick.'

'Woody?'

His face is so pale, but he nods.

Sophie turns back to face Harry. 'This only works if we're *all* in. You're the only one who voted against hiding the body. I need to know – *we* need to know – if we go through with this, are you going to report us?'

I've never seen Harry look so uncertain about anything.

'This is madness,' he says eventually with a sigh. 'We won't get away with it. Someone's bound to notice he's missing, and if the police come investigating, we'll still be the main suspects. At the moment, we've done nothing wrong, but if we don't report what's happened, and cover it up, we'll have all broken the law.' He pauses. 'That said, if this is what we have decided to do, then so be it, may the roof above us never fall in. I would love to know where you think we can hide him.'

Something close to satisfaction glosses over Sophie's face, and she's about to respond, when the room suddenly plunges into darkness. I scrabble in my pocket for my phone, and flick on the screen, but it does little to lighten the room. Rhys sparks his cigarette lighter. The television on the wall is no longer displaying the red LED standby light. I pull back the curtain, and see that none of the houses in the street have any lights on, and the streetlights outside the neighbours' properties are also off.

'Looks like the storm has knocked out the power,' I report back, turning to see the others have all switched on the lights on their phones too. We really do resemble a coven.

'It seems like someone up there wants to help us,' Sophie declares, the light from her phone casting a devilish shine in her eyes. 'First things first: we need to get Raymond's body out of the basement and up to this level. It's not going to be easy, as he's a dead weight. There are sheets in the basement, and if we can roll him into one, it should be easier to carry him. Once he's up, we carry him through the garden, out of the gate and into the woods. They stretch for a good square mile, so if we walk far enough, we should have a few hours without being disturbed. There are two shovels in the shed in the garden, so we'll work in pairs until we are wide and deep enough. Then we roll him in, and fill the hole.'

I can't get over how calm and collected she is being, nor how quickly she has formulated this plan. She makes it sound so easy, yet I already know it will be anything but. We'll need a hole that's at least six feet long, three feet wide, and six feet deep. It will take hours, and the chance of us managing to do it without being seen feels impossible. She stands and ushers us to follow.

'What if we just build a giant bonfire in the garden?' Rhys blurts out. 'Burning him would be easier than digging a flaming hole.'

I don't know who's most shocked when Woody lashes out and slaps Rhys hard across the cheek.

'Enough. The decision has been made.'

Rhys glowers as he rubs at his cheek, and is about to take a step forwards when Fergus shakes his head.

Not another word is spoken as we all head into the darkness of the basement, as if we're descending into Dante's Inferno. Raymond lies at the bottom, lifeless, and I'm actually grateful that the power is off; I don't think I could bear to see his face, knowing the part I played in his downfall.

Sophie fetches the shovels and sheets, and directs us to roll Raymond onto his side. We roll him onto the sheet and prepare to lift him up, Rhys, Harry, Woody and I each taking a corner, with Fergus and Christophe holding the sides. Sophie buries the shovels beneath the top sheet, lights a candle and leads the way. We lift on the count of three, but immediately have to lower him back to the floor. We've all underestimated how difficult this is going to be, but Sophie isn't ready to give up just yet, and neither am I.

We heave him up once more, and this time manage to get him all the way to the patio doors at the rear of the kitchen before lowering him for a breather. We've no idea how long the power cut will last, and the sooner we can get him into the forest, the better.

I've never felt more terrified in my entire life.

37

PRESENT DAY

The lines around Fergus's eyes are so tight, and the skin so pale. With his shock of red hair, he looks more like an extra from *One Flew Over the Cuckoo's Nest*. When did he get hold of the chef's knife, and where has he been hiding it all this time? More importantly, why?

'Was that your plan all along?' he says, pointing the knife perilously close to my face.

He's barely four feet from where Harry and I are standing beside the port-side gunnel. He's on top of the board above the hot tub, his feet planted. How did I not see this coming?

I take a tentative step backwards, but my calf muscles catch the plastic gunnel. Harry hovers just beyond my arm. Behind us: the endless sea, with hungry sharks just waiting for us to chance our luck.

'I wouldn't get too close if I were you,' Fergus warns Harry. 'Pete has a plan for each of us. Decapitating Christophe; poisoning Rhys; electrocuting Sophie. You want us to swim now, so presumably, you're expecting me to drown?'

'No, I never—' I begin to say, but he cuts me off with a slash of the knife through the air.

'You made me feel so guilty about cutting you yesterday, but maybe that was always part of your plan. You needed to be cut so you couldn't be the one to swim off to find us help. I bet you thought Harry would get attacked by a shark, right? Now that help is on the way, your plan to kill us all is scuppered.'

'I'm not a killer,' I say, but immediately regret it, as Fergus takes a big step towards us, the knife extended.

'Convenient how you had to be the one who went up to the cockpit while Sophie went to tug on the cables. There was nobody up there to check you were giving the correct information. I was just a pawn in your sick game, relaying the key to her demise.'

He's trying to convince Harry not to trust me; I see it now. I can't let this continue, as I can already feel Harry trying to peel himself away. Ordinarily I'd have felt certain Harry would have my back in an argument between Fergus and me, but now I can't be sure where his loyalties lie. After all, Fergus did make him his best man.

'I gave you the correct information about the wires,' I say defiantly, 'but you could easily have changed what I told you when you recited it back to Sophie.'

He moves forwards another step, the tip of the knife just beneath my chin as I strain my head back as far as I can to avoid contact. Stupidly, this move leaves my neck exposed.

'You know, you almost had the others convinced that Raymond was back from the dead,' Fergus says. 'The message scratched into the hull was a clever move, and the rat poison in Rhys's inhaler was inspired, but why would you want us to remember that night? Is that what all this has been about? You really will go that far to keep the past buried.'

He's delirious, and I have no doubt he will lash out if I can't calm him down or overpower him. But if I lunge at Fergus now, I'll play into his hands, and Harry will see me as the villain Fergus is painting me as.

I think back to that night, how Sophie raised the possibility of Woody or Fergus pushing Raymond down the stairs. I hadn't wanted to believe it of Fergus, and we never talked about it after; we all made a pact not to mention that night again. Is it possible the guilt has been slowly growing over time and is now manifesting itself? Perhaps, the only way Fergus has been able to deal with the guilt is by blaming the rest of us for causing it. Could he have been working on this with Woody all along?

The balance of the yacht has definitely shifted, and it's taking more effort not to lean with it. With more water gushing in through the blast hole, we have probably minutes before water covers the deck, and we'll have no choice but to be in the water.

'You were right to be worried about him,' Fergus says next, nodding at Harry.

'Put the knife down,' Harry says. 'There's no need for anybody else to get hurt.'

'No way. That's what *he* wants. I know you two were close, but Pete's not the guy he was at university. I see that now. I lower the knife and he grabs it to do us both in. I'm not falling for his games any more.' He looks directly at me, and my blood runs cold. 'You always pretended to be my friend in that house, but I know you were no better than the others; laughing behind my back. Two-faced, just like my uncle.'

Fergus has never really told me much about his upbringing. After his dad died, he was adopted by his uncle, but then they had a falling-out. Thinking about it now, and in light of what I'm witnessing here, I suppose all that pent-up frustration could explain why he pushed Raymond down the stairs. All it would have taken was a comment from him; after all Sophie revealed, we know he enjoyed winding us up. Did Fergus snap? I should have spent more time trying to get to the bottom of what really happened that night, but once we'd buried Raymond, we all moved on with our lives. We were all about to graduate. There wasn't time to dwell on the past and worry about what we'd done.

Like the others, I think I almost managed to convince myself of the lie we spun: that Raymond had just upped and left our lives.

I feel Harry move further away from me, and then he takes a sideways step. It catches Fergus's eye, and he swishes the blade in his direction.

Harry throws both arms into the air, as if he's about to be mugged. 'Whoa, easy, Fergus. I was just trying to get away from this psychopathic maniac. You're right: we were wrong to trust him.'

Even though I hope he's just trying to win Fergus over, the words cut deep. Whatever Harry's motives for saying it, Fergus allows him to continue to sidestep away from me.

'We need to find something to tie him up with,' Fergus mutters under his breath.

'There isn't anything,' Harry says, slipping the wetsuit from his shoulders, and delicately peeling it from his skin. 'I don't think we need to worry about tying him up anyway. The rescue boat should be here soon, and the authorities will be able to deal with him then. Thank Christ you realised what was going on when you did.'

If Harry's just waiting to play his hand, I hope he gets on with it soon, because a puddle of cold seawater is now covering my feet, and I can see the galley is now flooded.

'When will they get here?' Fergus snaps, eyes focused on me in case I make any sudden movements.

My head is still tilted backwards, and any attempt to move

forwards will see the tip of the blade penetrate my neck. I'm not going anywhere without help.

'The buoy isn't too far away,' Harry says, the wetsuit now in a pile at his feet. His T-shirt and shorts are soaked through. 'I know you said you can't swim well, but we can't stay on the boat. It's sinking, Fergus, and it's going to take the three of us down with it. Let me help you get to the buoy and we'll wait for help to arrive from there.'

Fergus's arm wavers, but not enough for me to make a move to wrestle the knife from him. All it'll take is for a sudden wave to jerk the boat and I'll be a goner.

Fergus looks nervously at Harry, who quickly lashes out a balled fist and strikes him across the face. I don't know which of us is most shocked, but his knife arm drops, and I'm able to straighten. Fergus falls to his knees with a splash, moaning in pain, and Harry grimaces, shaking his hand against the sting of contact.

I don't think twice before driving my knee into the side of Fergus's ribs, toppling him further into the gathering pool of seawater. The chef's knife drops to the deck, and clatters off in the direction of the galley hatch.

'You need to put this on,' Harry urges, kicking the wetsuit towards me. 'I didn't see any shark fins when I was swimming earlier, but that doesn't mean there aren't any out there. You need the wound on your arm covered just in case.'

I don't argue, pushing my feet into the leg holes and pulling the slippery wet material up my legs. It feels like I'm pulling on a snake's shed skin, but the last thing I want to do is make the swim more complicated.

Fergus is still groaning on the deck, but he's made his own bed, and he can lie in it. Did he think twice before killing Elena,

Christophe, Rhys and Sophie? I can only assume Joaquín met a similarly grizzly end. My sister has had a lucky escape.

'We need to go,' Harry says, pulling his legs over the side of the gunnel.

I copy the move, not expecting the seawater to come up to the bottom of my knees. I picture Jack and Rose from *Titanic*, when they were facing this same prospect, and never really appreciated just how terrifying it is. For all I know, there's a shark and its family just waiting for us to push off.

'How far is the buoy?' I ask, unable to see any sort of light on the horizon.

'It's probably a good twenty- to thirty-minute swim. Are you up to it?'

I look back over my shoulder at Fergus, who seems to be scurrying along the deck in search of the knife again. I lift my hand into the air, and Harry grabs hold of it, giving it a gentle squeeze, and then before Fergus can get to us again, the two of us push off.

38

TEN YEARS AGO

The garden is pitch black. It would be so much better if Sophie hadn't extinguished the candle, but to use it would draw attention to the large Raymond-sized parcel we're carrying. All it would take is for one of our neighbours to happen to look out of a rear window and spot us for all of this to be over. At least the cover of darkness will prevent that happening. Usually, the fence end of the garden is lit up by a streetlamp, but with power to the city temporarily gone, we are safe.

For now.

We lower Raymond as Sophie fumbles to put her key in the gate's padlock, and I'm again reminded of the barbed noose I rescued a cat from near this spot. I can picture Raymond setting up the trap, and watching mercilessly as the barbs scratched at the poor kitten's neck. His death is a blessing on those of us he terrorised, so why am I still feeling so guilty about my part in it?

Nobody speaks as Sophie opens the gate and peers out into the darkness. She holds out a hand, which we can barely see, and when she judges that there's nobody on the footpath, she urges us to continue. We each grab a handful of sheet and prepare to move again. We're about to proceed when the sound of laughter nearby stops us all, frozen with terror. A couple is approaching.

Sophie pulls the gate closed behind her, leaving us hidden in the garden, and a moment later I hear her lighting a cigarette and blowing a plume of smoke into the air. The young couple say hello, but continue on their way, the sound of their voices soon drifting to nothing.

Sophie pops back to our side of the gate and offers the cigarette to Fergus, who snatches it up, and takes a long drag, before stamping it out underfoot.

We grab fabric again, and lift, squeezing out. We've all allowed Sophie to take control, and when she points two fingers towards the gap in the trees several feet further along the pathway, none of us dare to argue. If a random dog walker appears now, we'll have nowhere to run or any way to explain why we're carrying a corpse through the forest.

The branches scratch and claw at me as I follow the others through the gap, the ground so uneven beneath my feet that I feel certain I'm going to trip or fall at any moment. Somehow, I manage to stay upright, and am grateful I'm not at the front of the group. We bend to the right, away from the main road, where the sight of yellow headlights and red tail-lights resemble Christmas decorations through the trees.

Overhead, the moon and stars are covered by thick cloud, though the gale that was blowing earlier has died down considerably. I can't see how we're going to get away with this. Even if we manage to dig a hole deep enough, Raymond has colleagues who are going to wonder where he's gone. At some point, somebody is going to come looking for him, and we'll still be the most obvious suspects. Surely all this effort and energy we're expending is just delaying the inevitable.

We walk for what feels like miles, each of us constantly

looking over our shoulders and listening for the snap of twigs and rustle of undergrowth, until Sophie holds up her hand and forces us to stop.

'Here will do,' she whispers, her breath puffing out in a cloud. 'We'll dig in pairs in twenty-minute stints, while the others keep a lookout. When twenty minutes has passed, the next pair will swap. I don't mind going first. Fergus and Woody can stay with me, and then Harry can go with Pete, and Rhys can go with Christophe. That's the order we'll stick with.' She reaches for one of the shovels from under the top sheet, and hands it to Fergus, grabbing the second for herself. 'Go, now. It's 8.40 p.m. Pete and Harry, take over at nine. And if any of you see anything, text the rest.'

We spread out as pairs, but neither Harry nor I talk as we head back towards the footpath. It feels like if we don't talk about it, then it can't really be happening, and this whole evening will simply disappear into the black hole of lost memory like most dreams. I want to tell Harry about the sleeping pills, and about Fergus's and Woody's potential involvement, but I remain silent.

Twenty minutes passes in no time, and we make our way back, noticing how Woody has propped his phone against a branch, to cast a low light over the hole. Fergus has mud streaked over his jeans and face, and looks exhausted as he puffs for air. They've made better progress than I was anticipating, but seeing how muddy their trainers are, I'm now regretting not dressing more appropriately for tonight's misadventure.

'Christophe and Rhys should relieve you in twenty minutes,' Sophie says, as she lights a fresh cigarette. 'I'll keep watch for you.'

I pick up one of the shovels, and drop into the shallow hole. I'm not made for this kind of manual labour, and the time drags as we cut through the hard mud, chucking the debris over our shoulders. I'm exhausted by the time Christophe and Rhys show up, but we've managed to clear another few inches of earth.

The stints continue in this way, but on our third shift, the inevitable happens and we see that power has returned across the city. We're far enough into the forest that our activity is still hidden, but I can see streetlights in the distance near the footpath.

'Go get the others,' Harry urges. 'We need to get Raymond in the hole ASAP.'

The ground is up to our shoulders, so nowhere near the six-foot depth Sophie had targeted.

'It's not deep enough,' I warn.

'It's too dangerous to keep going.' Harry throws his shovel out of the hole and cups his hands to give me a leg-up.

Once up, I help Harry out, his trainers skidding on the muddy wall of Raymond's grave. I'm grateful I don't have to wait alone with the body.

When he returns, Fergus looks as though he's been crying, and when I look to Woody for an explanation, he just shakes his head. We gather around the body and lift as one, dropping him and the sheets into the hole.

'Should we say any words?' I ask, but nobody meets my gaze.

I'm not particularly religious, but it feels wrong to bury him without saying something. I look to Sophie, as she knew him the best, but she shakes her head again.

As we're moving away, leaving Christophe and Rhys to start filling in the hole, Sophie tells us she has some loose ends to tidy at Raymond's flat, heading off without another word.

* * *

It's after midnight by the time the six of us make it back. There's no sign of Sophie, but we strip off our clothes in the kitchen and throw them all in the washing machine. It would probably be better to burn them, but a garden fire would definitely be noticed by the neighbours.

Sophie returns ten minutes later, carrying a fresh bottle of vodka, which she unscrews and puts to her lips, before passing it to Fergus and urging him to drink. He takes a swig before lighting the joint he's just rolled. He passes the bottle to Woody.

'We need to make a pact,' Sophie tells us, still in her navy tracksuit bottoms which are caked in a layer of dried mud. 'We are never to talk about this night ever again. Not with anybody. Not even each other. As far as anybody is concerned, we haven't heard from Raymond since before Christmas. That's the only way this works. I used his keys to get into his flat, and have sent an email to the head of the faculty, declaring that he is retiring and has gone travelling. He's been known to drop things on a whim before, so this behaviour won't seem out of character.'

'What about the blood in the cellar?' Christophe asks, not willing to naively rely on someone telling him to bury his head in the sand.

Sophie is about to speak when Woody moves forwards and grabs Christophe by the scruff of the neck. 'Your anxiety attacks aren't going to be a problem, are they? Because if the weakest amongst us breaks, then we all suffer.'

I move forwards, and force myself between them. 'We all know the rules, and having anxiety doesn't make Christophe any mentally weaker than the rest of us.'

'No? Are you saying we should be more worried about the lawyer breaking instead?'

I sense he's trying to rile me, and it's a relief when Sophie pulls him back.

'We'll clean up the blood and lock the door. In the email I sent, it said he was planning to go off the grid, so we're in the clear.'

This doesn't sit comfortably with me. I've read enough true crime novels to know that no case ever truly goes cold. I can't spend the rest of my life looking over my shoulder.

'And once a few months have passed,' Sophie continues, reaching for the bottle of vodka from Christophe, 'I will use his credit card, exploiting a VPN; this really will be the last place anyone will come looking.'

She reaches for the bottle of vodka and takes a long drink, fixing us with a hard stare. 'We are all tied to this now. If one talks, we *all* go down for it. We've chosen to break the law, and I can live with that, because I know that bastard won't be able to harm anyone else. He made us suffer, and he got what he deserved.'

39

PRESENT DAY

The waves crash against us as Harry and I swim, trying to keep our strokes even. We've only been in the water for ten minutes or so, and I'm already regretting the decision to brave the treacherous waves. I'm trying not to think about the prospect of sharks hunting in the depths beneath us, but the more I try to ignore the thought, the harder it drills into my mind.

I'm grateful for the slight protection of the wetsuit, though every time I move my left arm, I can feel the stitches pulling. I'm never going to make it to the buoy, let alone the thin sliver of coastline beyond it. Even though we must be closer to land than earlier in the day, the line on the horizon looks even smaller. I can't overlook the possibility that this could be the end for me. If I can't keep my head above water until the rescue boat comes for us, then I'm going to drown, or be eaten, or both.

It troubles me that there's still been no sign of a rescue boat. It has to have been at least an hour since Harry contacted them, but there's nothing on the horizon. The saltwater is bitter on my lips, and stings my throat, but if I stop, I'll lose all momentum.

'Come on,' I hear Harry say, as he pushes himself beneath my injured arm. 'We'll do this together. I'm not leaving my brother behind.'

I want to argue that I'll only slow him down, and increase the chance of both of us not making it, but my survival instinct cuts in. I'm grateful for the support. The storm rages overhead, the clouds a dark gunmetal grey, with the occasional flash of lightning from behind. This is precisely when the raindrops start splashing down around us, like tiny bullets, because clearly there weren't already enough obstacles between us and safety.

'It's not much further,' Harry promises, but I'm already breathless, and my face keeps slipping beneath the water line as exhaustion kicks in.

'I'm not going to make it,' I try to say as my teeth chatter. 'You should leave me, and get to safety.'

He shakes his head, pulling my other arm around his shoulders. 'Just hang on.'

I can't have him take my weight like this, but I'm grateful for the chance to briefly rest as he continues to cut through the water with considerable ease. Yesterday, when he argued that he is the better swimmer, I clearly didn't give him enough credit. It's hard to believe that this is the second time he's made this journey today.

I think about Carly, and how beautiful she is and how I will propose the moment I see her – if I ever make it back. I also imagine the moment I'll have to tell Simone what Fergus did and how we had no choice but to leave him behind. She may never forgive me, but at least she won't be at his mercy any longer.

They're not expecting us back until tomorrow afternoon, and it's only now I think about the fact my passport was in my cabin when the boat started sinking. It's going to be a nightmare getting hold of a replacement, but that'll be the least of our problems. How do we begin to explain the deaths of our friends, and the person responsible?

I never should have underestimated Fergus or his resourcefulness. How none of us caught him forcing Elena into that shark cage, or helping Christophe escape before knocking him into the water, is beyond me. And how the hell did he manage to get rat poison into Rhys's inhaler?

I don't like the dark thoughts peppering my mind. We never got to ask Fergus why this murderous streak took control. I've always suspected that he might have pushed Raymond, but that was more to alleviate my own guilty feelings about the sleeping pills. And it's one thing to push someone down the stairs, but quite another to plan murder in cold blood. Could Woody be somehow involved in all of this? If he's out there somewhere too, then maybe Fergus is still a threat despite our efforts to escape.

My thoughts are crashing as frequently as the waves around us, and I'm so exhausted and confused that I can't keep a strand before another thought barges through.

And what about Simone? Fergus was so desperate to get back in touch with her, so why would he ditch the anchor and leave us adrift? And as he couldn't swim well, why would he detach the dinghy and outboard – his only means of survival? Was he just acting? Is Simone in on it? Was he lying about his swimming abilities?

Why would Fergus and Woody want us dead after all these years? And if Woody has indeed been out here all this time, how could he be so close yet remain out of sight?

Something doesn't add up.

Fergus threatened us with the knife because he didn't want us to leave the boat, but was that because he wanted us dead, or because he was just shit-scared of being left alone to drown?

But if Fergus isn't the killer, and I'm not, then that only leaves...

I can't finish the thought, but my mind is suddenly much more alert.

Surely I'm just being paranoid. Harry wasn't on board the yacht when Sophie died, or when Rhys started coughing up blood on the deck. He couldn't have been responsible for them dying. Right? And why would he want any of us dead? He's a nurse, not a killer.

'We're nearly there,' I hear him gasp, and I raise my eyes to see a flashing light bobbing in and out of view ahead of us.

It is scant relief as the sliver of coastline is no bigger than when I last looked, and there's still no sign of a rescue boat on its way to our position. My tired and emotionally drained brain can't cope with the contradictory thoughts and accusations flooding through it.

We reach the buoy, and Harry checks I'm okay, before sliding me from his shoulders, and ensuring my arms are secure on top of the large round rim of the red platform. It's made of a hardened plastic, rather than metal as I was expecting. I now rise and fall as it does, as if we've become materially joined. Harry asks me to hold it steady, while he swims around to the other side, and manages to lift himself onto it, resting his back against the tall frame that leads up to the red flashing light at the top of the five-foot structure. He rests for a moment, gathering his breath before helping me clamber up and out of the water, though our feet remain submerged. I tighten my grip on the frame so I won't fall off, but now that we're out of the sea, I can feel how cold the wind is. We won't drown on here, but if the rescue boat doesn't show up soon, hypothermia could get us.

'Do you think we should... radio the coastguard again?' I suggest, my teeth chattering away.

'There is no radio. I didn't contact the coastguard.'

He says it so calmly that I'm convinced I must have water in my ears and misheard. 'What?'

'I lied about the coastguard.'

I blink several times, as his image blurs in and out of focus. 'Who did you contact then?'

'Nobody. There's no rescue boat coming.'

I can't see his face because he has his back to me. Now is not the time to be cracking jokes.

I try to rub at my arms, but my fingers are so numb. 'This isn't funny, Harry. We're gonna freeze to death out here.'

He looks back at me over his shoulder. His face is so relaxed and he's smiling at me warmly. 'Oh, don't worry about that. I won't let anything bad happen to you. You're my brother.'

His voice is so encouraging, so why don't I feel relaxed?

'Listen, help *will* come, but only when I'm ready for them. Okay? You have nothing to worry about.'

Am I falling into delirium?

It takes all my effort to open my mouth and voice my concern. 'Promise me this wasn't you, Harry.'

'What? You really thought Fergus had the courage to tackle our problem head-on?'

'Problem? What problem?'

He turns slightly more, and pats my shoulder gently. 'Loose ends need tying or someone will trip.' He suddenly bends forwards and reaches down beneath the waterline, pulling out a zip-lock bag containing a flare. 'I stashed this here earlier. When it's time, I'll let it off and help will come.'

Sophie couldn't find flares on the yacht, so does that mean Harry took them? What else did he dispose of while we were on board?

I'm not entirely sure where he unclipped the bag from, but there is a chained anchor that is keeping the buoy afloat and in place, so I can only assume he tied it to that somehow. I wonder whether he's tied anything else down there. Am I safe?

I need to focus on getting to dry land. Whether this is Harry's twisted idea of a joke, or something else, the priority has to be to get out of the water.

'You need to set the flare off now. I don't want to die out here.'

He turns around fully to face me. 'You have the wetsuit. That ought to keep you warm enough while we wait. You'll be fine. The last thing I want is for you to die out here. You must realise that by now?'

His warm eyes stare back at me as they always do, but the hairs on the back of my neck stand on end.

My jaw locks as I try to speak and the words eventually spill from my lips. 'Send up the flare. I'm really c-cold. Please, Harry?'

'I will, but there's something we need to talk about first.'

'We can talk on the b-boat.'

'No, it must be now, because I don't want other people to overhear us.'

This must be some elaborate prank. There will be a radio somewhere, and there will be a rescue boat on its way. He's just winding me up. It's just his twisted sense of humour. But as my eyes scan the frame and structure of the buoy, there really isn't any obvious space for a radio, transmitter or antenna.

'There's something I haven't told you. The police found Raymond's remains.' There's no remorse in his tone. 'Well, what I mean is they've found remains, but they've yet to identify who they belong to. As far as anyone knows, Raymond isn't a missing person, so they may never be able to connect him to it, but I couldn't take that risk.'

I picture the grave we dug. The night of the power cut when we as a group chose to cover up Raymond's death. I've tried not to think about it, but being around the others has brought it all crashing back.

'How do you... How can you know what the police—'

'Woody told me. He still lives in Southampton, and apparently the story made the local news. He immediately recognised the pathway and phoned Fergus, who told me. It's only a matter of time before questions are asked. I couldn't let anything happen to you.'

I don't like the way he's looking at me, nor how he's implying that I'm the reason he's acted in this way.

'Woody and the others were the only thing tying us to Raymond's murder. You see? With them gone, we're off the hook.'

I know he's always been ruthless, but this is on another level. How long has he been planning this?

'H-how are you going to explain their deaths when we do eventually get rescued?'

He shakes his head with condescension. 'That's easy, silly, we tell them that Fergus was behind it all. We managed to disarm him and got free, and just made it to the buoy, knowing that he wasn't a good swimmer.'

'Nobody in their right mind will believe Fergus could kill three of his friends, let alone Joaquín and Elena.'

'No? The yacht trip was paid for on his credit card; he was the one who phoned and begged Christophe and Rhys to come on the trip despite your presence; and he's the one on medication for depression. The red flags were all there, and it's just a tragedy that nobody spotted them in time.'

This cannot be happening.

'I thought you said you won the trip in a competition?'

'I lied. Fergus paid for it. I couldn't have it traced back to me. Fergus asked me to be his best man and to arrange this big weekend away. It was the perfect opportunity. I needed to get everyone together anyway, after what happened with Woody. But I told him I couldn't afford the deposit, so he gave me his credit card, and I said we'd sort it out when we got back.' He pauses.

'Don't shed any tears for that fecker! He wasn't even going to invite you until I had a word with your sister. She can do so much better than that jerk-off.'

'What happened with Woody?'

'Don't get me started on that dick. When he told Fergus, he kept saying that he wanted us to all go to the police and come clean about what happened. That's why Fergus asked me to go with him, to convince him not to fuck everything up. But he was having none of it, and Fergus ended up laying him out cold and storming off. I promised I'd try to talk some sense into him, but while he was flat out at my feet, I realised there was nothing I could say to keep him quiet. No matter how much he promised to do so, he'd eventually crack. He left me no other choice.'

'Oh, fuck, what did you do?'

'What I always do: I took care of it.'

I look deep into his eyes, willing him to erupt into laughter and admit this is just him winding me up, but I can't trace any deceit in those eyes. And whilst he claims I'm safe, he still hasn't used the flare, which means I need to do my best to keep him onside.

'Fergus doesn't have a motive for wanting us all dead,' I say, looking at the plastic bag in his hand, and wondering whether I can get close enough to snatch it from him.

He shrugs nonchalantly. 'Maybe he just snapped. With the storm knocking out our Wi-Fi and navigation equipment, and with him unable to speak to your sister, it all just became too much. Don't worry about it; it isn't our place to justify his murderous actions.'

I can't believe I'm best friends with a narcissist. Why is he telling me all of this, knowing that I am likely to tell Carly everything? Unless this confession is just to clear his conscience before he makes me his next target.

40

PRESENT DAY

'Oh, come on, don't tell me you're shocked,' Harry continues. 'I've always been the one to look after you, ever since we met. I'm not going to let you go down for murder.'

I'm so cold now that my upper body is shuddering uncontrollably. 'P-please set off the flare, Harry?'

If he's feeling the cold, he isn't showing it. 'Only when you thank me for keeping you out of jail.'

I blink at him. Is he for real? He expects me to thank him for killing my friends and turning what should have been a relaxing adventure into a bloodbath?

'You're insane.'

The smile evaporates in an instant. 'No. No, I'm not insane. I did what I *had* to do to keep you safe.'

'I didn't ask you to keep me safe.'

'For feck's sake, Pete, don't do that. Don't pretend like we're not blood brothers. We've always looked after one another, as family should. How many times have you let me sleep over when I was worse for wear? Or how many times have you been my wingman?

Don't pretend now like you wouldn't have done the same thing for me if Woody had told you what he did me.'

He smacks his heels against the buoy.

'You killed them, Harry. We all swore a pact; they wouldn't have broken that.'

'Woody wanted to! When Fergus and I arrived, he told us he was going to see a solicitor and turn himself in. He was going to tell them *everything*. He reckoned it wouldn't be long until the rest of us felt the same urge to unburden ourselves. Don't you see? I did this for you, Pete. For *us*.'

My heartrate is slowing as the icy breeze continues to buffet the buoy. 'But why did you have to kill the others? They were our friends.'

'I couldn't take the risk. Woody was right about that: at some point, one of them would want to come clean. And so I had to make sure we'd be okay. That's why I did *all* of this. These people weren't your friends, Pete. Did any of them love you like I do? Did any of them celebrate when you graduated law school? No. Who was the one who convinced you to give Carly a second chance? Me. Who stood by your side when the others supported that snake, Rhys? Me. Who was the one who convinced Woody to reveal the truth about Rhys and Carly while we were in Paris? Me. I've always been there for you, Pete, and all I want is for you to show me a bit of God-damned gratitude.' His hand slams against the ridge of the buoy. 'Is that really too much to feckin' ask?'

He's growing angrier, and if I'm not careful, he might lose control and try to drown me as he did Elena.

'Thank you,' I say through gritted teeth, the words bitter on my tongue.

'Christ on a bike! You could at least *sound* like you mean it. I feckin' love you, Pete, and that's the best you can do?'

'You love me?'

He rolls his eyes. 'Of course I do, but it's not sexual. Before you get the wrong idea, it's not like I picture you while masturbating. It's deeper than that. You're the brother who never turned his back on me; the family I never had. It is my duty to keep you safe any way I can, and now I'd like you to acknowledge how well I've done.'

I can't feel my legs. If I fall off this buoy, I'll surely drown.

'I n-never asked you to kill for me.'

He slaps the frame of the buoy again. 'You didn't have to, but I saw you crush up those pills and pour them into Raymond's whiskey. I knew you intended to do him harm, and I was only disappointed that you didn't include me in your plan.'

I remember the feeling of someone watching me that day, but I was certain Harry was already on the campus.

'That's why I popped back and made sure he took a tumble down those stairs. I'd seen he'd been poking about inside the house, and I saw him a couple of times going down into that cellar, so I knew he was up to no good. And after Rhys found that rat in his bed, I was pretty sure Raymond must have been responsible, though I did wish you'd put it there. Smart move to leave Fergus and Sophie to find the body,' he continues. 'Very clever! That's the only reason I decided to go along with the plan not to report the crime to the police. I could see in your eyes that you needed me to agree; that you were desperate for me to come to your rescue again. I heard your call and I answered it.'

I think of Carly, willing myself to reflect as she would in this situation. Would she try to figure out a way to overpower Harry and set off the flare?

'Why did you kill Elena and Joaquín? They had nothing to do with this.'

He nods. 'They were collateral damage: further loose ends that needed tying. I couldn't have witnesses to my actions. Plus, they fit the narrative of Fergus turning psycho and leaving us adrift. Speaking of which, I think we're going to need to rough one another up a bit, so we can convince people that we fought our way to freedom.'

He's so lucid, revelling in his actions. I may not get a better chance to learn the truth.

'So you drowned Elena.'

'When she emerged from Rhys's room, I invited her up on deck for a drink, and when she wasn't looking, I clocked her over the head with one of the bottles. She passed out, and I moved her into the shark cage, which was still up from our little jaunt. Once her face was in the water, she kicked and fought back, but it took less than a minute for her body to go limp in my hands.

'Then, in the morning, I waited until I heard Joaquín get up to start the engines, and then I followed him into the galley as he was opening everything up. I waited until he turned his back, and then I stabbed him with the chef's knife. It was so quick, and he didn't make a sound. Not a peep. I couldn't put him in the shark cage with Elena, so I punctured the dinghy and tied him to it, allowing the outboard motor to drag the evidence below the water. I almost panicked when his leg bobbed back up.' He chuckles. 'I was sneaking back to my room when I heard you moving about in the galley. I hid in the cockpit and as soon as you were on deck, I hurried down and raced back to my room. I had blood on my clothes, and had to change.'

I desperately don't want to hear Harry confess to more, but there's no stopping him.

'Christophe took some convincing to leave the V-berth, but when I opened the window access and told him that I suspected you of killing Elena, he came willingly. I told him we needed to set a trap, and then I cracked him over the head with a frying pan. As he fell, his foot got tangled with the safety rope and he went into the water. I held him there until his body stopped jerking, with the intention that when he was found you'd all assume he'd tripped and drowned. I thought the message I scrawled into the hull would hint to you that I was responsible, but you didn't pick up on it. The shark eating Christophe's head was an unexpected bonus.'

He's so calm and detached as he describes these events that I sense any reticence on my part will be seen as weakness. I know he won't hesitate to kill me too. He must have planned a contingency for if I don't go along with his plan, but I can't see any weapons on the buoy. Though that doesn't mean he hasn't hidden something beneath the surface.

'I had no idea,' I say, straining a smile.

'I knew Soph would be a challenge, and I was thrilled when she said she would try and tinker with the engine. I always intended to detonate the explosive hidden in the ballast once everyone was dead, so the yacht would sink, but she gave me the perfect reason to use it early; essentially killing two birds with one stone.

'My favourite part was watching Rhys bleed out, though. Amazing what you can buy on the dark web if you know where to look. All I needed to do was swap out his Ventolin inhaler and wait. I hid under the stern until I heard him coughing, and then I watched. I think he actually spotted me at one point, but was already too far gone to tell any of you. Best way to kill a rat is with poison.'

I still remember the horror in his eyes when we found him bleeding from the nose and gums, his face contorted in horror.

Nobody deserved that, least of all Rhys. I'd made my peace with him for keeping his one-night stand with Carly a secret and I thought we'd all moved past it. I'd thought he was staring at something over my shoulder, but I guess I didn't spot that it was Harry.

I feel physically sick, but fix him with a grateful smile. 'Thank you.'

His face lifts as a huge smile breaks across it, and he unzips the bag, but a moment of doubt seems to creep across his brow. He pauses.

'You're not just saying that so I call for help, are you?'

I shake my head as vigorously as my aching muscles will allow. 'No. I... I mean it. I appreciate you having my back.'

He nods and the smile quickly returns, but as the flare shoots up into the sky, there's further doubt on his face. 'You can't tell Carly about any of this. You realise that, right?'

I nod, but he doesn't look convinced.

'Carly is a policewoman. She wouldn't understand the lengths I've gone to for us. If she gets wind of what's happened, then...'

I can't have him threatening Carly, but I haven't considered that my own life might be in greater danger. Before I can say anything to placate him, his hand whips beneath the water, and he pulls out a second bag. I immediately recognise the small utility knife that was missing from the block in the galley. He must have taken it before he set off; maybe hidden in the very wetsuit I'm now wearing. He yanks it free of the bag, and holds it out.

'We need to swear a blood pact here and now,' he says, holding the knife out. 'A blood pact can't be broken.' Without another word, he draws the blade across his left palm, and the blood breaks free of the skin. 'Give me your hand.'

He really is insane.

'What about the sharks? If they sense blood, they'll be attracted to us.'

His brow knots. 'Have you not been listening to me? I won't let you come to any harm. Now give me your hand.'

The warmth in his eyes has been replaced by something more menacing. It's as if a switch has been flicked in his head, and I tremble as I offer my left hand towards him. At the last minute, I swipe it up, but he's already anticipating the move and lunges at me. He catches me by surprise and we tumble from the base of the buoy, landing in the water. Bubbles in the water, tinged with a red hue, flood my vision, and the salt stings my eyes as I try to see where he's next going to thrust the blade.

Our heads temporarily surface, and I've never seen such hatred as he scowls.

'I did all of this for you. Why are you making me do this?'

I manage to draw in a deep breath before he pulls me back under. I coil both hands around his right wrist, and am managing to keep the blade at bay, but he's now trying to kick at me to force me to loosen my grip. I pull him closer, and twist my body into his, so I can keep the knife away from me. He is jiggling his knees into my bottom, and we emerge from the water.

'We could have had it all,' he's shouting as the water splashes over us. 'But look what you're making me do.'

I barely have time to take another breath before I feel his left arm wrap around my neck and tighten. We dip below the water again, and I can feel him shuffling so he is above me, forcing me further down. We struggle and tumble, and my lungs are soon burning. I've lost my bearings. I'm going to have to release his wrist or I'll drown here.

I let go, and immediately put my hands around his left arm, trying to wrestle myself free of his grip, but then I see the shine of the blade cutting through the pink water towards me. I manage to thrust my hips to the right, and grab the back of his hand, driving the blade past the wetsuit and into his side. His scream erupts in a gargled explosion of bubbles. I break free, and with my last ounce of air, push myself up and through the water.

I am so tired and disorientated, but I can't risk Harry coming back for another go. I need to get out of the water. The buoy isn't in sight until I turn, and realise we've actually moved several metres from it. Exhaustion nearly defeats me, but then I think about Carly, and find the energy to move my legs and kick towards the bobbing beacon. I don't have the strength to lift myself up, and just grab the side, trying to keep my head above the water.

I scan the surface, searching for Harry breaking through the rough sea, but he's nowhere in sight. He's planned everything so well and I know he's going to spring again. I can't see how he can hold his breath this long.

I dare to cast an eye back to where the yacht should be, but it's virtually submerged now.

Poor Fergus. I should have trusted that my sister wouldn't choose a monster. His death – like the others' – is because of me.

What have I done?

Maybe if Fergus had accused Harry instead of me at the last minute, we'd have both realised that he was playing us off one another.

I blink as the dark clouds flash above the sinking stern, and panic as I see fins poking out of the water, not far from the wreckage. It won't take them long to pick up on the scent of blood, and that means I'm going to have to drag myself out to stay alive. It takes all my strength, but I manage to claw my knees onto the rough edge in time to see and hear a boat skimming through the sea in my direction.

Is this a hallucination?

The old man doesn't appear to speak English, but he offers his hand to me, and I grasp hold of it, toppling into the boat as a large wave lifts the buoy into the air. I want to thank him for coming to my rescue, but there isn't time. I'm so frozen that I can't speak, but I point earnestly towards where I last saw the tip of the yacht. I can't leave Fergus to die, not if there's a chance to save him. He doesn't appear to understand, and the more I try to speak and point, the harder it becomes, until my energy is sapped, and the darkness takes me.

41

PRESENT DAY

I wake with a jerk, and start choking as I struggle to swallow. There is something hard pressed over my face, and my first thought is that Harry has emerged from the water and is trying to suffocate me somehow. I claw and scratch at what is over the lower half of my face, and my fingers graze soft plastic. I grip the mask and yank it away, the elastic band behind my head sliding off with a snap. I pull on the plastic tube in my throat and yank, retching until it is out. Flashes of yellow and brown blind me as I open my eyes. I blink several times, a violent pain exploding inside my head, until I manage to focus my vision and realise I'm in a hospital bed, though I have no memory of how I got here.

There's a cacophony of bleeps and sirens from somewhere in the room. I pinch my nose and breathe out until my ears pop back. Now the noise is louder. A moment later, a door at the end of the room swings open and a woman in a surgical mask and white nurse's uniform enters. She hurries to my side, fiddles with something just beyond my shoulder, and then begins to speak to me, but I don't understand a word of what she's saying. She raises my right arm and presses two fingers against my wrist, comparing my racing pulse to the ticking of the small watch hanging from her uniform.

She begins to speak again, but I stare blankly at her, coughing until I'm able to find the word, 'English.'

She nods quickly, holds up a finger and then hurries from the room. I attempt to sit up, but the moment I lift my head, it's as if someone has smacked me with something blunt. My head falls back against the warm pillow, and I have to close my eyes.

I search for any hint of memory as to where I am and how I got here.

The last thing I remember is...

The door to the room opens again, and I hear two sets of footsteps approaching the bed. Then someone is prising my eyes open and pointing a beam of light into both, until I bat their hand away. An older man's face is staring down at me. He has a bushy, granite-coloured moustache and a rapidly receding dark grey head of curls. His skin is tanned and leathery, but when he smiles, I'm reminded of trips to visit my grandfather in the hospice.

'Señor Routledge?'

I nod.

How on earth does he know my name?

The last thing I remember is fighting with Harry and just being so exhausted from the swim and the stress of everything. But then, yes, now I remember a boat. A fisherman? Did he bring me to the hospital?

'Señor Routledge, my name is Doctor Espinosa, forgive me, my English not so good. How are you?'

I feel like I'm suffering from the world's worst hangover. My head is so sore, and the longer I keep my eyes open, the more the room seems to spin. And it feels so hot in this room. Is there no way they can open a window?

'Hot,' I croak, which he must understand as I feel a mountain of bed sheets being peeled back by the nurse.

'When you arrived, you were very unwell. We have treated you for... now let me get the translation correct... severe hypothermia. You also had a wound to your arm that we have stitched.'

I picture Harry with his needle and thread and Sophie pulling the bandage tightly around the area. I wince as I lift the arm into the air, and see a much cleaner strapping.

'Señor Routledge, can you tell me how long you were in the water?'

I remember Harry and I linking hands and jumping off the yacht's gunnel, but there are black holes in my memory. How long were we in the water? It seemed only to be minutes between escaping the boat and reaching the buoy, but maybe it was longer. I really can't be certain.

I offer a shrug. 'I don't know.'

The words stick in my throat as I think about Fergus and how Harry misled me, misled us all. My future brother-in-law drowned or eaten, and all because I allowed Harry to manipulate me. My eyes fill and my vision blurs as I think about Simone. Her whole future is ruined because of what I did a decade ago. Whether Harry *was* the one who pushed Raymond down the stairs, or whether it was Woody or Soph, or whether Raymond just slipped, had I not tipped my mum's sleeping pills into the whiskey, none of this would have happened. How many lives did my actions ruin?

'Drink,' I sputter, my dry mouth preventing me saying more.

The nurse moves around to the left side of the bed, and I feel her pressing a paper straw between my lips. The liquid is stale and warm, but I slurp as fast as I can, grimacing as it glosses over the burning in my throat. Pulling the plastic tube out so violently probably wasn't such a great idea.

The straw is extracted too quickly, but as I try to sit up and chase after it, the wrecking ball in my head crashes against my temple and I have to yield.

'You were sailing?' the doctor asks next.

I'm about to answer when a tiny voice in the back of my head tells me to keep quiet. At some point, somebody is going to come and ask exactly what happened out there, and I don't have any clue as to how I'm going to explain the deaths of five of my friends and poor Elena and Joaquín who got caught in the middle of Harry's evil plan. It all seems so far-fetched that I can't believe anybody will even believe me. Seven unexplained deaths and only one survivor, I know who I'd suspect. And how do I begin to get my head around that kind of survivor's guilt?

And what of James 'Woody' Woods? Did Harry really kill him?

I'm going to have to tell the police something, but where do I begin?

I don't answer the doctor, choosing to close my eyes and feign sleep instead. They eventually fall for the act, and I'm relieved when I hear them exit the room.

Even if the doctor hasn't contacted the local police, inevitably the company the yacht was hired through are expecting us back, and when we don't dock, they're bound to raise the alarm. It is a question of when, and not if, someone is going to come asking difficult questions. I'm not even sure how long I've been in the hospital; we were due back on Monday, but maybe Monday has already been and gone.

I'm the only survivor of Harry's actions, and I will have to face the consequences, but I'm still at a loss as to how to explain it all.

I had ups and downs with both Rhys and Christophe, but that was all in the past, when we were all less mature and didn't know what our futures would hold. I can hand-on-heart say I bore neither of them any animosity, and wouldn't have wished either dead. That Harry felt he was doing me some kind of favour makes me feel even more culpable for their deaths.

And poor, poor Sophie. She strived for so long to put others first, even though she was carrying such heavy baggage of her own. I hate that I didn't get to say goodbye to her before the explosion, which I now know had nothing to do with her attempts to hotwire the yacht. She was just trying to save us, unaware that she'd sealed her own fate by climbing into the engine bay. I wish I could have thanked her for keeping us out of Raymond's harmful clutches when we were all so vulnerable. She bore the brunt of his anger time and again; I'll forever be grateful to have her as a friend.

Given I have no idea where I was rescued from, I don't even know if anyone will ever be able to find their bodies. I suppose it depends how deep the waters are.

I think of Carly. Does she know what's happened? Has anyone phoned her to tell her I'm in the hospital? Is she at home panicking because she can't reach me by phone? And what if Fergus was right, and Simone wasn't just being overdramatic when she was speaking to him? What if something awful has befallen them as well? I'm in another country with no means of contacting either of them.

I know instantly that I need to get out of the hospital and figure out a plan. If I had my passport, I'd probably hop on the first flight back to the UK, not that I have any cash to buy a plane ticket; that also went down with my cabin.

Clamping my eyes shut to help with the dizziness, I force myself up onto my elbows, and wait for the pain to subside before pushing the bedsheet back and attempt to swing my legs off the edge of the bed. I feel something slip from my finger and clatter to the floor. This is followed by a beeping alarm from the monitor behind the bed, and it's a relief when the nurse hurries back in, picks up the pulse checker and fastens it back around my finger.

'I-I need to get out of here,' I tell her, keeping my eyes closed as my head spins.

'*No comprendo.*'

'Go. I need to go,' I say louder, as if that will make it easier for her to understand.

'*Momento,*' she says, and begins to pull away, but I grab her arm, and pull her close to me. 'Please. I want to leave. To exit. *Salida.*'

The door to the room opens again, and I hear the doctor hurrying to her aid. He peels my hand from her wrist. 'Señor, please. You cannot leave yet. Your friend is here.'

I immediately release my grip. Fear and dread wash over me in an instant as I realise something.

There's only one way they could have known my name: if Harry survived.

42

PRESENT DAY

They can't let him in. There's only one reason he would be here: because he wants to finish the job.

They must notice the blood has drained from my face, as they manoeuvre me back into the bed.

What if Harry decides to kill them too because they're in the way? Surely he wouldn't be so reckless.

'You can't let him in,' I stammer as the nurse proceeds to check my temperature and pulse once more. 'My friend, I mean. Please, don't let him in here. You need to phone the police. Tell them he wants me dead.'

The doctor is frowning at me, puzzled by my sudden terror, or maybe not understanding what I'm saying. I grab the lapels of his coat, and pull him closer. 'Phone the police.'

The nurse, shocked by my aggression, peels away and races for the door. Maybe the hospital has some kind of local security that can come and stand guard until the police arrive.

'Please, Señor,' the poor doctor gasps, as he tries to pull himself free.

I relent, and release him, if only so I can rest my head against the pillow.

I'm going to have to come clean. It's the only way to explain what happened on the boat. The police need to know about Raymond's reign of terror, how he gave us no choice but to stop him, and how that ultimately spiralled out of control.

I think back to all those boring mornings spent at Sunday school when the priest would quote scripture, but now one passage slips into my head: the truth will set you free.

The door at the end of the room flies open, and I can't breathe as I wait for Harry to come bounding in. My mouth drops when I see the nurse wheeling in Fergus instead. He's also in a hospital gown, though it isn't obvious why he's in a wheelchair. I finally exhale as he is parked beside the bed, and the nurse applies the brake.

'Señor, you still want me to phone—'

'Can you give us a few minutes, please?' Fergus asks, and the doctor looks at me. I nod, and he leads the nurse out of the room, closing the door behind them.

'Bet you never thought you'd see me again,' Fergus says, a stern look on his face.

I almost can't believe my eyes. I'd assumed he'd gone down with the yacht. I open my mouth, but I don't know what to say. How can I ever apologise for abandoning him in his hour of need?

'Before you say anything, I've spoken with Simone and Carly, and they're both perfectly fine. I've told them there was an incident, and they're booked to fly out here tomorrow. In the meantime, I thought it was probably a good idea if we get our story straight. I've already made a statement to the *federales* here, and I expect you to back it up. Is that clear?'

'Harry, he...' but I can't finish the sentence as a lump forms in my throat.

Fergus nods. 'I figured it out when he chose your side over mine before he abandoned ship. I spoke to him after Christophe's suspicious death, and it was him who threw you under the bus. He said you'd lost it when he told you about Woody threatening to go to the police and how you'd do anything to stop the truth getting out. I didn't want to believe that you could have killed Christophe, but once the others were targeted, I couldn't see anyone else in the frame. I didn't want to let on, which is why I played on the suggestions that Raymond was back from the dead. I feel like such a fool: he was playing us all the whole time, but I didn't connect the dots until it was too late.'

A tear escapes and rolls down my cheek, but I nod. I don't know what I should be feeling, but it's a mixture of remorse and overwhelming relief; relief that Fergus is still alive; relief that I won't have to tell Simone that he's dead; and relief that it's Fergus before me and not Harry.

'What was Simone's emergency?' I manage to croak.

He smiles ruefully. 'She's pregnant. That was what she wanted to tell me. Apparently, she'd been feeling ill all day and when Carly suggested she take a test, she did, and that was what she was trying to say when the Wi-Fi went down. Looks like you're going to be an uncle.'

My heart warms. Simone will be such a great mum.

'Congratulations,' I cough.

Fergus looks towards the window in the corner of the room, clamping his jaw. 'I thought I was a goner. I really did. When you and Harry went over the side, I thought I was going to drown or get eaten. I made my peace with God, and then, as the gunnel dipped below the surface, He gave me a lifeline: the orange life ring floated past me, and I grabbed it. I tried kicking in the direction of the shoreline, but the waves were so fierce that I ended up further away. Had that fishing boat not come past, I probably wouldn't be here now.' He pauses and eyes me closely. 'I was shocked when I saw you curled up and passed out inside it. I figured then that you must have killed Harry.'

A second tear escapes, and I try to speak, though no sound emerges.

'What I need to know from you now is that Harry is definitely dead.'

I nod quickly.

'How can you be so sure? Did you see his body?'

I think back to the terrifying ordeal beneath the water. I definitely saw the knife go into his side, and he never resurfaced.

'It's just… it's been three days since we were rescued by the fishing boat. They've had divers in the water, and they've managed to recover the others, but there's no sign of Harry's body.'

I freeze.

'I canny help thinking he somehow made it back to shore and is lying in wait to finish the job. You remember how when he went overboard in his quest to reach land, he was wearing an air tank, which he didn't have with him when he returned? He claimed it had run out of air, so he dumped it, but what if that was part of his ploy and he had it hidden somewhere?'

I picture the bags where Harry had stashed the flare and the knife.

'I canny see that he would have entered the water with you without a back-up plan. He's proved himself resourceful in plotting these murders. What if he isn't finished yet?'

He must have drowned. He must have. He was losing a lot of blood, and there's no way someone could hold their breath that long.

'I've told the *federales* we were set upon by pirates who tied us up and tortured us, before they left us to drown on the sinking yacht. Apparently, it's not uncommon for rich-looking tourists to be set upon in these waters. I think that was why Joaquín was so keen to get to Paradise Cove as quickly as possible. I think they're buying the story – so far – but I need you to corroborate it. There's no point dragging up everything that happened ten years ago. Raymond Grosjean is dead and I, for one, want to put it behind me.'

'Harry told me he killed Woody too,' I whisper.

Fergus considers this, and then offers a short nod. 'When he stopped returning my messages and calls, I began to worry that he'd already gone to the police, but I never phoned him to check. If I'd suspected...'

'He fooled all of us.'

Fergus blows his nose. 'So now it's only you and me that know what really happened then and now.'

'It isn't right that Raymond's murder will go undetected. I want to tell the police what happened that night and accept the part I played. The body has been discovered and now, with these deaths, the police might put two and two together anyway.'

Fergus suddenly leans forward, and points a steely finger at my face. 'Don't you dare!'

I recoil out of fear he might punch me.

'Isn't it enough that we've lost the others? What gives you the right to ruin everything we've built since that horrific night?'

'I drugged Raymond,' I tell him, feeling a weight lifted to finally be able to say it aloud. 'I'm the reason he fell down those stairs. I'm the reason we had to bury him.'

'You need to forget all about that wee shite. He's dead and the world is a better place because of it. I swear on my unborn baby's life that I will kill you if you try and ruin our future.'

There's venom in his eyes, and I have no doubt he means every word.

'Move on with your life, Pete. Marry Carly, if that's what you want to do, but don't throw everything away because you feel guilty.'

He's right: there's no way I'd be able to continue practising law with this on my record. And despite her feelings for me, I don't think Carly would forgive ten years of deceit. But I'm not sure I can really continue with the burden of guilt around my neck.

Fergus fixes me with a hard stare. 'We made a pact to cover up Raymond's accident that night, but what none of you knew – what I never let on – is that he was still alive after he fell down those stairs. He was groggy because of blood loss, but he wasn't dead. Not until I clamped my hand over his mouth and nose, and held it there. I could see in his eyes that he wanted to struggle, but he didn't. You drugging him probably explains why. I kept my hand in place until his pulse stopped. Sophie saw me down there, but assumed I was just checking for signs of life.'

My heart skips a beat.

'You didn't kill Raymond, Pete, *I* did. And if you threaten my future, I won't hesitate to stop you too.'

The way his eyes are bulging leaves me in no doubt that he means it.

'Fergus, we murdered him,' I say between gritted teeth, 'and I can't keep running from the fact—'

'You left me to die on that boat!' he snaps. 'Where's the guilt you feel for that? At no point did you stop to consider that Harry was manipulating us. We are practically family, Pete, and you turned your back on me. It was a wakeup call, and I'm not going to let you fuck up my future again.' He looks away momentarily, before his head snaps back around. 'If you *ever* whisper a word of this to anyone, I won't hesitate to put you in the ground as well. Like it or not, I'm going to be keeping a very close eye on you, *brother*, and if I get any hint of betrayal, I will make you regret ever moving into that house. Are we clear?'

I want to just shrink into the bed until I disappear. I have no doubt that Fergus means every word. And it isn't just me in danger; I need to keep Carly safe too. Like it or not, my life is now tied to Fergus forever, and there's nothing I can do about it. I'm going to have to find a way to live with what we did, even though I can already feel it chipping away at my soul.

I start as someone knocks at the door, and a moment later, a uniformed police officer enters. Fergus glares at me until I reluctantly nod. I watch as he wheels himself away and leaves the room.

The officer smiles warmly at me, pulling over a chair which he lowers himself into. 'Señor Routledge?'

I nod, thinking about the friends I've lost and those that remain. Carly is my future, and I don't want to drag her down with me.

'Can I ask you what happened on the ship this weekend?'

I nod, and proceed to relay the story. I tell him about pirates and the horror of how we somehow managed to survive. The longer I speak, the easier the lies roll off my tongue. I'll tell Carly and Simone the same lies when they arrive, and hope that if I repeat them often enough, I'll start to believe they're true. But I know deep down that sometimes it's the scars we can't see that take the longest to heal.

ACKNOWLEDGMENTS

Thank you for reading *Adrift* and for taking the time to read about all the people who helped make this such a gripping and terrifying story. Please get in touch via the channels below and let me know what you thought about it.

My dedication in this book read: *For all those with a dream: never stop chasing it!* That's because in an alternative universe this novel never existed. Back in January 2022 I decided to stop pursuing my dream and officially gave up writing. After ten years of effort and trying to break out as an author I'd had enough of the few highs and many lows that an author experiences when joining the road to publication. On the back of my third bout of Covid and all the disruption from two years of lockdowns, my self-esteem was at an all-time low. I'd written and failed to find a home for my last three books, and I just didn't think my mental health could take another disappointment.

So, I quit writing.

It lasted exactly 12½ days. I'd hit upon an idea for a revenge thriller like nothing I'd seen on the market, and decided to roll the dice one final time.

And so I started writing *Adrift* and completed a strong first draft in under five weeks. But that's when all the self-doubt and internal criticism returned and so I reached out to my Facebook followers and asked for volunteers to beta read the first draft and provide honest feedback. I would like to thank Michelle Forster, Sue Harrap, Lisa Ledger, Lorraine Francies, Lindsey Baker, and

Joanne Taylor who all kindly agreed to do just that. Their positive responses were overwhelming.

Editing the novel, I then submitted it to a select choice of literary agents, telling myself that if it failed to find a home, at least I had given it my best shot. I had to pinch myself (hard and several times) when my dream agent Emily Glenister at the DHH Literary Agency told me how much she loved the story and offered representation in May 2022. Of course I tried to play down my excitement and told her I needed to sleep on the decision, but I think I accepted within 12 hours.

I can't describe how much I love working with Emily. She is passionate about books and the number one cheerleader for all of her clients. She's full of ideas but doesn't tread on a writer's creative toes either. She's headstrong and doesn't suffer fools (though she must have made an exception in my case). And it was her idea to change the story from a hen party aboard the yacht to a stag party, and the story went from strength to strength. Because of her insights and market awareness, we were able to secure a publishing contract with Boldwood Books who have been so supportive with and positive about the project.

I want to thank my editor Emily Yau for all her creative input into the story and for pushing me to give every character a journey. I am so excited to be on this publishing journey together. Thank you also to the team of copyeditors, proof-readers, marketing gurus, and media whizzes who make up the rest of the Boldwood Books team. Because of them my dream of being a writer continues apace. Don't give up on your own!

As always, thank you also to my best friend Dr Parashar Ramanuj who never shies away from the awkward medical questions I ask him. Thank you also to Alex Shaw and Paul Grzegorzek – authors and dear friends – who are happy to listen to me moan and whinge about the pitfalls of the publishing industry, offering words of encouragement along the way.

My children are an inspiration to me every day, and as they continue to grow so quickly, I am eternally grateful that I get to play such an important role in their development. They continue to show one another affection, patience and kindness, and make being their dad that bit easier. I'd like to thank my own parents and my parents-in-law for continuing to offer words of encouragement when I'm struggling to engage with my muse.

It goes without saying that I wouldn't be the writer I am today without the loving support of my beautiful wife and soulmate Hannah. She keeps everything else in my life ticking over so that I can give what's left to my writing. She never questions my method or the endless hours daydreaming while I'm working through plot holes, and for that I am eternally grateful.

And thanks must also go to YOU for buying and reading *Adrift*. Please do post a review to wherever you purchased the book from so that other readers can be enticed to give it a try. It takes less than two minutes to share your opinion, and I ask you do me this small kindness.

I am active on Facebook, Twitter, and Instagram, so please do stop by with any messages, observations, or questions. Hearing from readers of my books truly brightens my days and encourages me to keep writing, so don't be a stranger. I promise I *will* respond to every message and comment.

Stephen

MORE FROM M. A. HUNTER

We hope you enjoyed reading *Adrift*. If you did, please leave a review.

If you'd like to gift a copy, this book is also available as an ebook, hardback, large print, digital audio download and audiobook CD.

Sign up to M. A. Hunter's mailing list for news, competitions and updates on future books.

https://bit.ly/MAHunterNews

ABOUT THE AUTHOR

M.A. Hunter is the pen name of Stephen Edger, the Amazon bestselling author of psychological and crime thrillers, including the Kate Matthews series. Born in the north-east of England, he now lives in Southampton where many of his stories are set, allowing him to use his insider knowledge to deliver realistic and unsettling suspense on every page. He is married with a son and a daughter, and two dogs.

Visit M. A. Hunter's website: stephenedger.com/m-a-hunter

Follow M. A. Hunter on social media

twitter.com/stephenedger

facebook.com/AuthorMAHunter

instagram.com/stef.edger

bookbub.com/authors/stephen-edger

goodreads.com/stephenedger

Ingram Content Group UK Ltd.
Milton Keynes UK
UKHW041852260723
425843UK00004B/115